A Graveyard for Spies

Readers are encouraged to go to www.MissionPointPress. com to contact the author or to find information on how to buy this book in bulk at a discounted rate.

Published by Mission Point Press
2554 Chandler Rd.
Traverse City, MI 49696
(231) 421-9513
www.MissionPointPress.com

ISBN: 978-1-950659-53-1
Library of Congress Control Number: 2020907236

Printed in the United States of America

A Graveyard
for Spies

J.R. Seeger

book 5 in the   MIKE4 series

UZBEKISTAN
DUSHANBE
TURKMENISTAN
TAJIKISTAN
CHINA
Balkh
Dowlatabad
Mazar-e Sharif
Kunduz
Eshkamesh
IRAN
Qal'eh-ye Now
Herat
Asmar
Asadabad
KABUL
Bagrami
Jalalabad
Azrow
AFGHANISTAN
ISLAMABAD
INDIA
Anar Darreh
Baghran
Uruzgan
Kandahar
Chakhansur
Darvishan
PAKISTAN
Rigestan

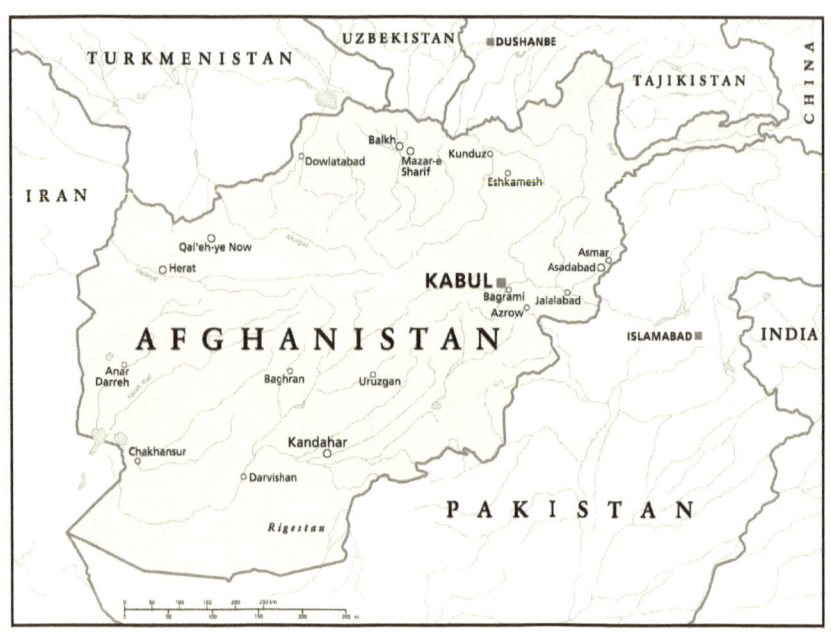

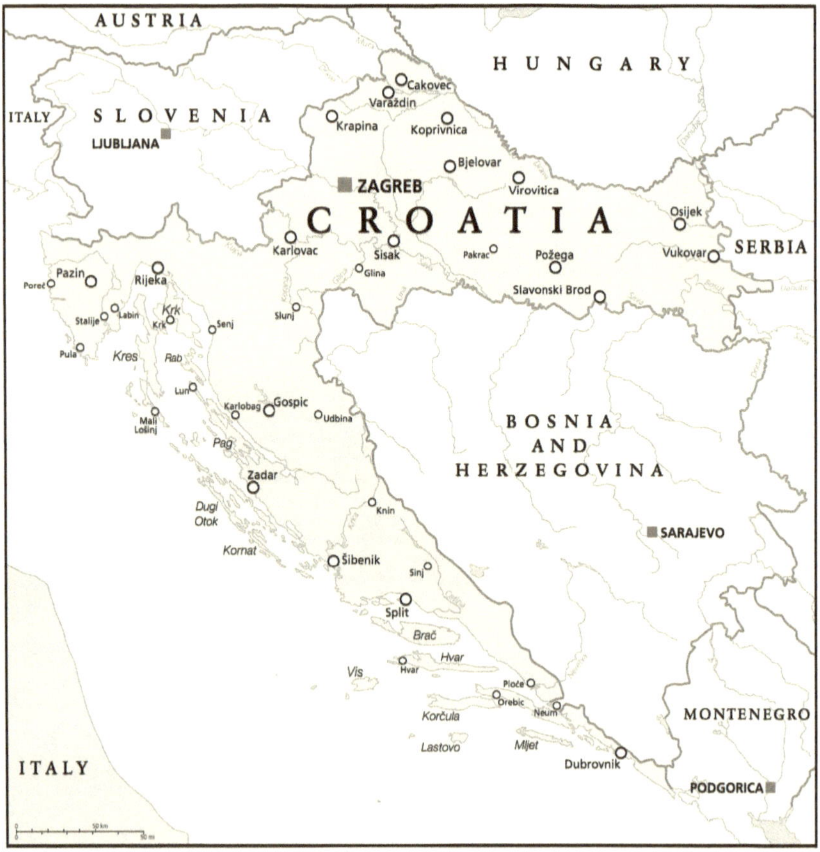
AUSTRIA
HUNGARY
Cakovec
Varaždin
ITALY
SLOVENIA
Krapina
Koprivnica
LJUBLJANA
Bjelovar
ZAGREB
Virovitica
CROATIA
Osijek
Karlovac
Sisak
Pakrac
Požega
Vukovar
SERBIA
Pazin
Rijeka
Glina
Poreč
Slavonski Brod
Labin
Krk
Stalije
Krk
Senj
Slunj
Pula
Kres
Rab
Lun
Karlobag
Gospic
Udbina
Mali Lošinj
BOSNIA AND HERZEGOVINA
Pag
Zadar
Knin
Dugi Otok
SARAJEVO
Kornat
Šibenik
Sinj
Split
Brač
Hvar
Vis
Hvar
Ploče
Orebic
Neum
MONTENEGRO
Korčula
Lastovo
Mljet
Dubrovnik
ITALY
PODGORICA

CONTENTS

Go out into the highways and hedges, and compel them to come in...

—Luke 14:23

>>>>>> A WALK IN THE PARK

Barbara O'Connell walked through the Christmas Fair trying as hard as she could to appear interested in the mix of wonderful smells, fresh Christmas sweets, small Christmas toys, and clothes of every shape and size. It wasn't that she didn't find the fair intriguing. She was working. And working for Barbara O'Connell meant meeting undercover agents, collecting intelligence, and delivering it to the CIA's Counterterrorism Center.

As the sun started to go down in the winter sky, Barbara was conducting a cleansing run to ensure she was not being followed by any one of a dozen different adversaries. She was on her way to meet a reporting source, code named *BRAKEDREAM*, who was a penetration of Lebanese Hizballah in Germany. At the last meeting, she had tasked *BRAKEDREAM* to provide any information he could on planning for a suspected Hizballah and Islamic Revolutionary Guards Corps (IRGC) attack on an Iranian Baluch exile living in Frankfurt. The last meeting with *BRAKEDREAM* had been in Istanbul. As an Iranian support agent, he traveled to Frankfurt with the IRGC team. Barbara had followed the same day on a different flight. He triggered the meeting for today in the park below the city that housed the old mineral Spa, the "Bad" or Bath of Bad Homburg. If *BRAKEDREAM* delivered, it could be the break that the joint US and German counterterrorism team had hoped for over the past month.

Barbara had been splitting her time on the road between meetings with sources reporting on Palestinian terrorists involved in the *Intifada* uprising on the West Bank, and Lebanese Hizballah sources reporting on the links between Hizballah and the IRGC. She had some Arabic, but most of the sources spoke either English or French so communications hadn't been a problem so far. Barbara was on the road at least two weeks out of every month working one of several sources while her husband, Peter, ran his station in Baku. It wasn't an ideal situation, but tandem couple assignments were hard to find and even harder to keep. If it meant traveling throughout Europe and the Middle East to run agent meetings, then Barbara was all about that effort. After all, she had two children in college.

A voice registered in Barbara's earpiece saying, *"Checkpoint 4, you are go. Time is 1620hrs."* Barbara's operation was being supported by a joint US and German surveillance team and they had been calling out her progress along the predetermined route in Bad Homburg: From the train station, through the main street, past the palace grounds and then a right turn down to the Spa and to her designated meeting site. Checkpoint 4 was the last surveillance position before the actual meeting site. Barbara had worked with German Station of the CIA in the past, but this was the first time she had worked with both station and the Germans themselves. Given the mission was to disrupt a terrorist attack on German soil, and since Germany was a trusted NATO ally, it only made sense to work with the German government. From the perspective of CTC at the Agency Headquarters it was all good. CTC had a long-standing relationship with their German counterparts in the counterterrorism world.

The biggest challenge for Barbara had been to work through the complex network of German intelligence and security organizations to determine which part of the government would work on this operation. From the CTC perspective, the normal connection would be through the US Special Operations Force (SOF) and with the German Police counterterrorism unit known as *Genzschutzgruppe 9* or more simply GSG9. This case was more about intelligence collection than a "finish" mission where a joint US-German assault force would conduct a raid on the terrorists. So, CTC instructed Barbara that it was up to Bonn Station to figure out which service, and which part of which service, would be her watchers.

Once she received that instruction, Barbara accepted she would work with whatever joint team showed up to the game. In the in-brief before the meeting, Barbara found out that the surveillance team would be a mix from the Frankfurt offices of the state police, the *Landeskriminalampt* or LKA, and the Frankfurt offices the national counterterrorism and counterintelligence organization, the *Bundesamt fur Verlfassungsschutz* or BFV. It was all alphabet soup to Barbara given her limited, high school German, but she noticed that the LKA team arrived at the meeting armed and the BFV team came to the table with technical surveillance capability, so it was all good. The CIA station lead was a young officer named Bert on his second tour in Germany after a tour in West Africa. He would be in the surveillance van with the two German officers and one officer from the US Army SOF liaison unit stationed in Frankfurt.

"If you hear a voice in your earpiece today, it will be me" Bert had told her. "I will count off the checkpoints and let you know when you are clear. There will be an observation point set up in the park near your meeting, so even after the last checkpoint, you will still be under our umbrella. The difference is that at that point, the team will be armed and ready to act if it doesn't look right or if you ask for help. Fair?"

"Perfect."

Barbara was not entirely pleased to be going into a meeting with a terrorist without her standard sidearm, but rules were rules, especially in Germany. Of course, they hadn't said anything about a collapsible baton or a switchblade, so Barbara started her route with both in the pockets of her heavy wool loden coat of forest green with blue trim. Along with her navy blue wool beret, her dress boots over her jeans, and the loden coat, Barbara hoped she looked as inconspicuous as possible. The cold weather made the multiple layers credible and those layers covered the communications gear and the Second Chance body armor she was wearing under her coat. The meeting was going to be outside, so she wasn't worried about being cold with that many layers. In Bad Homburg in December, it was cozy.

Barbara walked across the main street that separated the city from the Spa and the park. The meeting was set for 1625hrs and she could see *BRAKEDREAM* making his way across the park along a separate path that would lead to the 19th century entrance to the spa. Their meeting would be a brief encounter just past the entrance. He would pass her a small concealment with any information that he collected and she would pass him a German cellphone. The US-German team assumed the IRGC would have gathered all of their own phones and secured them in some safe house in Germany when they arrived. As part of the team, albeit only a support asset, *BRAKEDREAM's* phone would have been secured as well. After this meeting, *BRAKEDREAM* would have a way to get in touch with Barbara and the Germans would have a way to track *BRAKEDREAM*.

Barbara knew from her years as a street agent, these last few minutes before a clandestine act were always the "give away" time. The intelligence officers and their agents would show signs of increased adrenaline in their system. Some were nervous and would show it in their hands, usually clenching and unclenching their fists. Some were calm but they would show it still in the fact that they would increase their pace toward the act. The least experienced would give the act away by taking that one last look to be sure they were not being followed. Barbara used these last few minutes to take deep breaths and run a series of multiplication tables in her head as her method of calming down. The deep breaths would wash out some of the adrenaline and prevent these natural "tells" from giving away her impending contact.

BRAKEDREAM definitely did look nervous as Barbara came closer to the site. He was demonstrating all the tells. He was fidgeting, he was walking too fast for the rest of the crowd moving to and from the bath house, and he made that last look over his shoulder before he made the turn that would obscure their brief encounter. Barbara could understand his actions. *BRAKEDREAM* was the one who would face Hizballah retribution if he was caught. They had decided months ago to use Bad Homburg as a meeting site, but *BRAKEDREAM* most probably hadn't considered the size of the crowd for the Christmas fair. The brush pass should take no more than a few seconds, but Barbara hoped she would have enough time to give him some praise for his actions and leave him feeling more comfortable with the operation. The best news to *BRAKEDREAM* would be Barbara telling him that the bank account where he received his pay now had a thousand Euros more than when he started his train ride this morning.

The moment arrived and *BRAKEDREAM* delivered the concealment with a degree of precision that impressed Barbara. He appeared to jostle Barbara as they walked past each other. The concealment went into her pocket before she even realized he had accomplished the act. With equal precision, she put the phone in his hand. There was no opportunity to give him praise, but Barbara knew she could send him a secure message between their mutual dead letter drops. Nothing secret, just a thank you would do. Barbara continued to walk up the hill away from the city while *BRAKEDREAM* walked past the bath house and toward the city.

After waiting for a green light at the crosswalk, he started across the street toward the city and the train station when a black Opel Astra made a hard-right turn at the intersection and hit *BRAKEDREAM* just before he completed his crossing. The aerodynamic front end of the Astra and the acceleration immediately broke both of *BRAKE-DREAM's* legs and launched him over the Astra. Behind the Astra was a black panel van that ran over *BRAKEDREAM's* body and sped away from the scene.

From across the park, Barbara had heard the first attack and, as she turned toward the city, she had a chance to see the second vehicle complete the murder. *"Blazer, I say again, blazer."* Barbara was certain that she was yelling into the body microphone, but at this point, it wasn't as if anyone would notice. All eyes in the park were focused on what the average German citizen saw as reckless drivers and a tragic accident.

"Roger. We saw the entire incident. Our colleagues are already in pursuit." Barbara noticed Bert's voice on the radio was calm. He probably had seen worse in Africa. Shortly after his transmission, Barbara heard the distinctive German police sirens which were described in German magazines and comic books as "tah too, tah too, tah too." Two police cruisers plus two LKA motorcycle police officers in their

green leather gear were accelerating down the road in the direction of the two assailants.

"Move to Turm for extraction." The turm was a small tower at the end of the park in opposite direction of Barbara's planned travel. She cut across the park to change direction and headed toward the tower. When she arrived, a black Volkswagen van was waiting with the sliding door open. She climbed in, and before she belted in and before the door closed, the vehicle was on the move toward the autobahn and the Frankfurt headquarters of the LKA.

From his post on the rear bench seat of the van, Bert looked at her with sad eyes, "Barbara, I'm sorry. The ambulance service has reported *BREAKDREAM* didn't make it. He was dead after the first car strike. The van was just a stupid bit of violence."

Barbara was fighting back tears. She knew from the beginning of her service that the trade put both agent and agent handler in harm's way. She just had not seen the proof of that statement so directly. She said, "Can we get these guys? Where are they going? Can we join the pursuit?"

Bert shook his head. "Barbara, from the German perspective, this is no longer an intelligence operation. It is now a pure law enforcement investigation of a murder. If they capture the creeps, we may or may not get a chance to interrogate them. German law is pretty clear about that."

"Well, German law is crap then."

"Unfortunately, my German colleagues agree with you. They regularly point out some of their most restrictive regulations are based on laws that we forced into their constitution back in the 50s. I actually looked it up. They are right. We didn't want to recreate the Gestapo and definitely didn't want to have a West German Secret Police like the East German *STASI*. For now, we are going to have to wait and see what happens."

"I've never been real good at wait and see."

"I heard."

Bert handed her a cup of coffee from a thermos as they drove back to Frankfurt. Barbara took it and thought about *BREAKDREAM,* his family and his hopes. Part of the job of a case officer is getting to know your agent, what makes him happy, what makes him sad, and what motivates him to commit espionage. *BREAKDREAM* had a family who would never know why he was a victim of a car accident. She would make sure they received compensation for his courage. For their own safety, that compensation would be structured so that they would not know he was a CIA source. It would require some work, but she knew the Agency would do the job. Still, as she drank the strong, black German coffee, Barbara started to quietly cry.

The IRGC major sat on the edge of his chair in the safe house apartment near the Frankfurt train station. He leaned across the desk littered with paper, money, a Beretta pistol, and an ashtray filled with cigarette butts. He was dressed in a white shirt and a dark suit. An Irishman was sitting on the other side of the desk. The Irishman was not happy about his current situation. The major had spent the last ten minutes shouting at him in a mix of poor French and even poorer English. Brian Boru had been through more than his share of interrogations with the IRA, the PFLP, and now the IRGC. He knew this could go very badly, very quickly. He wanted to be certain that he could get to the pistol before the major, so he leaned forward, offering the Iranian his most subservient face, and said, "Sir, I did as you asked and ran the tout over. The plan was for your men in the van to stay clear and follow me to the drop-off point where we would torch the car and come back here. None of your men were even supposed to be on the street. They didn't follow your orders. It is not my fault that they are now in a German jail."

"Mr. Boru, you are free and they are not. Why?"

The Irishman used the "Brian Boru" alias when he was working with any of his Middle East contacts. They didn't seem to realize he was claiming to be a descendent of a mythical king of Ireland. When he was working with the narco-traffickers he used Michael Collins. Again, they didn't seem to know he was claiming to be one of the founders of the IRA who had died 60 years ago. The Irishman started again to outline the events leading up to the assassination, beginning with the pre-operation briefing, the agreement on what the Hizballahis were supposed to do, and his own job of killing the Lebanese traitor. He could see it wasn't going well with the major and he lowered his eyes, as if to be even more subservient but mostly to keep his eyes on the major's hands and on the gun at the table. Just as he finished his description of buying the car from a Kurdish car thief, he saw the major reach for the pistol. A suppressed pistol fired and filled the room with the smell of gunpowder and blood.

"O'Connell, you did your part today and this Iranian couldn't see that the problem was with his own men."

The Russian mafia contractor walked out of the shadows in the back of the room where he had been standing throughout the interrogation. He was holding a small Beretta pistol with a three-inch suppressor attached. He was unscrewing the suppressor as he came forward. "You are too valuable an asset for us to let him salve his ego by killing you. We only loaned you to him because of our long-standing relationship with the IRGC. It was a business deal. I suspect now our contract is terminated. Don't you?"

The Irishman realized that this had been as close to death as he had been for years. The last time he was this close was when an adversary in the IRA leadership decided to accuse him of treachery. It was at that point he left the IRA and started taking on contracts as a mercenary. Russian organized crime found him training a Libyan assassination team and offered him a permanent contract to work for them. Permanent so far meant lucrative, and today it meant dangerous. He might have to reconsider his options. Still, he nodded and said, "Sasha, I'm certainly glad you were there."

"We take care of our people, Michael. That is what the *siloviki* do. Now, we have to clean this mess and leave. Let the Germans sort out the rest." The two men started to work through the apartment, cleansing the rooms of any sign of their role in the operation and leaving the dead body in the empty room.

A s dead bodies go, the one face down in the marsh was not exceptional. Older man. Slightly overweight. Grey pants. Lightweight nylon jacket. Shoes with worn soles.

Terry Reimer had seen plenty of sad deaths in his years as a patrolman and detective with the Buffalo Police Department before he left the city and joined the village police force in East Aurora. Most resulted from substance abuse mixed with harsh Buffalo weather. Some were due to creeps with guns or knives. No dead body found on a city street was pretty.

In this case, the old man lying next to the boardwalk on Major's Park looked as if he could simply have fallen asleep in the marsh grass. A heart attack? A stroke? It would be up to the local coroner to figure that one out. In the meantime, Reimer had to stand guard until the coroner arrived and confirmed this was not a suspicious death. Reimer looked at his watch and noted the time in his notebook. He wrote: 0625hrs. Arrived on the scene.

Reimer understood the charm of East Aurora. It was green, it was quiet, and it had a tradition of public parks. His patrols in the Buffalo PD had never included any of the various city parks. Instead, he was familiar with the neighborhoods of South Buffalo that were a strange mix of run-down and well-kept houses built in the 1920s and 1930s when Buffalo was a booming industrial town. Industry left and so did the union jobs. Most South Buffalo neighborhoods had yet to see the "gentrification" of other parts of the city. They were a time capsule of what made Buffalo one of the classic stories of a failing "Rust

Belt" city. Overall, the city had recovered and in the 21st century was thriving. Much of South Buffalo had been bypassed by that parade.

Reimer was born in Buffalo. His father was a union man at Bethlehem Steel Company who retired just before the first economic hardship hit the city in the mid-70s. By that time, they were living in West Seneca. Reimer finished high school and went to Erie County Community College, earning an Associate's Degree in criminal science. He joined the Army in 1980 and, in one of the few times he saw the United States Army do the right thing, ended up assigned as a Military Policeman. He spent his first tour as an MP in Germany, reenlisted and became a Special Agent in the Army Criminal Investigative Command. His second assignment wasn't exactly the high-speed job he expected since most of the crimes he investigated were sad, little tales of soldiers doing stupid stuff in Germany. But it did give him more training, kept him in Germany for another few years and delivered a leg up when he left service as a staff sergeant and joined the Buffalo Police Department.

He had a good career in the Department. But one day, after Reimer had passed what was called the "kiss my ass" status making him eligible for retirement, he had a very bad day that made him decide to retire. He was investigating the death of a small child who had been neglected by her parents. The parents were both methamphetamine addicts and didn't notice that their child had wandered out of the house and fallen into the Buffalo River. When the small body washed up two days later, Reimer was the detective assigned to the investigation. It took days to identify the child, and when the parents were notified they seemed not to care at all. It was just too much for Reimer and he grabbed the father with the full intention of beating him to death. Two uniformed officers pulled him off the man before he did any serious harm, but after he closed that case and served as the witness for the prosecution, he pulled the plug on the Department and the city of Buffalo. He moved out to an old farmhouse on a hillside in the township of Aurora.

Six months after retirement, he realized that at 55 he needed a job. He was too young to focus just on hunting and fishing and too poor to live on a pension that had been reduced though a divorce settlement. When pressed by his sister, who lived with her husband in Elma, he admitted he missed being a lawman. She jumped into older-sister mode and offered advice, actually instruction, to get a new job in law enforcement somewhere in the southtown suburbs of Buffalo.

The East Aurora Police Department took him on as a reserve patrol officer. His part time status meant traffic control and serving as a backup School Resource Officer at the high school. It was just the right amount of work and pay. Everyone on the force realized he wasn't competing with them for promotion. And the patrolmen used him as an informal mentor, which allowed them to get smarter without asking stupid questions to the chief. Reimer was more experienced than anyone on the force except the Chief of Police who was a retired New York State Trooper. Both Reimer and the Chief knew it was a good deal for everyone. Of course, that "good deal" also meant that he did many of the duties no one else wanted. That included answering a call on a Sunday morning when a jogger found a body in the park.

Major's Park ran along Cazenovia Creek and was about as pleasant a place to wait as could be expected on an early spring day. It was a favorite of early morning joggers and dog walkers in this town of gardeners, joggers, and dog walkers. The 30-something jogger who found the body was standing by Reimer. He looked cold and just a bit angry that the body had disturbed his run. Very stylish long hair and equally stylish, very short beard. No doubt someone who made his fortune in the city and then retreated to East Aurora on the weekends. Since it was easy enough in East Aurora to find anyone, Reimer jotted down the jogger's statement and contact information and sent him on his way.

When he arrived on the scene, as a matter of habit, he had gloved up with the nitrile gloves from one of the pouches on his duty belt. After releasing the jogger, Reimer checked the body for identification and any sign of foul play. Identification was there, evidence of foul play was not. The man face down in the marsh was carrying his wallet with his New York State drivers' license. Michael A. Polchak.

Date of Birth: March 12, 1943. Residence: 114 Harrison Place. East Aurora, NY. The wallet had $42, two credit cards, a grocery store shoppers' card and a picture of a woman taken sometime in the late 1960s. Wife? Sister?

Well, someone would have to tell the next of kin, and Reimer figured it was going to be him. That was the sort of thing he had done often enough in Buffalo. The general rule of thumb on any patrol was: "Your mess, you handle it." That was especially the case in a small town police force where everyone on the force had something to do every day: covering traffic, handling occasional bar fights, and dealing with the various misdemeanors that happen everywhere there are people. Humans were relatively predictable and villains even more so. Policing a village of 6,000 souls didn't require Sherlock Holmes. It required diligence, experience and caring for people. "To Protect and Serve" is a motto on every police cruiser in America. In East Aurora, it was more than a motto. It was a way of life for every officer, whether in the Police Department, the Sheriff's Department or the nearby State Police barracks.

Once the coroner arrived and took the body away in the ambulance, Reimer's job was done at the park. He was cold from the hour that he had been waiting for their arrival. Another cup of coffee and breakfast at one of the half dozen places in town would be money well spent, but first he had to make the notification to Mr. Polchak's next of kin. Once that was completed and he had sorted out which churchman needed to be called to console the family, he could grab that breakfast. When he got to his old jeep, he pulled off his rubber boots and put on his black trainers. He reached into the back seat of the jeep and pulled out his blaze yellow EAPD jacket with the embroidered badge on the front and POLICE with reflective stripes on the back. Not exactly a spit and polish transformation, but he wanted to look more professional than his jeans, long sleeve polo shirt and sweatshirt offered. No one deserved to receive the news he was going to deliver. The least he could do was not track mud into the house or look like he was just some Joe off the street.

Reimer shut off the "wig-wag" blue and red lights front and back of the jeep and looked again at his notebook. 114 Harrison Street. After eighteen months working in the village, he thought he knew every street in town. Harrison Street wasn't one he knew at all. As the "new, old guy" on the force and as a reserve officer, Reimer was not about to call dispatch and admit he didn't know the town. He pulled out his smartphone, checked the digital map and found the location. Not much more than an alley way running along the railroad tracks on the north side of town, past the old Fisher Price factory and just before Sinking Ponds Park. The other side of town from Major's Park, probably a good three miles of a walk. Quite a distance for a 65-year-old man. It was certainly a puzzle. He wondered if Mr. Polchak had dementia and wandered off and couldn't find his way home. That would be an even sadder story than the one he considered when he first saw the body.

"Dispatch, 2-4. 10-24 at Major's Park. I am going to 114 Harrison to inform next of kin."

"Roger, Terry. I copy you are leaving Major's Park. Coroner and the Ambulance are at the scene, correct?"

"Roger, dispatch. Come and gone. No sign of foul play and I figured I should let the next of kin know before anyone else told them."

"Thanks, Terry. Let us know if you need anything."

"Roger, out."

He started the Jeep and pulled away from the park entrance. On a Sunday, he figured it would take him about five minutes to get across town, another ten minutes to talk to the next of kin, and another ten to log in his report. He should be eating breakfast at Charlie's Diner in less than an hour with his duty belt, firearm and raid jacket back in his sports bag.

When he joined the East Aurora police force, he told the chief he would prefer not to tie up their limited number of vehicles for any on-call dispatches. His jeep was already outfitted with the wig-wag, radio and siren from his days as a detective in Buffalo. It wasn't much to look at, but he knew its quirks and he didn't expect to have to use it in any high-speed pursuits, so, good enough. The Chief agreed and thanked Reimer for understanding that as a reserve officer, he wasn't going to get much in the way of admin support from the department. Badge, credentials, uniforms, radio, and lapel camera were all issued. Everything else, reserve officers had to buy. Reimer reminded the Chief that he had his original duty belt, two pistols and a pump shotgun that he bought as a patrolman in the Buffalo PD. After he qualified with his firearms and signed the paperwork for the rest, it was all good.

Reimer drove along the east side of the old Fisher Price factory heading toward what his GPS said was Harrison Street. As he downshifted to climb a small rise on the street he was waved down by a teenager. Reimer noticed the kid was wearing a bright orange parka and leather hikers that cost more than Reimer's jeep. His jeans had stylish slices in them which made them nearly useless for anything other than strolling down Main Street. Reimer's years on the force in Buffalo told him the young man, perhaps 16 or 17, was high.

Reimer rolled down the window. The young man smelled of beer and marijuana. A long night out on the town. "What can I do for you?"

"Dude, can you give me a ride home? I'm late for church."

Reimer hated being called dude or buddy or anything else that implied he was "just a guy." Still, he was on duty and he figured grabbing the kid by the collar and shaking him until the earring in his ear fell out was probably not the right solution. "Young man, did you notice what I am wearing?"

Glazed, hungover eyes tried to focus. "Hunh?"

"Listen, are you going up this hill or down?"

"Up."

"OK, I will give you a ride until I get to Harrison."

"That's my street."

"Perfect."

The kid walked around the front of the Jeep, opened the passenger door and started to climb in when he finally noticed Reimer's duty belt, sidearm, radio and peeking out from his back, his handcuffs. "Ah…I think I'll walk."

"Too late, genius. Get in. I will take you home." Reimer now noticed the distinct odor of old vomit along with the other blend of smells. He immediately regretted trying to be a good civil servant. "Here's the deal. Don't puke in my jeep and I don't ask any questions about where you were or what you did last night, K?"

The boy nodded and said, "Is this your car or some sort of undercover vehicle?"

"Yes."

Silence from the kid. That was a good start.

"You live on Harrison?"

"Sometimes I stay with my grandmother when my folks are out of town."

"Sometimes you come in late when your folks are out of town."

"Sometimes."

"OK, what's the house number?"

"112 Harrison."

Reimer nodded. This might work out well for both of them.

Two minutes later, he was in front of 112 Harrison. He encouraged his young passenger to get out and go to the front door of his grandmother's house and tell her that he was home and that there was a policeman waiting for her. Reimer suspected this kid normally would sneak in the back door, climb the stairs to his room, and crash until sunset. Not today.

Reimer waited on the front porch of the 1930s house, listening to what was certainly a dressing down by grandma. Eventually, she came to the door. She was in her seventies, grey hair cut short, dressed in a set of sweats and running shoes. She said, "I'm sorry for the delay but I had to give Mickey a piece of my mind. I was headed out for my daily jog, so it was good that you caught me before I disappeared for a half hour. Thank you for giving him a ride home. I hope he isn't in trouble."

"Ma'am, he isn't in any trouble with me, if that's what you are asking. I was driving up here anyhow and he looked like he needed a ride." Reimer figured there was no reason to add to the kid's upcoming confrontation with his grandmother, so he just left it at that.

"Coming up anyway? What brings EA's finest to Harrison Place?"

"I am going to visit the folks at 114 Harrison. The Polchaks."

"Only one person lives at 114 Harrison. Mike Polchak. I haven't seen him this morning, but he is also an early riser and often goes out for a walk."

"Mrs…?"

"Beacher. Hanna Beacher, Officer…?"

"Reimer. Terry Reimer. Mrs. Beacher, I'm sorry to tell you, but I found Mr. Polchak at Major's Park this morning. That's quite a walk from here."

"Major's Park? Nope. That can't be Mike. He has arthritis and doesn't get along all that well. Major's Park. That's an easy five miles round trip, maybe more. Even I won't do that sort of run on a Sunday."

"Mrs. Beacher, Mr. Polchak is dead. I can confirm it is him. Do you know if he has any family here in East Aurora?"

Hanna Beacher paled. After a moment she said, "I'm sorry Officer Reimer. I think the only living thing that cared about Mike was his cat. Oh my goodness, his cat! We need to find his cat." She stepped off the porch and headed to 114 Harrison. She turned back to Reimer and said, "Well, come along. This isn't going to be easy." Reimer nodded. The breakfast at Charlie's was going to have to wait. Terry Reimer: lawman, cat wrangler. Perfect.

Mrs. Beacher had a key to the house, so they went immediately to the front porch. She opened the door, and waiting for them at the entrance that led to the living room was a thin, old Siamese cat. At the sight of Reimer, the cat made a deep throated howl, turned and ran deeper into the house. The windows had thick drapes and the early morning light had yet to penetrate. As Mrs. Beacher followed the cat, attempting polite cat conversation with Natasha, Reimer opened the drapes and looked at the living room. What he saw told him that his breakfast at Charlie's was cancelled.

It was clear that someone had spent more than a few minutes searching the property. Drawers on tables were opened, furniture tipped to show the bottom wooden frames, pillows cut open, and framed pictures, including what appeared to be a number of Russian icons, were pulled off the wall and on the floor. Reimer pulled his sidearm and using his best police officer command voice said "Mrs. Beacher, I need to see you. Please come back."

As she returned to the living room, Hanna Beacher gasped at the sight of Reimer, firearm at a low ready and in a slight crouch. He said, "Mrs. Beacher, someone has been in the house and may still be in the house. I need you to go outside, go home and call 911. Tell them where you are, where I am and tell them there has been a break in. Can you do that?"

The woman put her hands on her hips and said in her most reserved, elementary school teacher voice, "Of course I can, young man. It is not as if this is the first time I've seen trouble."

With that comment, she turned and walked out. Reimer decided there was a story there, but now was not the time to find out. Instead, he proceeded into the rest of the house, past a dining room and a small bathroom also suffering from a search. From the dining room, he could see the small kitchen, with every drawer pulled out and dumped on the floor, as well as a paired staircase. One side up to the second floor and one headed down to the basement. Which to choose first?

The howl from the cat upstairs helped him make the decision. If the cat was still upstairs and annoyed with him, it seemed less likely to have additional perpetrators in residence. He headed down the basement stairs, with his pistol in his right hand and the surefire flashlight from his duty belt in his left. Once he found a light switch, Reimer illuminated the entire basement. It looked like his own farmhouse basement: stone walls, cast iron sink, washer, dryer, water heater and furnace. A small work bench was near the stairs. Every tool and every container of nails, screws and bolts were spilled out. No perpetrator, so it was time to go up the stairs.

He climbed the stairs to the sound of the Siamese cat calling out from the far corners of the second story. Reimer checked the two bedrooms and a small bathroom for an occupant. All he found was more evidence of a search. The cat continued to cry, but he didn't see it anywhere. Finally, he realized the cat was crying from the attic.

How in the world did it get up there? Reimer looked up at the ceilings in each room and couldn't find any hatch or access door to the attic. Finally, he noticed the back wall of a closet, behind old clothes and shoe boxes, had a small hinged door, about four feet by four feet, already opened by the cat.

"Natasha?" Reimer had been confronted by scared house cats as a young Buffalo Police officer, so he knew if he wanted to avoid blood and tears, he would have to slow down and find a way to coax the cat out of the attic. He peeked through the door, and using his flashlight he found both a light switch and a small ladder leading up. "Oh, swell," was all he said as he crawled through the door and started to climb.

Reimer found more than a cat in the attic.

>>>>>> MISSED OPPORTUNITIES

Barbara O'Connell looked around her at the remainder of a spymaster's life. She was surrounded by antiques and four separate file boxes of paper in a small bungalow in Chautauqua, NY. After months of procrastination, she was going through the last of the material existence of Peter O'Connell, World War II veteran, Cold War spy, and the father of Barbara's long-dead husband. While alive, Peter Senior had been polite but distant from Barbara. That was true even as she progressed along an unconventional and dangerous career track at the CIA, much closer to his own adventures than his son's work against Soviet and Russian intelligence services. After working with the OSS, Peter O'Connell, Sr. conducted multiple European operations in the early Cold War as well as paramilitary operations in Laos. After his time in Laos, he served as the Chief of Station in Bangkok, returning to a more conventional career blending tours in headquarters with tours overseas. He ended his career as chief of the Farm. Was he jealous or angry that his son had chosen a more conventional route to target Soviet and eventually Russian spies? Did he blame Barbara for her husband, Peter Jr's death? Did he blame himself for his son's death? After all, Peter Senior managed the Russian program and it was Russian poison that killed her husband in 1999. She would never have all her questions answerede, since it was a Russian assassin's bullet that killed Peter Senior in this house in December 2005.

Peter Senior had always been much closer to his grandchildren than he had ever been to Barbara. He had a house on the Potomac River and regularly hosted both her son Bill and her daughter Sue.

This was while they attended college in Virginia and while Barbara and her husband Peter served their final field tours. Barbara always assumed Sue's choice of an Army special operations career was due to her grandfather's guidance. The same might be said for her son's service in the Marine Corps and now the FBI. Both her children were serving the country, but neither was in the CIA. Well before he died, Peter Senior deeded his Georgetown townhouse to her son and his rambling farmstead on the Potomac River to her daughter. It wasn't until the will was read that Barbara found that she was the owner of his last home on earth, this bungalow on Chautauqua Lake.

It was small. It was a smaller version of her own bungalow south of Chicago. One thing was certain: She would never have been able to afford Chicago lakefront property on her retirement income. Now, she had lake property in New York, a bungalow, and even a vintage wooden ChrisCraft motorboat in a small boathouse. Peter Senior never visited her place in Illinois and they never talked about a mutual interest in the Arts and Crafts design movement. Yet, here she was surrounded by a collection that was a near mirror image of her own. There was a critical exception. In Illinois her furniture was made up of Arts and Crafts replicas. Here, every piece was the real thing. All Roycroft and Stickley furniture of dark wood and brown leather. Roycroft copper and pewter, Tiffany lamps, Rookwood art pottery and dozens of leather-bound books, including English first editions of Russian novels and poetry. It was a side of her father-in-law she had never known. Barbara wondered if this was the Peter O'Connell that existed before the death of his wife, Judith.

Barbara was going through file boxes of paperwork from a closet in an upstairs dormer room. Along with the boxes, there was just enough space for an armchair, a lamp, a small desk and a glass-covered bookcase. The space looked to have been the most used part of the house. Unlike the leather-bound books downstairs, the books in the glass covered bookcase across from her chair included first edition memoirs and histories of special operations in World War II and the early Cold War. Long ago, the closet in the study was used as a small clothes closet. Now it served as the filing cabinet for Peter O'Connell's life. Barbara was sitting in the well-used leather club chair with the boxes of Peter's life. Old tax returns, correspondence with lawyers and stockbrokers, and letters from Agency and military colleagues. Some of the correspondence appeared to be from the Cold War founders of US and British Special Forces. Most were from individuals who Barbara had never known or heard of in her twenty-five year career in the Agency. All of the letters were sorted and held together with rubber bands. To the very end, Peter O'Connell kept his world orderly.

Barbara knew that her father-in-law had built a number of concealments into his Potomac River House. She was certain there were little hiding spots in this bungalow as well. So far, she hadn't found them. When she left her house in Illinois, she called her son and daughter to let them know where she was going. Her son, Bill, serving on a counterintelligence squad in the Washington FBI field office, offered to take leave and help. Barbara thanked him, but wanted to do this herself, if only to get a better understanding of Peter O'Connell, Sr. and, perhaps, her own Peter. Her daughter, Sue, was on another TDY in Afghanistan so it hardly mattered if she knew where Barbara was currently located. That said, Barbara did engage an old contact who was now one of the Agency officers assigned to the SOF headquarters at Ft. Bragg. He promised that once Sue resurfaced, he would to let her know where Barbara was.

Barbara decided to go through the "administrative" side of Peter O'Connell's paperwork first. She reckoned it would be the easiest to sort into piles to toss and piles to keep. After all, old bills and utility contracts were no longer valid. Even some of the Agency retirement paperwork could easily visit an incinerator with no worries. The current box she was working through was filled with exactly this type of paperwork, which she moved from the file box to an empty box, file by tedious file.

At the bottom of the old file box was a crumbling legal envelope addressed to Peter and Barbara O'Connell. As she pulled the envelope out of the box, its seams failed and a letter and what appeared to be an architect's drawing of the house fell out. Barbara opened the letter carefully and read the note in a faded blue/green ink she recognized immediately as her father-in-law's handwriting.

12 June, 1999

Chautauqua, NY

Dear Peter and Barbara,

If you are reading this letter, it means you are going through my effects after my death. I want to start this note by saying how proud I am of both of you and your careers in our Agency. I am now long since out of the picture, but I am sure you are carrying on in a manner that is sure to be far more successful than my own career.

There are many things to say that I didn't say in person. For that I apologize. I hope by now you know that I have done my best to take care of William and Susan while they were in college and to leave a small legacy for them.

Please review the architect's drawings in this envelope. I think you will find more than a few surprises.

With all my love, Dad

Barbara recognized Peter's efforts to reach out in a way quite different from the brusque style that she knew. After years of keeping secrets, perhaps he just never could come out and say how he felt about the family. Either way, the letter offered a curious puzzle with regard to the architect's plan. Barbara set the letter aside and carefully opened the architect's drawing of the Chautauqua bungalow, stretching it out on the floor between the boxes. This was by no means the original plan from 1910. Rather, it was a drawing from 1972 with a notation at the bottom that it was prepared at the request of Peter O'Connell. Attached to the drawing was a second page of what appeared to be a photostatic copy of the original 1910 plans. The blue lines of the original were fading fast, but the 1972 plan was as clear as if it had been drawn in the past month. Barbara looked at the copies side-by-side. She realized the differences right away. She spoke to the ghost of Peter O'Connell, "You old devil. Of course you would build concealments. I just never expected so many or for them to be so large."

Old paperwork would have to wait while Barbara went on a treasure hunt. Just because she knew where to look didn't mean she would find the concealments or, for that matter, be able to open them. Still, it was a great diversion from the dust in the study.

The first concealment was nearby. It was behind a false wall in the closet previously filled with the file boxes. Barbara moved the rest of the boxes out of the space and looked at the seams of what was the apparent back of the closet. Somewhere there would be a small release. It might be a pressure point, it might be a slight opening in the seam that you accessed with a knife, it might be something associated with the left and right walls of the closet. After five minutes of careful study, followed by another minute using her Surefire flashlight, Barbara found the access point. She reached into her purse and pulled out a 3-inch clip knife. Barbara took the thin carbon steel blade and pushed it through the small opening. A satisfying click, followed by the false wall sliding to the left. Barbara used the flashlight to see what was hidden in this space. It was Peter's Chautauqua arsenal.

Set into the original wall of the closet was a narrow gun cabinet. Inside the cabinet were two long guns wrapped in oiled cotton t-shirts and one pistol in its own cotton sleeve. She unwrapped the first t-shirt to find a Swedish K submachine gun. Barbara had fired the Swedish K in training. It was a heavy beast, all milled steel with a folding stock. The gun could fire 9mm bullets at 600 rounds per minute from a twenty-round magazine. Hard to hit much at any distance, but a fearsome weapon in a house. It was used by the Agency paramilitary operators in Southeast Asia in the early 1960s. This one had a heavy barrel with an integrated sound suppressor. Very, very illegal.

Next came a Remington pump shotgun that looked remarkably similar to the Remington 870 that Barbara had seen in the concealed armory that Peter O'Connell kept at the Potomac River House. Finally, she unwrapped a High Standard pistol with a specialized barrel that doubled as a sound suppressor. This was once standard issue for OSS field officers. Barbara had never seen one except in the Agency museum. They were supposed to be destroyed when the OSS was disbanded. Well, this one wasn't. Also in the cabinet were two empty slots for pistols, with an oiled rag balled up in each slot. Barbara remembered that Peter had passed a Colt revolver to Sue before he died. When they responded to the 911 call on the day of Peter's death, the police found him with a Browning High Power in his hand. Sue still had the Colt and the Browning was still in FBI custody since Peter's murder was considered unsolved. On the floor of the gun cabinet were boxes of ammunition, also wrapped in oiled rags, and two stick magazines for the Swedish K. The ammunition included 9mm for the Swedish K and Peter's old Browning, 12-gauge rounds for the Remington, .357 rounds for the missing revolver and .22 caliber hollow-point rounds for the High Standard. While the guns were old, the ammunition was new. He had planned for a gun fight. It was a gun fight that killed him.

Barbara had travelled to WNY in her old Range Rover. The hidden compartment in the Range Rover carried her equally well-travelled arsenal, including a pump shotgun and her Smith and Wesson Model 60 .357 magnum revolver. On arrival in Chautauqua, she transferred the guns to the upstairs bedroom. She didn't need any more weapons, so she returned Peter's guns to their slots and pulled the false wall back in place. After she heard the click telling her she had locked the concealment, she decided that it was probably worth the effort to put some of the boxes back in the closet just to hide the concealment. One down and at least one more to go.

The second location was smaller and even better hidden. In small bungalows, architects couldn't afford dead space. The stairwell to the second story and the stairwell into the basement were located against one of the exterior walls of the house. When you walked down the stairs to the basement, you could see the frame of the stairs going up to the second story. That was true except for the space directly above the entrance to the basement stairs. Barbara saw a small triangle of unfinished ceiling sheetrock approximately the width of the stairs. According to the plans, the second concealment was in this small space. This time it took Barbara the better part of an hour, a step ladder, and a flashlight to identify the latch. It was really nothing more than a hinge in the bottom of the triangle, controlled by a latch release at the top. Once released, the bottom of the triangle dropped to reveal a small metal box fixed with spring clips to the now-horizontal piece of sheetrock. Barbara opened the metal box and found a 3-inch barrel, Colt Commando revolver from World War II, a small bag of gold coins, a World War II era Bulova watch on a worn leather strap, and five leather-bound journals. Barbara wound the watch and it started immediately. She put it on her wrist. After returning the revolver and the gold coins to the box and closing the concealment, Barbara took the journals back upstairs. She looked at the new reading material and said to herself, "This is going to take a pot of tea."

Tea made and back in the study, Barbara looked at the journals. All hand-written. The consistency of the handwriting and the ink argued these were not daily diaries as much as autobiographical notes on specific parts of the old man's career. Perhaps summaries from real diaries? Barbara wondered if those diaries were buried somewhere in the boxes in the closet or in some other concealment in the house. She looked at the journals one at a time. On the front page of each was a title and a date. The first said *Italy-France 1944*. The second said *India, SE Asia 1944-1945*. The third said *Hungary, Berlin 1956-1962*. Number four said *Indochina, Bangkok, Headquarters 1963-1973*. The last one simply said *Family* with no dates. Barbara knew these were the personal and likely secret thoughts of her father-in-law. The administrative filing would have to wait.

Barbara had never been a good history student, even though that had been her major at William and Mary. When asked by her parents if she intended to go on to graduate school in her subject, perhaps at her father's alma mater, she insisted that nothing was more brain killing than working with archival material. Now, she was facing a challenge far greater than archival research on some moment in European history. It would not be brain killing. Given the title of the first journal and her most recent experience the previous year with the Beroslav family and their vendetta against the O'Connells, Barbara knew she had to start there.

She opened the journal to find a date, 1953, and a place, Washington DC. She flipped through the first pages that described Peter's time in the 82nd Airborne and then his OSS training and deployment to Italy. The subjects were interesting and certainly something she would read eventually, but Barbara wanted to know about Beroslav.

After working through a year of his first deployment in Italy, Barbara finally came to a description of his deployment in France. The mission was to ensure that French Resistance fighters supported the allied invasion forces in Southern France. This included building something resembling a coalition effort among the various resistance groups made up of Free French, Communist French, and foreign fighters to harass the German troops while the allied conventional forces made their way off the beaches. Barbara was left with the question: Why spend so much effort writing about these events years after they happened and then not talk about the same events at all to his son or, for that matter, to his daughter-in-law, when they both followed him into the intelligence trade? It wasn't until she got to the end of the journal that she found out why Peter felt he had to capture the events on paper and why he didn't want his son to know.

July 1944, Southern France.

It all starts with the insertion. The smell of aviation gas permeated every-thing inside the plane. I'm traveling with a British officer from the SOE named Clive Barker and a French officer named Francois Broumand and we are crammed into the back of a Lysander aircraft filled with rucksacks, weapons and ammunition. Only a small piece of the pilot's windscreen visible to give any sense of where we were. Mostly, that view was of black night sky. I looked at the luminous dial on my Bulova: 0230hrs. If the pilot briefing was correct, our Jedburgh team named CRANKCASE was on its way to engage with the French resistance near Avignon in support of the invasion of Southern France, OPERATION DRAGOON.

The Jedburghs were new to me. Prior to this, I worked only with other OSS agents from the special operations side of the outfit. We worked with the locals, lived with the locals and generally dressed like the locals. During my time in Italy, sometimes I was the only American living with the Partisans. Now, we were serving as the representatives of the three allies, pathfinders for the invasion. We Jedburghs were in country to show the resistance that the allied armies were on their way and to encourage the resistance to attack specific, strategic targets to assist the conventional campaign.

I hadn't been in a Lysander before. It was far better than my other insertions: A parachute jump through a troop door in a Dakota into Sicily or through a hole in the bottom of a Liberator aircraft known as the Joe Hole. For security reasons, we weren't allowed to tell the crew our names, so all of us were "Joe." The Lysander had long range, though long range at a slow speed. It could land on farm fields. Our aircraft had seen some hours in combat. The control cables that ran along the length of the aircraft were dripping grease. I thought I could see through the skin of the aircraft where either machine gun fire or shrapnel had cut the fuselage. The plane smelled of oil and sweat. The sweat was from me and my two colleagues on the Jedburgh team.

We landed with a bounce, the pilot feathered the prop while hitting the right wheel brake. One final skid and a 180 degree spin and then all movement stopped. He turned back to us and said with a smile, "All present and correct?" A dozen men approached in the dark. In the dark, they looked almost exactly like my memory of Wyeth illustrations of Stevenson's Treasure Island. Not so different from the Italian partisans I had worked with before, though certainly less exuberant. The largest of these pirates grabbed me, hugged me, and kissed me on both cheeks.

Barbara closed the journal for a moment and thought about what she had heard from her husband Peter about his father. He knew that his father was first a paratrooper and then in the OSS Special Operations. If he knew his father was in Italy and France during the war, he never told Barbara. She thought he had spent the entire war in Asia. Reading the journal was going to remind her of opportunities lost with both Peter Senior and her husband. She would never have a chance to grow old with her husband and now all she had of her father-in-law was his written word. The tea was cold and the room was dark as the sun set over the lake. It was time to make some dinner and have a glass of wine before she returned to the story of Jedburgh CRANKCASE.

Over a dinner of pasta, fresh bread and a glass of red wine, Barbara thought about the journals and Peter O'Connell. Her introduction to Peter Senior had been just after she and Peter had graduated from the CIA Farm. Her image of him was as a taciturn loner in a dark suit and a severe, 1950s haircut. He didn't spend much time with either his son or with Barbara when they were first married. Their CIA foreign field tours prevented any consistent contact except for the annual home leave broken up by a few days in Headquarters. Always a few days at the Potomac River House where Peter Senior "held court." The talk around the table during these visits focused on their operations and never on whatever he was doing for the Agency. Once Barbara asked how his work was progressing. His response was curt. "It's just fine. Thanks." Now she was reading his story in his own words.

After dinner, Barbara cleaned the kitchen, poured another glass of wine, and headed back upstairs to the study and the journals. Unlike a novel, Barbara already thought she knew the end of the story, so she couldn't help herself and decided to flip the pages until she found something, anything, that talked about Beroslav. It showed up near the end of the journal and Barbara had to backtrack a bit to make any sense of the tale.

14 August 1944 Southern France

Ten years after this night, I still have nightmares. Clive and I were going to drop the only two bridges in the region that could hold heavy vehicles. Previous resistance attacks were designed to move the Germans away from the bridges. If they were gone, the German response to DRAGOON would be limited to whatever force was available on the day of the operation. Tanks, tank destroyers, half-tracks and virtually any wheeled vehicles would have to stay north of the canal and by the time alternative routes were available, it would be too late.

We finished working on the second bridge and were walking back to our rucksack cache with nearly an hour to spare and less than a kilometer back to the RV. Barker went down like he was punched in the jaw. I heard him say, "Mate, I'm shot." I dropped and crawled over to Barker to render first aid.

We both heard the slow approach. A hunter's stalking approach. Careful, slow and deliberate. Another bullet passed near my head, another silent round. I heard the crack as it went by, but not the shot. A suppressor? Germans didn't need to use suppressed weapons. So who? I remember Clive looking at me as I puzzled over this. He whispered, "Will you go kill him for goodness sake?"

I rolled on my left side and pulled out the High Standard .22 fitted with the silencer. Another round cracked through the space between me and Barker. I pulled the slide and put the pistol into battery. First, I had to find the bastard. Clive decided to help.

As a new bullet fired, Clive shouted, "You bastard. You blew his brains out."

"That was the idea, Britisher. Now I will come to make sure you are done as well." Out of the darkness, I finally saw a man in an all-black camouflage suit appear briefly against the shadows of the trees.

Clive continued to do his part, "What are you waiting for, froggy? Come visit me."

"I am no Frenchman, you fool."

"German then…"

The sniper appeared convinced I was dead. He started to walk toward his kill shot. He brought the rifle up to his cheek and said, "Wrong again, Britisher. Soviet Special Services. I am here to ensure our French communists win after the Germans leave. You and your dead friends were in the way."

The suppressed round smacked into the skull with no more sound than a dart hitting a dart board. It was the first time I had ever killed a man at close range. I over-reacted by firing two more rounds into his back and then kicking him over and firing another into his face to be sure. It wasn't pretty.

Barbara flipped through another few pages outlining the days before and after DRAGOON and Barker and Peter's return to England. Finally, she found what she was looking for in his writings about his debriefings in England. She noted the last paragraph was in the same handwriting but different ink with a new date.

20-22 September 1944, debriefing in England

The first debriefing on 20 September had gone as well as could be expected. OSS and SOE debriefers focused on our operations in advance of DRA-GOON. Both headquarters were pleased with the results. After that, we were confronted by two men from counterintelligence. Kim Philby and James Jesus Angleton. They accused us of making up the story of the assassin and of working for the Soviets. At that point, I pulled out the identify card of the Soviet assassin named Boris Nicolai Beroslav. I will never forget the name and never forget what was left of his face after I killed him. Anyhow, delivering the ID card shut them up. But Angleton didn't like it and he definitely didn't like me.

Barbara noted the change of ink that followed. It was clear that Peter Senior had added the next piece well after his initial effort to capture his memories of World War II.

Addendum – February 1963

I've had more than one confrontation with Angleton since. He says I have an Irish cousin working for the IRA and that means I must be a traitor. I have no Irish cousin, so he's wrong about that. But, after all I have done, he is still hounding me and has put me on a watch list that is keeping me from the field. I just found out, the real irony in this is Philby was a spy for the Soviets. He must have reported me to the Soviets.

They never forgot that I had taken out one of their own and disrupted their operation in Southern France. I'm not certain they would have controlled a post-war France, but at the time the communists were the best organized resistance in the area. If Beroslav had been alive to continue guiding the program and killing those in the way, who knows? That OSS operation in Southern France created more tragedy in my life than I could ever have expected. I always thought it was because I was working the Soviet target. Now, I know I am the target of the Soviets. Did they kill Judith?

It took Barbara a while to digest the tale. She had always considered Peter's obsession with the Russians as something that was not entirely rational. When she heard that the KGB used that obsession to guide him into creating the LABYRINTH double-agent operation that ended with her most recent contact with the Beroslav family in Greece, she felt sorry for Peter but still didn't believe there was much to the obsession. It hadn't made sense until now. The vendetta started in a forest in southern France. Barbara knew it ended in 2006 on a ship in Black Sea when Russian commandos killed Anastasia Beroslav and when, shortly afterwards, the Russian penetration of the CIA was arrested due to the work of her daughter and an old colleague named Mary Sanderson. Peter Senior was killed in this house because of the vendetta, and her husband was poisoned because of events in 1944. Personal tragedies generated by superpower conflicts.

When Sue O'Connell had heard that her unit, the Special Operations Forces Humint Intelligence Collection Unit (SOF/HICU) was moving its headquarters from Ft. Bragg to a warehouse facility at Camp Ederle in northern Italy, she knew she would have to close up her condo at Ft. Bragg, put it up for rent, and split her household effects into two shipments. One shipment would be moved to Italy, courtesy of the US Army. She chose to pack up the rest of her belongings and move them to what she still considered her grandfather's house on the Potomac River. When he died, the house became Sue's. Now, she was driving a yellow Penske van of books, a few clothes, and personal memorabilia to the house. The boxes would fill one room in the house, but at least they would be safe, sound and not stuck in a self-storage lot in Fayetteville.

After her last mission in Afghanistan and arrival at Camp Ederle, her commander, Colonel Jedediah Smith, authorized her 30 days leave to get admin issues, known as PCS or permanent change of station paperwork, accomplished at Ft. Bragg before returning to Italy. During her last week at Ederle, the SOF/HICU established its cover office in a warehouse area on the same road as the parachute-packing shed used by the 173rd Airborne Brigade. At this new location, the fenced compound had a small sign reading "Regional Support Logistics Unit." When Sue arrived at the headquarters, she found everyone pronouncing their cover office name as "Real Sue." It wasn't funny the first time and it became less funny every time Massoni, Marconi, or any of the "brain trust" analysts used the term.

Sue was more than happy to catch a military hop aircraft from

Ederle to Ft. Bragg and start her PCS paperwork, hoping the joke would wear itself out by the time she returned. On arrival in Fayetteville, Sue called her mom to tell her she was back in the US. Her previous email exchange with Barbara on her return to Europe had been cryptic at best. Reference to "family business" came up several times, but with the caveat that they could only talk about these unspecified issues when they were face to face. Previous discussions of family business had included a Russian vendetta against the family, double agent operations, and the murder of both her father and grandfather. Sue was in no hurry to explore the next chapter in this saga. There would be no avoiding the discussion because Barbara planned to be waiting at the Potomac River House when Sue arrived.

The good news was that her brother Bill had taken leave from his work at the Washington Field Office of the FBI to help with the loading, driving and unloading. The last time they had anything resembling a conversation, Bill was recovering from a shoulder wound from an assassin hired by a Russian double agent working inside the CIA. Her focus at the time was his health and recovery. This time, they would have hours together on the highway to shout over the roar of the Penske truck. As they headed north, Sue opened the conversation by asking, "So, life better now that you are on the foreign counterintelligence side of the Bureau rather than serving on the Gang Task Force?"

Bill shook his head, "I liked the work on the Gang Task Force and I really liked my boss. Of course, once a guy saves your life from a gunshot wound, ya kinda have to like him, no?"

Sue paused to think over her response. Did she want to reveal to Bill her most recent adventure rescuing the man who saved her life in Afghanistan? Well, why not? "I spent the last month rescuing the man who saved my life, though not my leg. Yup, it is kinda hard not to like him."

"Love interest?" Bill said with a smirk, knowing the answer.

"Hardly. He is just shy of mom's age. More like the best uncle you could imagine."

"So, time for an adventure story, no?"

Sue nodded and began the story of the kidnapping of Bill Jameson, the fact that he was then auctioned off to Nicolai Beroslav, the man she thought had died in Cyprus. This former Russian special operations officer and now mafia smuggler hoped to use Jameson to trade for his defection. Sue closed with the story of the gunfight in a 2,000-year-old monastery in Pakistan, where the Russian died and Jameson survived.

Nearly an hour later, Bill said, "Uh, Sis. You ever realize that your life is more than a little complex?"

"Really, I never noticed. Now, how about you? Remember, you are the one who had an assassin's bullet lodged in your shoulder." Sue shifted the conversation as Bill responded with a rude finger. "OK, so what sort of counterintelligence work are you doing? Remember, I have the clearance tickets so 'need-to-know' won't let you avoid my questions."

"It's more complicated than I expected. As the new guy in the various CI squads in DC, I'm not involved in the Russia stuff. That's only for the more experienced foreign counterintelligence or FCI guys who have been working the target for years. After a series of classes at Quantico, I was assigned to the Iranian target. In one sense, it's harder because they don't have a diplomatic mission. On the other hand, they tend to pal up with the Lebanese Hizballah types in the area. That's good news 'cause those Hizballah guys are basically crooks at heart. They self-fund through crime. Extortion. Smuggling. Car theft. Whatever. I'm more comfortable on the Iran squad than I would be anyplace else because the vast majority of the informants we have are villains and we have leverage over them. Not so different from the gang-squad work. What surprised me was the Iranians have two services just like the Russians: one civilian, one military. The military guys are killers, so that makes it all worthwhile."

Sue nodded and said, "When I was in Cyprus, my focus was on Iranian efforts to help the Iraqi Shia militias who were killing our troops. The Iranians were all Revolutionary Guards."

"Those are the guys. They have the deepest contacts with the Hizballah anyhow because they have been helping since the creation of Hizballah in Lebanon nearly before we were out of elementary school."

"I think Mom did her share of work against those guys back in her day."

"Always amazing to me that I never knew her dangerous life."

"Wait until you see her handle firearms. You will definitely be a believer."

They pulled over at a rest stop and changed drivers. Bill took over and Sue had a chance to relax her left leg and its prosthetic by moving the seat forward and angling the seat back so she could relieve some of the tension on her back. After a quick stop to get fast food at Bill's insistence, they continued the drive.

After another twenty minutes of silence, Bill said, "Sue, you have anybody you're seeing? Man? Woman? I'm not judging, just asking."

"Nope. And just 'cause I'm not man crazy, that doesn't mean I play both sides. I just haven't been able to get serious since I lost my left leg. I haven't been able to get my head around how to explain the missing part." Sue smiled in an attempt to make the comment appear more comic that she felt it to be. While she might have grown used to the scar tissue just below her left knee, she wasn't looking forward to the first time she showed it to a man she was dating. "Plus, the reality is that when I'm downrange, it is all adrenaline all the time. It is exciting, it is focused, and there isn't much time to do anything but work, work out, eat and sleep. I hate to say it, but it is when I feel most alive."

Bill said, "I certainly remember the time downrange in the Corps. As strange as it sounds, it is a beautiful, simple, distilled life. Just down to the minimums. A single duffle bag of field kit. Weapons to maintain. Focusing on my guys' health and welfare. Planning the next op. I liked it and hated it at the same time. You have to hate it, especially when your guys are killed in combat."

Sue nodded, "Exactly. When a rotation is finished, you fly back to CONUS. You are exhausted. You are thrilled to be back home. Then, long before leave is up, you miss being back in the fight. You miss the guys. You miss the adrenaline. Just like you said, you miss the simplicity. I don't know what will happen when I won't have a warzone deployment. Will I fit into something resembling a normal life? Is that when I will find a guy? The only men I know are inside the SOF community. The quickest way to get tossed out is to start playing house inside the community. It just doesn't work right now. I would rather be as celibate as a nun than lose my job. It's who I am as well as what I do."

"Roger. Just wanted to know. I'm trying to sort out how I'm going to date Molly Norton. She's the duty relief in the Gang Task Force, former Texas cop, and good people. It's just hard to find the time. Work seems like 24/7/365. It's hard to find time for coffee, much less dinner."

"But you can take time to drive me to the Potomac River."

"That's different. We haven't had much of a chance to talk over the last couple of years and I'm happy to take the time. Plus, I reckon it doesn't hurt to have an armed driver."

"Who said I wasn't armed?"

"Sue, I hope you are at least street legal here in Virginia."

"Umm, maybe. But we aren't going north of Quantico and you can vouch for me, no?"

Bill shook his head. "O'Connell women are seriously dangerous."

"Count on it."

Command Sergeant Major Jim Massoni walked over to a bay of computers where five analysts sat facing multiple screens glowing with a mix of green and blue light. As the senior enlisted man in the HUMINT detachment, he spent as much time as he could focusing on the day-to-day lives of his people. Years in the Special Operations Force (SOF) world, starting as a young Green Beret, then a member of the Ranger Regiment, then the Surveillance and Reconnaissance Squadron, had convinced him that the tactical analysts were some of the most important but certainly the most neglected in the community. They were also the most introverted, so he had to be careful on how he approached them. To an outside observer, his approach might have appeared more as stalking than simply walking over to his analytic team.

Sarah Billings, known to the staff as Flash, was the sole female analyst. She had short jet black hair, was wearing black t-shirt, black sweatpants, and black high-top sneakers. She spun her chair around when Massoni reached ten feet from the analysts. "Jim, when are you going to learn that we installed a camera looking back toward your office so you can't sneak up on us?" Flash was not an introverted analyst. Flash was a great linguist and equally adept at complex analysis and sniper rifle operation.

Massoni frowned and said, "I suppose it is hard wired to your gizmos so I can't just unplug it?"

"No dice, Sergeant Major. We aren't telling."

"OK, Flash. For now, you need to come with me. The boss wants to talk."

Flash stood up, came to the position of attention and said, "Yes, Sergeant Major."

"Give it a rest, Flash."

They walked down the length of the RLSU spaces toward the office of their commander, Colonel Jedediah Smith. In the original Warehouse 171 spaces, Smith and Massoni shared a space identified only by a bare wood frame and sheetrock. In the new space, Smith had his own office separate from Massoni. Early on at Camp Ederle, Massoni pointed out to the crew that now that he had real walls in his real office, he could do real wall-to-wall counseling if required. Nobody on the team wanted to find out what wall-to-wall counseling looked like from a sergeant major from the Ranger Regiment. Massoni knocked on the half-opened door at Smith's office. Smith responded, "Enter."

While Jed Smith rarely demonstrated a commitment to Army protocol, one thing Massoni and Flash knew was you did not take a seat in the boss's office unless invited. They did get the invitation with a simple greeting from Smith, "Get in here and sit down."

As was his usual way of doing things, Smith started without preamble or any social greetings. "We finally got some take from Bragg on the data we collected from Beroslav's concealment. He was one serious character when it came to keeping electronic files. He probably thought it would save his life."

Flash was with Smith, Massoni and Sue O'Connell when Nicolai Beroslav was shot in the back by a Russian sniper. She said, "It didn't work for that cat, Boss."

Smith looked up. He was never sure if Flash was just wicked smart and didn't care for normal military protocol or if, like Massoni, she liked to pull his chain. Over time, he had accepted that Flash was Flash and nothing he said, good or bad, was going to make a difference. He definitely intended to keep Flash on his team as long as he was in command.

He offered a flat response. "That was certainly true. It looks like he gifted us critical information on the nexus between Russian paramilitary contractors and the Iranian Revolutionary Guards. They are using a set of Afghan smugglers to deliver heavy weapons to both the Taliban and to their Shia adversaries in Central Afghanistan. He also had evidence that the Rev Guards are getting high-end Russian and Chinese electronics as payment for their part of the deal."

"Hence, why you are here, Flash." Massoni wanted to cut to the chase before Flash offered her advanced assessment of the Russians, the Iranians, the Taliban or modern electronics. She could go on and on to the annoyance of Smith.

"Check, Sergeant Major."

"So, Flash, it looks like another trip to Afghanistan. You able to break free for a brief trip to Mazar-e-Sharif?"

"Boss, I have a couple of reports from Cyprus, but once those are done, I don't think I have any intelligence coming in from our folks in Beirut or Akrotiri for a month. After that, I better be back in my seat. But…," Flash paused to see if Smith was willing to take a question. Since his countenance didn't change from his normal angry self, she figure it was worth asking. "Boss, why isn't Pluto going to northern Afghanistan? He's our Afghan guru."

Smith shook his head, "I think the setup could be as much as two weeks, not counting travel time, and I can't spare Pluto for that long. You know as well as I do he is our guy when it comes to the nexus between the Taliban and Al Qaida. Right now, the guys in Jalalabad and Khowst are tracking a series of new sources and he is their brain trust. You are used to working with O'Connell and she's going to be the handler for this project. Check?"

Flash nodded.

Massoni chimed in, "You can catch a cargo flight to Bagram. After that, you are going to Mazar-e-Sharif on an OGA bird. It might even be approaching spring by the time you get there, so you won't have to pack your woolies."

Flash knew that OGA or "other government agency" meant a CIA aircraft. It wasn't really some secret code. Everyone in the SOF community knew that if you said OGA or referred to "the Klingons" you were talking about their CIA partners. Perhaps it might even mean another chance to spend some time with her favorite Klingon,

Jamie Schenk. "Thanks, Sergeant Major. Just when I was thinking my first spring in Italy would be flowers and cafes, you are telling me I'm going back to a war zone and mountains. Perfect."

"Think of it as an opportunity to excel."

Smith was used to this sort of back and forth between Massoni and his team, but it did wear him out. He said, "Jim, get Flash up to speed and get her down range by 15 May. I will contact O'Connell and tell her that her 30 day leave has been compressed. I will have SOF headquarters make those arrangements. Clear?"

Massoni was already out the door headed into the RLSU bay. He said over his shoulder, "Check, Boss. We are on it."

"**N**ow, Mom. Let me get this straight. You are a bodyguard for defectors? And you are doing it out of Grampa's house in New York?" Bill O'Connell was always perplexed at the intelligence side of his family history. He was especially puzzled that his mom was still in the game. This newest revelation came over a perfect lunch made by his mother and set at the table in the dining room overlooking the Potomac River.

"Bill, it's not bodyguard work. For the last few years, I have been helping debrief emigres and defectors once they are relocated in the US. Of course, if they get into trouble, I try to help. Basically, it is a simple mission. Establish contact when they arrive, debrief them if it makes sense, and help them if there is any trouble. I did this in Chicago and now I'm doing the same sort of work in western New York."

"Is this like Micah in Chicago?" Sue had met one of her mother's former assets in December 2005 when Sue and her mother were on the run from a Russian hit team. Micah was an Iranian Kurd who was exfiltrated out of Iran, relocated to the US, and now ran a small deli near Barbara's residence near Chicago. Sue met Micah when his restaurant served as a temporary safe house as they sorted out their options.

"Well, Micah was one of my cases when I lived in Illinois. Now that I'm moving into your grandfather's place in Chautauqua, I will be taking responsibility for western New York and western Pennsylvania. Basically, Buffalo and Pittsburgh. In fact, the reason I'm taking this job is because it was your grandfather's responsibility until he was killed." Barbara turned to her son and said, "If an 80-year-old

World War II veteran can do the job, you have to know it isn't about car chases and gun fights."

Bill was still baffled. His personality was tuned to hard facts and straightforward missions. It had made him an excellent Marine platoon commander and an even better FBI Special Agent. The ambiguities of espionage annoyed him, plenty. "So, you do…what?"

Barbara O'Connell was used to Bill's perspective and realized part of the problem was he had never really understood what his mother did for the CIA. She said, "We are called the Safe Keepers. The name is appropriate because that is what we do. First, we debrief individuals when they arrive in the States. If, and only if, they have some trouble with the law or, if there is any trouble from their former country, we are responsible for keeping our cases safe from the time of the threat until Agency resources can be brought on board to get them out of trouble. I think of the work as something like an insurance agent. I meet with my small number of clients in the region so that they know who I am. I make it clear what we can and can't do. Then, if there is a compromise focused on one of my clients, I work with the Agency to move the client and, possibly his or her immediate family, to a safe location I have already identified. After that, we wait until another part of the Agency or the FBI handles the admin side of the program for a new, permanent home."

Sue O'Connell was more used to her mother's style of telling but not telling a story. She could imagine how it must be adding to Bill's confusion rather than making it easier for him to understand. She decided to intervene, "Bill, Mom debriefs the emigres and defectors and will use her tradecraft skills in an emergency to get a family from wherever they are living to a safe house. She makes them disappear and then the Agency provides them with another identity. And, if there is trouble, they call in the FBI. Get it?"

Bill nodded. He didn't like it, but he was beginning to understand. "So, this is an Agency WITSEC? Why not just put them in WITSEC?"

Sue was shaking her head. Barbara could see that her daughter was about to say something she would regret. Instead, she entered the sibling fray, "The US Marshal Witness Security Program is structured with very clear, very legal restrictions on who can and should be in the program. As it is, the marshals have more than enough problems to handle. Further, our former assets do not have the legal status for WITSEC. They never were and never will be witnesses in any trial. This is more about a moral obligation rather than a legal one."

"So, the Agency does this because it needs to, or because it has to?"

"It is a relatively new mission that it has to do. In the old days of the Cold War, there was an unspoken rule between hostile services that you didn't conduct kidnappings or assassinations in the enemy homeland. Both sides accepted there would be traitors and defectors. That changed some years ago and now we face threats even in the US. Rare, but still possible."

"I guess I understand the concept. Are you working with the field offices in Buffalo and Pittsburgh?" Sue smiled as she heard her brother ask the question. He had become a true blue FBI agent. Jurisdiction and turf were two things that were central to the successes of the FBI. Turf battles were also central to potential conflicts between services and between law enforcement organizations throughout the US.

Barbara answered, "I have met the folks in Buffalo. I haven't made a face-to-face linkup with the Pittsburgh office. I reckon I will make that my first stop when I go down to meet my…clients."

Bill nodded and said, "If you need any contact info, please let me know."

Sue laughed and she could see that laugh had hurt Bill's feelings. "Bill, I'm not laughing at you, but I'm just imagining how many contacts Mom has in the Bureau at this point. I suspect she has a couple of SACs in her contacts list."

Barbara decided to sooth her son's ego. "Actually, I could use a focal point inside the FCI squad in Pittsburgh. Let me know as soon as you get back to DC, OK?"

"Will do, Mom."

They spent the rest of the weekend unpacking Sue's boxes and putting them in the various upstairs rooms that would serve as temporary storage until she returned to an assignment in the US. None of them knew when that would be, so they carefully unpacked the Fayetteville boxes and then repacked them in larger foot lockers and standing cabinets. The majority of the boxes were books from Sue's time in college and her early assignments in the Army. Text books, books covering regions where she had worked, and novels used to pass the time while "downrange." The bookcases were hardly filled with her books when the boxes were empty. A complete contrast to the collection of beautifully bound books that her grandfather left her along with the house.

Barbara was pleased to see that neither Sue nor Bill had focused on the fact that the last time she had been in the house, in 2006, she and Max Creeter had been fighting for their lives. That attack at the Potomac River House resulted in the death of Max Creeter, SOF legend, family friend and, briefly, Barbara's new lover. Afterwards, the Agency "cleaners" had come through to manage the relationship with the FBI and local law enforcement. They went through recovering the bodies and the equipment left after the firefight. When that was completed, Barbara worked with Agency-cleared contractors to harden the Potomac River House again with alarms, steel doors and bulletproof windows. She found a local housekeeper who would make sure the house was always ready when one of the family came to call. The housekeeper's husband, a retired Navy Petty Officer from Naval Special Warfare, was hired as the groundskeeper just to make sure the house didn't look abandoned. The word got out in the community that the house was guarded by a thoroughly dangerous man. Basically, the Potomac River House would serve as the safe house for the O'Connell family whenever it was needed. No bullet holes in the plaster or signs of broken window frames from the fight. It was Sue's house without any reminders.

Monday arrived and Barbara and Bill said farewell. Barbara would drive Bill back to DC and then head north on US15 until she hit the New York State border. After that, she would head west back to the Chautauqua House. There was plenty of room in the Range Rover for Bill's kit and her overnight case. After mid-morning breakfast, they headed North on I-95 hoping to make it to DC between the morning rush hour – bad – and the afternoon rush hour – worse.

Sue was left in the house and began to explore, again, the various nooks and crannies and special modifications that her grandfather had made. She ended up in the basement where, behind a false wall, her grandfather had his "ops center" including an ancient desktop computer and equally ancient printer. Against one wall was a file cabinet filled with heaven only knows what since he emptied some of his files before leaving for Chautauqua.Against the other wall, a gun cabinet had held some of his collection. Sue walked up to the cabinet and returned a Colt Python to what appeared to have been its home in the past. The last time Sue saw her grandfather, he gave her the revolver as a gift. It had served as her home defense weapon in Fayetteville and traveled north with her in a deep concealment holster on her hip. Now, it would return to its position in the cabinet and stay there until Sue returned…home.

Sue realized for the first time that she had begun to see the Potomac River House as her home. Her past and future assignments were intervals, distractions or just temporary places to stay. The last time she had called anyplace "home" was when she lived with her parents in Reston after they moved back from one of their many overseas assignments. Both she and Bill had the good fortune to finish high school in Virginia and spend time in a three-bedroom house in a DC suburb. Sue thought about what a home might be like when she decided to retire from the Army. Would she be single at that point? Would she do contract work like her mother? As she sat down in a large leather chair that faced the concealment door to think about this new perspective, her phone rang. The caller ID on the screen said "No ID" which could mean only one thing to Sue: It was SOF headquarters reaching out. She answered.

The voice on the other end said: "Chief O'Connell?"

"Who is calling, please?" The Warehouse 171 team was more than a little security conscious after the last two years of operations. Sue knew that just because the person on the other end knew her name didn't mean that person wasn't a hostile.

"75778." The caller was providing the daily operational code that SOF headquarters sent to Sue via her SOF email account.

"Yes?"

"Chief, this is Master Sergeant Baker. Your leave has been cancelled. You need to get back to your unit as soon as you can get there by commercial air. It must be serious because the orders say first class authorized if necessary."

Sue remembered Baker from her return to SOF after her injury and the rehabilitation to get her used to her prosthetic leg. He worked in the SOF personnel shop, the J1, and was another wounded warrior still in the fight. He had served as her jumpmaster on her first parachute jump after losing her leg. It was a no-equipment drop, known as a "Hollywood" jump, out of a Blackhawk on Sicily DZ, probably the largest sandbox in NC. A perfect way to return to the fight. For a moment, Sue's inside voice crept out and she said "Shit."

The voice at the other end of the line said, "Chief, that's what I thought as well. Anyhow, I'm sure you have everything you need to RTB, so I'm going to leave it to you to get there. Check?"

"Check, Master Sergeant. I am on it. Thanks."

"Out here." The line went dead and Sue closed up the office, secured the concealment so that the wine racks covered the door, and started up the stairs. Sue was pondering the caveat of first-class travel authorized for a return to base. Administratively that translated into a Jim Massoni Ranger acronym, "RFN" meaning get back to Ederle "right fucking now."

>>>>>> A HOME AWAY FROM HOME

11 May 2007. Camp Marmal, Mazar-e-Sharif airfield
FOB Hairatan, Balkh Province

Sue O'Connell stepped off the ramp of the German Air Force C-160 Transall and onto the hot tarmac of Mazar-e-Sharif airfield. She was wearing her "cargo aircraft uniform," a sage green flight suit with no unit markings and modified jungle boots that looked like normal boots but fit the prosthetic on her left foot like a glove. She had her nylon duty belt with drop holster, and was carrying in her left hand a long gun case for her M4 carbine and in her right hand a nylon kit bag with three sets of clothing and her body armor. Over her shoulder was a nylon aviator's helmet bag that served as her field briefcase. It carried two Moleskine notebooks, an Army-issued mechanical pencil and pen, a paperback to read on the flight, her RLSU issued satellite phone, a computer tablet, and all the annoying wires and connectors to make things work. As she walked away from the noise and the smell of the Transall's turbine engines, she smiled and thought to herself that she was carrying everything a modern woman needs on vacation in a war zone. As she walked toward the airfield tower and base operations, a tan four-door Ford Ranger pickup pulled up. The driver's door opened and Flash got out.

"Took your time, Sue."

"Hey, Flash. Nice to see you as well."

"Yup. Always nice to see the Flash. Throw your kit into the back and we'll head out of here to our home away from home. By the way, pull your M4 out of its case. This isn't as much of a resort as it appears."

"And I was considering talking to a real estate agent about condos here in the north."

"Yeah, well, it turns out property values aren't what they used to be. Let's go before the German Air Force police realize that I'm on the tarmac. I didn't want you to have to walk through the base looking for me, so I found a gate manned by a less-than-diligent Afghan."

"Nice." Sue opened the right rear door of the armored vehicle, threw in her kit bag and the aviator's helmet bag, pulled out the M4, and joined Flash in the front. Before she had closed her door, Flash had put the pickup in gear and was rolling along the taxiway toward a side gate. The heavy armored door slammed shut.

Sue was surprised as they headed east from the airfield. "I thought Camp Mike Spann was west of the city."

"It is."

"I take it we are not going to the U.S. Camp."

"Correct."

"Are we going someplace special?"

"Very."

"Are you going to tell me where we are going?"

"Nope. Just relax and listen to some tunes." Flash turned on the CD player in the vehicle. The exterior noise of the pickup truck was minimized by the vehicle armor but it was still very loud. Flash shook her head and turned the CD player up even louder.

At that point, Sue said, "Is this a copy of Jamie's CD? I hated it in Iraq, why should I like it in Afghanistan?"

"Because it is the only music we have since this is Jamie's truck."

"I suppose we are going to another Jamie safe house?"

"And the guys at Real Sue say you aren't a trained observer."

"I hate that name."

Flash smiled and said, "I know."

They drove east for an hour and then turned on a better paved road heading north. As soon as they turned north, they joined convoys of heavy truck traffic heading north and passed truck convoys heading south. As they accelerated on the better road, Sue said, "Are we headed toward Termez?"

"See, if I told you up front we were going to the border, it would have spoiled the surprise."

"Jamie has a safe house on the border?"

"The better to find, fix and finish bad guys, don't you think?"

"OK, so you are going to punish me because you have been here a week without me?"

"Yup."

"Didn't Jamie keep you company?"

"Up to a point."

"Up to a point?"

"Up to the point when he didn't."

Sue decided that she wasn't going to get much out of Flash between the mix of the engine noise and the rock music from the 1970s and 1980s. She decided to focus on the terrain. Sue couldn't remember if this was her fifth, sixth or seventh TDY in Afghanistan. They all seemed to run together. For certain this was only the second time she had been here since she lost part of her left leg in a gunfight in Jalalabad. All of her previous trips to the country had been either in river valleys or over mountains separating river valleys. After her flight over the Hindu Kush and the approach to Mazar-e-Sharif on the German Air Force aircraft, it was hard to imagine that anyplace in Afghanistan could be as flat as this terrain. Sue was neither a geographer nor a geologist, but she suspected that this terrain must be a geologic feature related to the natural gas deposits the Soviets developed in Northern Afghanistan in the 1960s and 1970s. The terrain looked like pictures she had seen of the Arabian Peninsula, except colder and higher.

After an hour following convoys, they turned off the main highway and bounced along a dirt track for five minutes before arriving at a sand-colored walled compound on a slight rise overlooking on the Afghan border town of Hairatan and its Uzbek sister city on the opposite side of the Amu Darya, Termez. The bridge over the Amu

Darya was just visible, as was the truck traffic passing through customs checkpoints on both sides of the bridge. As they approached the compound, Flash grabbed the radio microphone and said, "Sesame. I say again, sesame." The double gates of the compound opened and they entered without breaking speed until they reached a set of Hesco blast walls.

Sue turned to Flash and said, "Sesame. Really?"

"Hey, I didn't make this up. It was their code before I got here."

"Special."

Two well-armed, bearded Americans approached the truck. They checked the underside of the Ranger with mirrors, checked in the engine compartment and finally opened the two rear doors of the four door truck. One of the men said, "Flash, welcome back. I suppose this is Superwoman?"

"Yup. MIKE4 in the flesh."

He held out a gloved hand and said, "Chief, welcome to Trail's End."

Sue took his hand and said, "I hope you mean that literally and not figuratively."

"We all hope so. Anyhow, that's what the boss calls it, so that's what it's called."

"The boss?"

From the other rear door, a familiar face, shaved head, mustache and white teeth poked his head into the vehicle. "You called?"

Sue said, "Since when do you get to run operations with Americans?"

"Since you ruined my operations in the Konar."

"It wasn't my fault."

Jamie Schenk turned to his colleagues and said, "She always says that."

Flash said to Sue, "I keep telling him that it wasn't your fault, but he holds a grudge."

Sue looked at Jamie and said, "You don't really blame us for the loss of the compound do you?"

"Yes, I do. But, it meant they moved me to another garden spot and this time, I get to work with Tajiks and Uzbeks as well as my Hazara folks. Kind people. Very sociable and happy-go-lucky, right Davey?"

The bearded officer nodded and said, "Happy-go-lucky as long as they get paid and we don't ask them to work together."

Jamie nodded and said, "Not so different from you and not so different from me."

Sue had to admit, her previous experience with OGA forward operating bases contrasted with US military FOBs. Military bases were usually dusty, temporary affairs of large green tents and smaller green tents that served as shower and toilet facilities. HESCO barriers and barbed wire surrounded the tents. Once they were through the security checkpoint and entered into this compound, the Agency facility looked more or less like what she imagined a warlord might use as his home away from home. A large, brown two story house with a dozen antennas sticking up from the flat roof. The dirt yard was surrounded by 10-foot-high brown walls reinforced on the inside by Hesco Blast walls. No guard towers and no barbed wire. Three other Ford Rangers were parked in a row, with room for the Ranger Flash was driving and two more slots for "guests." Behind the parking lot were a series of solar panels and a large diesel generator inside a separate building to mask the sound. There was even a small vegetable and rose garden irrigated by water captured from the roofline. So far, hardly impressive, but certainly more permanent than the military FOB's.

Entering into the building changed her perspective. The rooms had a second set of modern walls built on top of the local adobe brick, and the floor was a raised platform off the original foundation. Air conditioned, of course, and with real lighting. Flash took her up the stairs to their quarters. The second floor had a total of eight bedrooms with two beds per room and four shared bathrooms. Not exactly a five-star hotel in Europe, but the rooms didn't look like anything you would expect downrange. More like a hotel along some US interstate.

Flash watched as Sue looked around. She said, "Yup, I thought Jamie's digs in the Konar were pretty nice, but these are seriously nice. There is even a gym downstairs as well as the SCIF. You look at the outside and you see a smuggler's nest. You live inside and you think, hey, this isn't so bad a TDY. Of course, we have to cook our own food which means you can have any microwave dinner that you like. Still, it's nice. Plus, for the last week, I have been surrounded by five American men who are not inside the SOF community. So, sooner or later these guys are going to rotate out and I'm hoping for a linkup somewhere in Italy."

"Flash, you are one piece of work. Here we are in the middle of a war zone and you are working the crowd to find the next man in your love life."

"Hey, a girl has to have a hobby."

"OK, I'm going to get rid of two days worth of body *schmutzig* and change into whatever duty uniform is appropriate here. Any recommendations other than the standard Flash black?"

"Black is always appropriate, but most of the guys are wearing jeans and t-shirts when they are inside the compound."

"Check. See you in 20."

"Roger, Roger," Flash said over her shoulder as she left.

The sensitive compartments information facility or SCIF was a box inside a box inside the building. It was a steel framed fiberglass space with banks of computers, three plasma screens, a plexiglass "whiteboard" filled with notations, and a detailed map. At the end of the room, a six-foot-long work table covered with note papers and ground photography. Sue walked into the space that was alive with energy and some excitement.

Jamie was the first to greet her. He was wearing a pair of black high-top sneakers, tan nylon gym shorts known in the SOF community as "Ranger panties" and what looked like a homemade green T-shirt that said "Special Feces." It was the first time Sue had seen Jamie's bare legs. His left leg was covered with a long scar from just below his knee to mid-thigh. The calf on his right leg had a star-shaped scar that could only be from a bullet wound. She wondered for a moment what Jim Massoni's legs would look like if she ever saw him in shorts. Probably much the same.

"So, I'm asking you up front to let me live here in peace this time. In Iraq, we got blown up. In the Konar, our compound was destroyed by mortars and helicopter gunships. This is by far the nicest place I've had downrange since I joined the Agency and I would like to finish the rest of this rotation in this nice place. Do we have a deal?"

Sue could see he was joking, mostly. All she could think to say was, "I will do my best."

"Oh, thanks, O'Connell. I understand that may mean we face Armageddon here. I will tell my team to prepare accordingly."

"So, Jamie, now that you've finished with your welcome, can you please tell me why I'm here. I am supposed to be on my PCS leave."

"Hey, Sue, you have to ask Flash. I'm just the landlord here and doing my best with six guys to destroy the Taliban and Al Qaida infrastructure in four provinces. Flash and your crew in Italy sent you here. Not that it isn't nice to see you." He turned to the SCIF and said in a parade ground voice, "Isn't it nice to see O'Connell, guys."

The four men in the SCIF said in sarcastic unison, "Yes, Boss. It's great to see O'Connell."

"See what I mean? Where else are you going to get this sort of enthusiastic welcome?"

"An al Qaida detention center?"

"Cruel, but accurate. So, I'm going to leave you to Flash. Coffee and tea are brewing in the corner and the fridge has a bunch of bottled water, iced tea and sodas. We don't serve hors d'oeuvres inside the SCIF. Actually, we don't serve them at all. Food is in the kitchen when you are hungry."

"Thanks. By the way, what's with the shaved head?"

"It makes it easier to wear a turban when I go out to enjoy my people in Hairaton. I am considered quite a well-dressed and well-groomed man on those mean streets."

One of the other SCIF members said, "Yeah. You should see him driving down the streets in his 60s Cadillac convertible."

Jamie offered a hurt face, "Cadillacs are a sign of sophistication. I heard that somewhere from someone. I had one for a while, but Kabul heard about it. Now, I'm forced to drive in an up-armored Ford Ranger. My guess is the word is out that when we worked together in Iraq, I was blown up."

"I told you, that wasn't my fault."

"Sure."

Sue decided she had played the punching bag for long enough and walked over to Flash who was sitting in front of three plasma screens, working two keyboards and listening to heaven only knows what on her Bose headphones. She saw Sue approach in the reflection of one of her screens, turned her chair to face Sue and pulled down her headphones. She said, "Get tired of the Jamie show?"

"Kinda like the Massoni show. Do you think it's part of Special Forces indoctrination?"

"Could be. I dated an SF medic one time and..."

"Let's not go there, K?"

Flash stuck out her tongue and then said, "So, you want to know why you are here?"

Sue smiled what she hoped was her most sincere smile, "That would be nice, thank you."

"OK. So, if you remember Nicolai Beroslav..."

"I don't need to go that far back, Flash." Sue remembered the Nicolai Beroslav that shut her in the trunk of a car filled with explosives in Cyprus as well as the Nicolai Beroslav who died in Pakistan as he was trying to defect to the US. None of these were good memories.

"It took the big brains back at Bragg and at OGA to decipher the data he had in his watch. He kept track of the entire smuggling network that he ran from its origins in Russia in the town of Merv, through the Uzbek corridor to Afghanistan and Iran. People, places and what equipment went where. Probably the most important data for the gurus in CONUS were his descriptions of the financial transfers between Russian oligarchs and Iranian Rev Guard leaders. Everyone made money along the way. He documented it all for the last year. For our purposes, he also had a list of his primary smuggling contacts on both sides of the Amu Darya. If we are going to track and eventually disrupt the gun running, we need to get these guys to start working for us. Of course, when I say we, I really mean you."

"I'm going to recruit Afghan and Uzbek smugglers?"

"And why not? You speak the lingo. You are an agent handler. So, use the magic they taught you at the Farm and make it happen."

"And why is this our mission and not the OGA mission?"

Flash said, "Well, I asked Jamie that and…"

Jamie stepped in and said, "Mention my name and I appear like magic."

Jamie was standing behind Sue when he said this. Sue spun around and accidently but gently shot an elbow toward Jamie's groin. He dodged, just in time. Sue said, "Oh, sorry."

"I offer you a roof over your head and this is how I get treated. Seriously, the Commanding General of SOF said he wanted a SOF intel presence as we developed the targets. My COS says what we all know: What the CG wants, the CG gets."

"And he sent me?"

Flash said, "Really? You think the CG tracks the mighty O'Connell's work? No, Jed Smith sent you because you know the case and our guys south of the Hindu Kush are hunting different bad guys."

Sue decided to surrender and get to work. "Any idea how to get started?"

This time is was Jamie who said, "So Flash and I think the best way to do this…"

>>>>>> DEAD SOULS

Barbara was eating breakfast oatmeal when her mobile phone rang. The screen on the phone said "No Caller ID." There were several possible reasons for this. It might be Sue calling from a satellite phone or from some SOF headquarters building. It could be Bill calling from his FBI offices. It could be the Agency. It could also be a sophisticated telemarketer. The only way she would know for sure was to answer, so she answered using the last four digits of her telephone number. "6793."

"Nice to hear from you too, sister." Mary Sanderson's voice was unmistakable even through the digital speaker.

"Sorry, dear. I wasn't sure who might be calling at 7am."

"Well, it is me and that's because I need your help."

"Mary, you know I am a mere, wretched federal pensioner."

"Who is still on the books as a contractor."

"Only as a debriefer for defectors. And the Agency hasn't asked me to do that for a while."

"You have been busy with your own operations in the US and Europe, but we won't go over that ground again. Let's just say we really need your assistance on another program. In CONUS and near your new digs in westernNew York."

"Who said I have moved to western New York?"

"Your realtor, dear. You have your place in Chicago up for sale. Once I realized you were moving to western New York, I wanted to get in touch. I've been trying to track you down for about a week. I didn't really want to just call up, but I finally decided if I was going to find you, the best way was to find out where your phone was located."

"You geo-located my phone?"

"National requirements, dear."

Barbara was peeved that Mary had tracked her phone. Still, given Mary's new senior job in the Counterintelligence Center and Barbara's agreement nearly thirty years ago to allow government surveillance forever, including work and personal life, it was certainly legal if not polite. She said, "So, what are those requirements exactly?"

"Can you drive up to East Aurora to meet me?"

"When?"

"Wednesday would be nice."

"I am trying to clean up Peter's dad's house so I can live on a lake in my dotage. I wouldn't mind a small diversion. I can drive up on Wednesday. Where?"

"I will send you some directions to another location. 1000hrs?"

"See you when I see you."

"Ciao bella."

16 May 2007, Hairatan, Balkh Province. Afghanistan

It took some time to get the necessary agreements from all the players in northern Afghanistan. Eventually, the US military command known as RC NORTH, US SOF leadership, and Britain's UKSF Task Force leadership in country, and the station in Kabul agreed: Jamie and Sue could start a surveillance operation on two of the Afghan smugglers identified by the Beroslav intelligence. After they got the approval, Jamie and Sue worked out the resources needed and sent the requirement up their respective chains of command. US SOF resources assigned to RC NORTH area of responsibility were stretched thin. There was one company of US Special Forces working across multiple provinces in the AOR. Sue was familiar with the program of Village Stability Operations or VSO based on the operations in the Konar. SF teams worked with village and district governments to defend against the Taliban. The alternative offered was a section of UK Special Forces from the Special Boat Service. UKSF operations were primarily focused in Helmand in the southwest of the country, but their teams rotated in and out of Helmand from a UKSF base of operations in Bagram airfield.

Based on Jamie's request, the Chief of Station in Kabul offered to send a 10-man team of Hazara tribals known as the Tomahawks from the Konar, trained by Jamie. They would serve as close security for any operations on the street. Suddenly, their operation went from bare bones to an abundance of riches. They would be able to house the UKSF operators inside the compound and Jamie had a separate safe house in Hairatan, really little more than a warehouse, for the

Tomahawks. He would have to acquire transportation for the Tomahawks, but that wouldn't be too much trouble in a town of smugglers.

When the UKSF team arrived in two sand-colored Land Rover Defenders and the gates to compound closed, the Brits unloaded their gear and walked up to Jamie and Sue. It only took a minute for Sue to realize she knew the four-man team walking toward her.

"George, what in the world are you doing in Afghanistan? I thought you were in Basra."

"Sue, it's good to see you too." After hugging Sue, George turned to Jamie and said, "Mate, you do know she is a bullet magnet."

"Brother, you don't know the half of it. Anyhow, welcome to our little bit of paradise on the Afghan plain. I'm Jamie. You've already met Jerry and Don at the gate. Dave, Mitch, Keith and Terry are inside. Terry is our commo guy so he may be your first stop. We have rooms upstairs. Take any open beds."

"Jamie, the fact that you have rooms and beds and not cots in an aircraft hangar, we are already in dreamland."

As George and his team headed inside, Sue caught the arm of the largest of the SBS team. She said, "Dozer, it's great to see you. Where's Paddy?"

"He isn't with us any more Sue. Killed in an ambush in Basra. Just four of us now, George, Brian, Mac and me."

"Dozer, I'm sorry."

"Me too." Sue let Dozer continue to head into the house.

Jamie said to Sue, "I hope we find something good, because our bosses are really giving us no excuse if we don't."

Sue nodded. "No foolin.' The UK forces down south are in a serious fight, so we have to be a high priority if they released any SBS operators to play up here. The real good news is that I know George's guys are both shooters and surveillance guys, so we will be safe."

"Until we aren't," was all Jamie said over his shoulder as he walked back into the house.

B arbara O'Connell arrived in East Aurora after receiving the directions from Mary Sanderson. This was followed by a contact at the Buffalo Field Office of the FBI, Special Agent Ellen Jones. As she drove up from Chautauqua, she wondered why she was instructed to support an FBI investigation. What Barbara could do in an FBI investigation was not in the least bit clear, but Mary wanted an Agency officer on the ground as soon as possible. Since Barbara was nearby, she was Mary's choice.

Mary said, "Keep the fires burning there for another day and I'll be working the case. Please." Barbara was unwilling to argue. This was the first time she was asked to help Mary since they uncovered the GRU penetration of the Agency nearly a year ago. Just in case there was no real work to be accomplished, she brought the last of Peter O'Connell's notebooks focused on his time running a team of Soviet double-agent operations. That team had included her husband. It was one notebook Barbara hadn't opened. Her concern was that the notebook would reveal more about her husband's death than she wanted to know.

She pulled up in front of the East Aurora Village Hall, parked her aged Range Rover on a side street near the Boys and Girls Club and walked into the hall. A sign inside the entrance directed her to the Police Department. It was 1000hrs exactly, so she was right on time for what was supposed to be a meeting with Jones and a local police officer to talk about heaven only knew what. Barbara hoped this would be simply a courtesy meeting that would give her enough time to get back to Chautauqua and avoid a night in a hotel. Just in case, she had packed her overnight bag.

As she walked into the small office, she saw Special Agent Jones and a uniformed officer sharing coffee at the large coffee maker. Barbara had met Jones when she did a courtesy call on the Buffalo FBI Field Office. The Special Agent in Charge tasked Jones to be Barbara's point of contact for anything Barbara might do in Buffalo. Barbara suspected Jones saw the tasking as yet another crummy job for a new Special Agent: handling some federal pensioner who would do nothing but cause more paperwork.

Jones was a young, fit woman who didn't fit any standard plan for FBI agents. In the initial introductions, Barbara realized that in the entire history of the FBI, only in a post 9/11 FBI under Director Mueller would Jones have been accepted as a Special Agent. She had a Masters in Criminal Justice from the State University of New York at Albany and a PhD in organic chemistry. In the FBI before 9/11, at best she would have been an FBI forensic scientist working in the labs at Quantico. Instead, she was a Special Agent with a scientific background. She must have been a dedicated runner. She was whip thin, with long black hair pulled into a pony tail. Adding to her persona as an outsider inside the FBI, Jones dressed in what could easily be considered high fashion and not the standard special agent uniform: navy blue pantsuit, white silk shirt, black leather flats, a men's Omega watch. One thing was certain about that fashion: She didn't buy those items on a special agent's salary. Obviously, there was money somewhere in the family. Barbara did notice that Jones had her clothes tailored after she joined the Bureau. Her Glock pistol was not visible under her suit jacket.

Barbara wondered what it must have been like for Jones going through the Academy with men like her son and trained by men who might still have pictures of J. Edgar Hoover on their desk. The only saving grace would have been the commitment to reform by Director Mueller and his seniors. Over a glass of wine in Old Town Alexandria in 2006, Barbara compared the CIA and FBI glass ceilings with her old friend Janice Macintosh. When they talked, Janice had been the squad supervisor for the FBI FCI office in DC and her son's senior supervisor. In March 2007, she was promoted and became a section chief in FBI headquarters supervising Russian cases across all the field offices of the FBI. Barbara heard from Mary Sanderson that by 2008, Janice would be offered either a job as a Special Agent in Charge in one of the 56 FBI Field offices or as the Legal Attaché in one of the many FBI offices abroad. Janice was definitely on the fast track.

Janice's descriptions of fighting to succeed in the FBI in the 1990s matched Barbara's own experiences in the CIA in the 1980s. The difference was that Barbara's demonstrated skills on the street and her language skills resulted in successful terrorist cases. That sort of success in the Agency meant promotion. The system was forced to accept her. Janice said the FBI didn't accept her as a skilled agent until she volunteered for the Dallas field office's SWAT team and passed selection, leaving half of the male applicants in her dust. Based on this background, Barbara knew that, for now, Special Agent Jones was going to have to accept whatever cases were assigned to her. And, those cases were going to be strange and probably less-than-critical ones. Those assignments might simply be a way of teaching her the lesson of how to be a team player.

After Barbara shook hands with the FBI agent, Jones said, "This is the Chief of Police, Marty Benzinger. He is going to sit in on our meeting with the police officer who is handling the case."

The Chief was in his summer uniform, white short-sleeved duty shirt, navy trousers, highly shined black shoes. He looked to be a very fit man in his late 50s or early 60s. He shook Barbara's hand with a grip that was neither too hard nor too soft. He was used to working with professional women and he looked Barbara right in the eyes as he said, "My pleasure, Mrs. O'Connell. Welcome to East Aurora."

"Thanks. It is my first time in your village."

"But not the first time an O'Connell has visited. I met your daughter my first day on the job. She was in the Roycroft when we arrested Mary Sanderson after she assaulted your daughter."

"Chief, sometime in the future, I will have to tell you the rest of the story. For now, let's just say, like most Agency stories, it is complicated. I will let Mary explain some of the story when she arrives tomorrow."

The chief looked puzzled but kept his sense of humor by saying, "We can return to the scene of that crime anytime you like. The Roycroft has a terrific restaurant and I would be happy to host you both. Just name a day and a time. Meanwhile, Terry is waiting in our little conference room that doubles as the file room and the copy machine room. He has set up the case files for you."

They followed the chief down the hall to a room which was slightly larger than a closet but certainly smaller than any conference room Barbara had used since she returned from the foreign field. Waiting in the room was Terry Reimer, also dressed in a summer uniform, leaning over a small conference table and three folders each marked with a serial number and labeled *POLCHAK, Michael. 05 May 2007.* Barbara was surprised to find Reimer across the table. She said, "Terry, the last time I saw you, you were chasing a Libyan down a German street."

Reimer looked up and said, "Chief, if you told me yesterday that I had to work with Barbara O'Connell again, I would have taken a week of unpaid leave."

Both Benzinger and Jones were confused by this exchange. Barbara explained. "In the early 1990s, I was working in Germany on a number of terrorist cases. This is just after the Wall came down and Germany was still going through the challenges of unification. The US military was the major US player in Germany and most of my cases were coordinated through the Germans and the Army. Army CI and the Army Criminal Investigation Division were not always the best of friends and neither one liked the Agency. My work almost always made me a visitor in someone else's jurisdiction, and that meant lots of coordination. Terry was my CID focal point. "

"I'm not going to point out that I left Germany and military service shortly after meeting Barbara O'Connell."

Barbara raised her hands in surrender, "Not my fault. Well, not entirely my fault."

Terry nodded, "Not her fault, but take it from me, working with the Klingons is not career enhancing in the US Army."

Jones said, "Klingons?"

"You know, Klingons from Star Trek. Cloaking devices? Just like the cloaks and daggers favored by Barbara's outfit."

"Old outfit, Terry. I'm retired. Well, mostly retired."

"Uh huh, and that is why you are involved in this case. Because you are...mostly retired?"

Benzinger decided it was time to gently show who was boss, so he said, "Folks, it's always great to see old friends have a reunion, but I think we need to spend some time looking at the case and sorting out how we solve this murder."

Barbara said, "Murder?"

Reimer responded, "We didn't think it was murder until we had a coroner's report. We just thought the geezer's death was either a heart attack or a stroke. Then we thought it was related to the break-in at his house. Now, it is clear he was murdered, most probably in his house, and then transported to the park. Some sort of exotic poison according to the coroner. Open the file and let's get going on this case."

Reimer's briefing lasted just over a half hour. First, crime scene photos from Major's Park where they found Polchak and then photos from his house. Details from the Buffalo County Coroner and follow up reporting from both the FBI and the Department of Homeland Security analysts on the chemical compound used to kill Polchak. He had been killed by lethal injection from an alkaloid agent based on a plant toxin, gelsemium. The analysts said it was a close relative to strychnine and in the proper doses had medicinal use as a cardiac depressant. Reimer said if the coroner hadn't noticed the injection site, he would have assumed Polchak died of a heart attack.

Finally, Reimer showed them another photo which made all the other details of the case seem even more improbable. The label of the photo said "114 Harrison, attic." It showed the normal beams and joists you would expect from an attic, but at one end of the space was a complex antenna. The antenna cable ran to a small platform in the attic where there was a metal frame and a car battery. Reimer said, "I asked our local ham radio guys and they said it was clearly a radio rig for sending and receiving HF radio messages. The metal frame would have held a radio transmitter/receiver and the car battery would provide the power for the rig. The local amateur radio operators said the antenna was directional and pointed to Canada. They use omni-directional antennas because they want to talk to the world. Polchak used this antenna to talk to someone in Ontario."

Reimer and Benzinger turned to Jones, expecting her to offer an answer. In her previous meeting with Jones and her SAC, Barbara noted Jones was more than willing to demonstrate to anyone who would listen that she was the smartest person in the room. Not an endearing trait for a young agent, but Barbara assumed that, sooner or later, Jones would realize that the law enforcement was a team sport. More likely than not, she would learn that lesson well before she finished her tour in Buffalo. If not, she would be encouraged to leave the FBI. Jones said, "Back in the Cold War, the Soviets ran some of their US agents out of their consulate in Toronto. They weren't supposed to travel outside the Toronto city limits any more than the Soviets based at the UN were supposed to travel outside Manhattan, but they could and did break free from surveillance both here and in Canada."

Reimer was the first one to respond. "A spy?"

Jones raised her right hand to say stop. Again, Barbara wondered how long it would before Jones realized that this was not polite, especially with lawmen. She said, "Gentlemen, Vasily Andropovich, also known as Michael Polchak, was a Soviet military intelligence officer from the GRU. He defected to the CIA in Vienna, Austria in 1988. He was repatriated to the US and worked with the FBI on multiple cases in New York City in the 1990s. He disappeared in New York in 1995. He was listed as presumed dead, most probably murdered by the Russian mafia since he was helping us in organized crime. Until your report, which included fingerprints, was sent to the FBI, we had no idea Andropovich was living under the assumed name of Polchak or, for that matter, alive at all. The real question now is what was he doing here for the last twelve years and what was he doing with an HF radio?"

Barbara turned to Jones and said, "Well, you definitely have a case now. What I don't know is why I am involved."

Jones turned to Barbara and said, "I have the answer to your question. Your headquarters and my headquarters want you involved. I suspect you know, that's really all it takes."

Barbara said, "I guess that means we are going to have to wait until Mary arrives to tell us what is going on in DC and how this case has become both a murder and a counterintelligence case."

Benzinger turned to Barbara and said, "So, that means a dinner at the Roycroft?"

She said, "I think it also means I need a room for the next couple of days."

Reimer said, "We can get you a room at the Roycroft Inn. Perhaps we can even review the scene of the last O'Connell crime."

Barbara said, "I told you it was complicated."

Benzinger said, "We have all evening."

The Roycroft Inn was everything that Sue said. An Arts and Crafts gem carefully and lovingly restored to its heyday at the beginning of the 20th century. Beautiful furniture and oriental carpets, with murals on the walls framed by dark wood paneling. As Chief of Police, Benzinger had a bit of influence at the Inn and he had no problem getting Barbara a room that evening. The Inn was in the center of the village and Terry Reimer volunteered to take Barbara on a walking tour. They walked along streets named after old trees that created a canopy stretching over the streets. Oakwood, Sycamore, Walnut, Willow. He showed Barbara the oldest houses, including a house built by President Millard Fillmore, a church with the largest surviving collection of sacred Tiffany stained glass windows, and a series of parks that provided green space inside the village limits.

They returned to the hotel in time for Barbara to shower and change into a new set of clothes and join Reimer and Benzinger for dinner. They had dinner al fresco along an extended porch known by the architectural feature name of the Peristyle. Late afternoon light was filtered through the trees on the quiet street. It was one of the better "work" meetings Barbara had in years. But, as she expected, it was work and she was going to be debriefed whether she liked it or not.

Terry started first, "Barbara, what are you doing in Chautauqua? The last time I heard from you, you and your husband were returning to Reston and going to work in Headquarters."

"Years ago, Terry. Years and miles ago." Barbara hadn't been forced to describe her life story for a while. She decided to offer the short and highly edited version of the tale. "We returned to headquarters with two kids: one son and one daughter. They went to college and shortly after 9/11, my husband died of cancer. I retired. My kids went to war. My son served as a Marine in Iraq. My daughter in the Army in Afghanistan. My son got out and is in the FBI. My daughter stayed in and is based in Italy. Marty Benzinger had spent more than his share of time listening to half-truths and outright lies as a New York State Police patrolman, so he could see they weren't going to get too much out of Barbara O'Connell, at least not right away. He decided to change tack and asked, "Did you say Mary Sanderson was coming up tomorrow from Washington? The same Sanderson we arrested in December 2005?"

"Marty, I mentioned Agency stories can get a little complicated."

Reimer interjected, "Hold onto your wallet Marty, she's about to pick your pocket."

Barbara smiled and said, "Seriously, the story is about as byzantine as it gets even by Agency standards. None of us knew at the time that Mary was under deep cover working as a double agent. The confrontation with Sue was part of that cover operation. In the long run, courtesy of Mary and Sue's work, we identified a real Russian spy working inside the Agency. Mary was brought in from the cold, as the spy books say. She is now a senior in counterintelligence in

DC. I kinda work for her on another project associated with handling emigres and defectors. I still don't know why I'm here on this murder case. My cases are all living emigres and defectors trying to make a new life in western New York and western Pennsylvania."

Benzinger asked the question that both he and Reimer wanted answered, "Any more spies in our life in East Aurora?"

Barbara laughed, "Marty, I didn't know anything about Polchak until this morning. I can tell you for certain that none of my cases live in East Aurora. They live in Buffalo and in Rochester."

Reimer said, "Marty, now you know why I left CID. I hate these sorts of cases."

Barbara nodded and said, "Terry, you sound like my son. He hates this sort of stuff."

Benzinger said, "He sounds like a good Marine and a good lawman."

16 May 2007, East Aurora, NY

Barbara woke early, and just as the sun was coming up she went for a run retracing her steps from her walking tour with Reimer. The meeting with the two East Aurora policemen went as well as could be expected given the fact that she still didn't know why she was involved in any of this. It was certainly a joint case between the FBI and the local police department, but why the CIA was involved and, more importantly, why she was involved remained a mystery.

Once again, they held the meeting in the police department conference room. This time, Jones was accompanied by her squad supervisor, Nate Chason. He was definitely what Barbara expected to see. He was a fit 50-year-old, greying hair cut very short, navy blue suit, white shirt, red and white striped tie. She noticed he was wearing a large, gold Marine Corps ring. She wondered how well Special Agent Jones enjoyed working with a man who might still have a picture of J. Edgar Hoover in his office. Still, looks can be deceiving and during their brief introduction, Barbara found out that Chason served as an assistant legal attaché in Poland right after the end of the Cold War, spoke Polish, and had been in the counterintelligence world for nearly a decade. As Barbara said to him later, "So, not just a pretty face."

Chason laughed and said, "Well, they do keep me around for press releases and photographers, but only when I am helping to arrest spies and terrorists."

Mary Sanderson arrived a half hour later and listened to the next set of briefings from Benzinger and Reimer. After the East Aurora police finished their review, Chason tried, unsuccessfully it turned out, to explain how Andropovich had dropped out of sight in New York and reappeared with full documentation as Michael Polchak. Jones added a detailed description of the FBI review of the antenna system in Polchak's house on Harrison Street. That included a discussion of capability including range and, possibly, data transmission. It seemed clear the Andropovich/Polchak story had more questions than answers.

Mary opened her briefing by saying, "I have been working with Janice Macintosh, who is the FBI section chief focused on Russian operations in the United States. What I am offering is a joint FBI-CIA assessment of this case. Most of what you are going to hear is conjecture. We honestly don't have any more data than what you offered this morning. What we might be able to provide is context." She paused to see if anyone wanted to speak.

When they didn't, Mary continued, "First, we believe Andropovich was a legitimate defector when he arrived in the States and when he first worked with the FBI. However, we think sometime before he disappeared in 1995, he was approached by the Russian services and given a choice: return to work for Russian intelligence or die. Both the Agency and the FBI had a series of defectors in 1996 and 1997 who talked about the GRU reviving what they referred to as "dead souls." At that time, both services assumed these were sleeper agents who had been in place in the US and Canada for decades. While we can't say for sure, it looks like Andropovich was one of those dead souls. The FBI is still trying to sort out that part of the story, but as you might imagine, after twelve years that trail is very cold."

Mary stopped to take a sip from the coffee offered by Benzinger and said, "What we can say for sure is that the FBI folks at Quantico and our tech folks at Agency headquarters are certain that the Polchak documents are excellent forgeries. They are consistent with the work of the Russian secret services and, most especially, of the current Russian counterintelligence service, the Federal Security Service or the FSB. The analysts are still working on the documents, but if that is the case, then the GRU or the FSB decided to send Andropovich to western New York to serve in some intelligence capacity. And, when that mission, whatever it was, was completed, they killed him."

Reimer said, "What sort of missions could he have had here?"

Chason interjected, "western New York has always been a center for high tech industries and especially for avionics and missile systems. Plus, the Niagara River provides power to a good chunk of the East Coast. If the Russians had or have sources in these industries, Polchak might have served as a deep cover principle agent allowing the Russians to get the information without ever meeting their sources. I realize it is a big if, but that's what we think is the likely explanation."

Reimer said, "And, they killed him after he worked for them for twelve years?"

Jones decided to add, "It seems hardly logical to do so after all of this time."

Barbara said, "Sadly, the story is not so hard to believe. First, when he defected in 1988, he was considered a traitor. Forever. Treason for a GRU officer means a death sentence. If they told him in 1995 that he could work his way out of that sentence and he believed them, he was delusional. Secondly, it is entirely possible that this case was handled not by the GRU or the FSB but by some cutout like the Russian mob. If that is the case, at some point they decided he was too old or too troublesome to keep. And, they probably didn't want him to be able to reveal any information on their people or their tradecraft."

Jones seemed unconvinced and said, "Doesn't that seem like something out of spy novels rather than the logic of an intelligence operation? No offense, but you have been out of the game for a while. This isn't the Cold War anymore and this certainly isn't Berlin."

Mary could see that Chason might do something rash if Jones decided to say anything more. Instead of allowing her FBI supervisor to engage in what might turn out to be verbal "wall-to-wall counseling" inside the East Aurora Police Department, she looked at Jones and said, "Special Agent Jones, I think you need to take my word that Barbara O'Connell knows precisely what she is talking about and is very familiar with the current tactics of both the FSB and Russian organized crime."

Jones seemed ready to enter into the debate based on her understanding of the current activities of Russia in the US when Chason said, while looking at Jones, "I know some of this background and I can say for sure the Bureau agrees with your comments and Mrs. O'Connell's assessment."

In an effort to reduce the tension in the room and change the subject slightly, Barbara asked Mary, "So, why am I involved in this at all?"

Mary said, "Barbara, you are involved in this because Janice thinks and I agree that the likely murder suspect for this is a contract killer who travels under a number of aliases and may have been involved in the murder of a CIA asset in 1994. Barbara, we think it was your asset killed in Bad Homburg."

Barbara took a deep breath as she sank in her chair. She hadn't thought about that case in years. The Germans never found the assassin. They arrested the Lebanese men who drove the van over her asset, and convicted them of reckless driving and manslaughter. They never found the driver of the car that killed *BREAKDREAM*. What they did find, two days later, was a dead Iranian who was identified as a Revolutionary Guard officer. Dead, with a bullet in his brain. As far as the German services were concerned, case closed. Barbara and the Agency never gave up on the hunt for the killer, but there were no leads. She looked at Mary and said, "Are you sure?"

"Well, our search back in the 1990s identified a man traveling on an Irish passport under the name Brian Delaney. He left Frankfurt the same day as the attack and flew to Vienna. He travelled on a Lufthansa flight sitting next to a Russian passport holder. Perhaps not proof, but certainly suspicious. A cold case from 1994, but we believe Delaney has been a foot soldier for the Russians for years. Delaney crossed over the Peace Bridge into Canada the same day as Andropovich's murder."

Barbara sank further in her chair. She had seen more than her share of tragedies and heard more than her share of counterintelligence twists in over twenty-five years in the Agency and another five years as a semi-retired Agency officer. She had focused much of the last year hunting and being hunted by the Beroslav mafia family. Still, the information Mary showed them was probably the most disturbing.

Mary pulled out a file from the National Counterintelligence Executive which was the most senior counterintelligence organization managed by the Director of National Intelligence. She read from the file, "Brian Boru Delaney. Additional alias names include Brian Patrick Kelly, William Kelly, and Sean O'Reilly. Passport data from each of the aliases has a date of birth of 10 September 1956 and a place of birth as Dublin, Ireland. British intelligence reporting has him suspected of being the son of some senior member of what the British called an IRA Active Service Unit operating in Northern Ireland during the troubles. We don't know much about Delaney until the late 1980s, when he is identified as an IRA enforcer hunting informants that the Northern Ireland Police and the UK Special Forces used in their counterterrorist programs."

Reimer asked, "How do we know this and why do we care?"

She countered, "Give me a minute and I'll explain why we care, but we know this because the British Security Service shared this information with us about ten years ago."

Benzinger gave Reimer a look that said, "Give it a rest."

Sanderson said, "In the mid 1980s, two things happened to our target. First, in his diligence to eliminate any CI threats to the IRA, he crossed the wrong people in the IRA leadership in Northern Ireland and they decided he was the real threat. They put out a kill notice on him. This is during the height of The Troubles, and killing in Northern Ireland and on the UK mainland was horrific. It would seem that Delaney realized that if he stayed in Ireland, he would be killed by someone."

Mary took another sip of coffee and continued, "Now, here is where it applies to our current story. We have reporting that in 1988, the East Germans brokered a meeting between Delaney and the KGB.

They were interested in building a cadre of contract killers who were not affiliated with the USSR or any of the East Bloc countries. An Irishman would be a good choice given his freedom of movement on an Irish passport, especially if they could get him appropriate documentation. It was at this point that our target assumed the Irish alias of Brian Boru Delaney."

"Now where does that come from?" Reimer was not willing to accept the information as given. He wanted to know the sourcing. In law enforcement talk, he wanted to know the precise predication for the accusation that Delaney was the man they wanted.

Sanderson was used to people, especially men in authority, asking her to back up her statements. After years of living a double life, this was an easy challenge for her to handle. In fact, she knew if someone from another agency was trying to tell her this story, she would be asking the same questions. "The file on Delaney is based on twenty years of reporting from virtually every part of the US intelligence community, the British Security Service, the UK Special Forces community and the Israelis. Some of the details of Delaney's missions for the KGB were documented in the East German Stasi files and some from KGB files that were…acquired…after the collapse of the Soviet Union."

At this point, Barbara had finally recovered from her surprise and offered her thoughts on the background. "Terry, as you know, I spent most of my time on the counterterrorism target. While the IRA was not part of my portfolio, I do know that in the late 1980s, there were a number of former IRA mercenaries supporting terrorist organizations, including Palestinian terrorists like Abu Nidal, Black September, and even the FARC in Columbia. The Brits put so much pressure on the IRA in Northern Ireland, and the Irish Republic put pressure on the IRA safe havens on the border that many of the gunfighters of the IRA decided there was money to be made selling their trade to clients outside of the UK or Ireland."

Benzinger asked, "So, Delaney was a hit man for the Soviets and then the Russians?

Sanderson nodded and continued, "At one point five years ago,

Delaney was wounded as he escaped from a warehouse he was using prior to an assassination attempt in Paris. The French police put the forensics into the Interpol database when they set up a Red Notice for his arrest. The British Metropolitan Police Special Branch identified the DNA as belonging to an IRA terrorist, name unknown. The FBI received the material and the Red Notice. They checked to see if there were any matches given the Delaney name was an alias. It is only in the most recent forensics from 114 Harrison that Quantico found Delaney's DNA on a cup he used to make tea while he was searching the house. The FBI is reviewing the DNA on other Russian cases."

Reimer said, "Pretty sloppy."

Jones said, "True, but did he even expect the FBI to do a full forensics sweep of the house when he made it look like a burglary?"

Barbara said, "Villains over time convince themselves they are smarter than anyone else. Terrorists, and especially terrorist bomb makers, think they are brilliant. It almost always ends up they aren't so smart."

Mary said, "These days, the Russians really want us to know they are the ones eliminating their enemies. So, perhaps that's the reason."

Benzinger put on his chief of police role and asked, "So, do we know where the murderer is right now? I want to catch this creep."

, "We aren't entirely certain," Sanderson said. "We don't know the name on his travel documents. But, we have an idea what email address he used in this most recent contracts and negotiations, and we do have a plan to draw him out."

Barbara could see where this was going, "And you want to use me to do so."

Jones said, "Well, that's what Janice recommended."

Barbara smiled and said, "She always was a pal."

Benzinger offered to arrange for Barbara to stay at the Roycroft Inn and to get a room for Mary. But Mary said she needed to get back to

DC to work with the FBI on this case and, she admitted, a dozen other cases shared with Janice Macintosh from the FBI. Barbara opted for a return to the Chautauqua house. Barbara explained that if she was to draw out the assassin, she would need more information. She wondered if that information might just be sitting in some notebooks kept by Peter O'Connell. Chason and Jones agreed that it was unlikely that their villain had stayed in the area after dispatching his target. There was no time-sensitive action required. Benzinger and Reimer accepted their perpetrator was probably across the Peace Bridge and into Canada before the jogger even found Andropovich during his Sunday morning jog. While neither of the East Aurora lawmen was ready to let the case go, they acknowledged that some additional work would be needed before anyone had a chance to bring their man to justice. As Barbara walked out of the Village Hall, Reimer stopped her for a second.

"I know you are a square dealer. My experience with the FBI in Buffalo has been mixed. If you need something from this end, give me a call." He passed a business card with his name and a mobile number.

"Thanks, Terry. I may need help sooner than you think." Barbara was already crafting an idea in her head and it seemed likely that it would require some participation from East Aurora's finest.

Special Agent Jones decided to continue the conversation. So, after Chason left for the field office, she followed Barbara in her FBI sedan as they made the hour drive down to Barbara's house on the lake. The house had a detached two-car garage and Barbara pulled her Range Rover into the second slot. Peter O'Connell's 1964 Austin Healy was still parked in the primary slot. Covered in canvas and nearly two years' worth of dust, it was another piece of the O'Connell legacy yet to be sorted. Once she closed and locked the garage, Barbara invited Jones into the small bungalow for a drink and a strategy session. Jones told Barbara up front that she had to be back in the city by dark. She had a cat and a boyfriend, in that order, to handle. Barbara nodded and asked if Jones wanted coffee or tea. She was pleased to hear Jones liked Earl Grey tea, so Barbara made a pot and took it into the living room that overlooked the lake.

"Are you OK with continuing?" Jones was offering her most sincere look, probably taught at Quantico and practiced ever since with interview subjects and informants.

Barbara stifled a laugh and said, "Ellen, let's agree to play nice and not try to case officer each other."

"Case officer?"

"CIA case officers are taught to manipulate folks every way that is humanly possible. We are taught tricks used by con men, politicians, journalists, and psychologists to get our targets to agree to commit treason and give up secrets. When one case officer tries to manipulate another one, we say…"

"'Don't case officer me.' I get it now."

"So, here are some rules of the game for you to consider. This is serious and we are playing for high stakes. No offense, but I was playing this game before you were born and my father-in-law was playing this game before I was born. I expect that for thirty years, this Irish assassin has been playing an even more serious game just to survive. I am in this because Mary and Janice are convinced he killed one of my assets years ago. This isn't about revenge, but I wouldn't mind helping bring him to justice. We need to look at this from a set of cold expectations. No matter how interesting the approach, the target is going to smell a rat. We are in the USA and that means we are in your jurisdiction and I am obliged to work with you. It is the right and proper thing to do. That doesn't mean I'm going to do anything dopey to advance your case and it also means that if this case goes abroad, many of the rules will change. Clear enough?"

Jones looked up over her tea and put on a different face, again one taught at Quantico. She decided to engage as Special Agent Jones, FBI. "Do I need to remind you that I am the federal officer in charge of this case?"

Barbara smiled her most motherly smile and said, "Dear, I certainly recognize your authority and jurisdiction. Perhaps I need to remind you that I have colleagues in FBI headquarters, the CIA, and they are the ones who pulled me into the project. If you want to know my full story, feel free to call them. If you have decided I am simply a federal pensioner who needs to be handled and then discarded, I can make some calls for you so that we are on the same sheet music sooner rather than later. I think it would be better for *your case* if we agreed to work together as partners and not as adversaries. However, that is entirely up to you."

This wasn't the first time Barbara had lived with a turf battle, but she was a bit surprised that her FBI contact had decided so suddenly to throw down the gantlet. Barbara wondered if Jones really thought she was going to run this case after she just heard how important it was to both the FBI and CIA headquarters. Chason had enough time in the FBI to see how this was going to work, but apparently Jones did not.

Barbara saw this through another lens as well. Jones was very much like her daughter Sue: smart, aggressive and willing to do things on her own based on her own sense of what was right. Barbara's contacts in the Special Operations community had pointed out that Sue was injured in Afghanistan because she charged ahead when she should have been patient. Barbara hoped Jones understood what she was trying to say, but she did have both Mary Sanderson and Janice Macintosh on speed dial on her phone.

"Mrs. O'Connell, I think you are going to either follow my instructions or make that call."

Barbara nodded. She pulled up Janice Macintosh' number and dialed. Two rings and then the crisp voice from inside FBI Headquarters answered. "Macintosh."

"Janice, I'm sorry to bother you but an FBI colleague out of the Buffalo Field Office would like to talk to you and I said I would make this happen. I hope you have time right now."

A laugh at the other end of the line and then, "So, he has decided to use the G-man approach with an old lady, eh?"

"Actually, she."

"Name?"

"Special Agent Ellen Jones."

"This has to do with the Andropovich case, right? We want you to help find, fix and finish his killer."

"Yes, dear."

"Are you willing to do it?"

"Yes, dear."

"She doesn't understand the game, does she?"

"No, dear."

"Check. Put her on the line, please."

The initial conversation was short and Barbara could see from Jones' face that the discussion was more than a bit puzzling. As Jones was handing back Barbara's phone, Jones' own mobile rang. This conversation was equally short, but, given Jones' demeanor and her rather stiff responses, apparently the call was from some supervisor in the Buffalo Field office. She hung up and Barbara offered her another cup of tea.

"Biscuit?"

"No, thank you." Jones was obviously hurt and angry. She had just learned her first lesson from Barbara O'Connell. Never underestimate the Sisterhood.

Barbara now had to make it clear to this Special Agent that she wasn't the enemy. She smiled and said, "So, are we good with working together or are you going to drop me like a hot rock?"

"It would appear that I don't have much of a choice."

"Ellen, over time you will learn that I am an existentialist at heart. I am a firm believer in free will and taking responsibilities for our actions. I think you have choices. You can either pursue the case on your own or we can work together. Both choices have consequences. Honestly, the truth of the matter is that I will be perfectly happy with whatever you choose. I just hope you don't see me as the enemy here. I was asked to help you and I'm trying to do so."

"By arranging for the SAC to call me and chew my ass? By the way, that was the first time I have spoken to the SAC since he welcomed me to Buffalo."

"You were the one who said I needed to make the call."

"Who did you call anyhow?"

"Just as I said, an old friend."

"Agency?"

"Bureau. You heard about her during the briefing today. Janice Macintosh. She is a section chief at FBI headquarters."

Jones carefully put her tea cup and saucer back on the tray. She stood up and straightened her suit. Barbara stood up from across the table. She was the same height as Jones. Jones looked about the same age as her daughter. Barbara noticed that Special Agent Jones had decided to look her directly in the eye. She offered her hand and said, "I have to get home. I will be in touch."

"I certainly hope so. I look forward to working together." Jones nodded and then walked out the door.

Barbara watched as she drove away. Barbara said to the empty house, "I hated to do that to you, Ellen. But, you haven't realized yet how dangerous a game we are going to be playing. I suspect you are very smart and will be a good field agent soon. Our target is a killer. If we face him, he is not going to surrender, and I'm not going to be involved in a plan that I can't control."

Barbara watched the sunset on the lake with the last of the Earl Grey tea. She took the tray back to the kitchen and washed the dishes. She went out to the garage and opened up the deep concealment in her Range Rover. She retrieved her Smith and Wesson Model 60 and its inside-the-waistband holster. She checked the revolver to be sure it was loaded, put the weapon in the holster and put the holster on her hip. The assassin may be long gone, but there were plenty of villains still around.

After checking all the locks on the bungalow doors, Barbara went back to the kitchen and made dinner which consisted of a tray of sliced meats, cheese, olives and a glass of wine. Tonight, she would determine what, if anything, Peter O'Connell knew about any Irishmen who were murderers for hire. First, she had to ask a favor from Mary Sanderson and then an indulgence from Marty Benzinger. She wasn't sure which would be harder.

Barbara used her newly issued encrypted phone to call Mary Sanderson at her home number. After Mary initiated a secure line, their conversation was cordial and productive.

"Didn't I just spend the day with you. Can't you let me have a little peace at the end of my work day?"

"Mary, it is 8 p.m. Why are you still in the office?"

"Because I have more than just your case in the works. By the way, I heard you had a little run in with our Special Agent after I left."

Barbara had to laugh. The informal Beltway network was as fast as ever. Alternatively, this case was far more important than she understood. She said, "Special Agent Jones tried to play the role of the G-man in charge."

"OK, shame on her. I understand Janice sorted that out."

"Not without some heat on Jones' backside."

"Well deserved no doubt. So why are you calling me at 8pm?"

"If you want me to proceed, I'm going to need something from you. I have an idea, but I will need additional data. Some you may not want to give up."

"Speak and you shall receive an answer. Of course, the answer may be no."

"I need an email address for Mr. Delaney or whatever his true name is. Ideally one that the Russians use to get in touch."

"And you intend to use it in western New York? How exactly?"

"I intend to berate our man and tell him he didn't complete his most recent mission. I intend to tell him Andropovich survived."

"And then?"

"And then I intend to get him back here."

"And then?"

"And then I will see what happens next."

"Clever, but a little dangerous."

"Remember, for a change, I have the FBI on my side."

"As I said, a little dangerous."

"Mary, don't forget young Bill is a special agent and Janice is our pal."

"Barbara, don't you forget that you had to punish a Special Agent today."

"Only because she is inexperienced and hasn't realized I can bring some skills to the table."

"And that is why it is a little dangerous. This is probably her first big case on her own. She will be overly enthusiastic."

"She reminds me of Sue. I think I can work with her, but you are assuming she will still want to work with me in the morning."

"They always want to work with you in the morning."

"Hush."

"OK, I'll give you a call tomorrow. It's not like I have the file on my desk."

"Yes, you do."

"OK, yes I do. I surrender to your astral projection skills. Hold on." A rustle of papers filled the telephone receiver for a moment. "I can't say this is the one they used for Andropovich, but it is one he uses for his business dealings. Ready to copy?"

Barbara responded with a slightly sarcastic, "Yes, dear."

"OK, wiseguy. I spell Bravo, Oscar, Romeo, Uniform, Mike at EUNET.NET. It is some sort of proxy server in Romania. Happy?"

"Roger. I copied BORUM, at sign, EUNET.NET. I will let you know how this works out."

"Yes, I hope you will. Are you going to engage the locals before you do anything rash?"

"Please. When have you seen me do anything rash?"

"Perhaps when you decided last year to use a mercenary army to hunt down the Beroslav family."

"Hardly an army. Just four good men plus our friend from State."

"Beth counts as an army on her own."

"Too true."

"Anyhow, I don't really care much about the locals, but I would like to think you will let me know and I can let Janice know. Otherwise, we are the ones who will be in the shit."

Barbara had been typing a message to the suspect email address as she talked to Mary. "Not to worry. I will be happy to keep you in the loop."

"Right. Just so long as the loop doesn't end up around my neck."

"You worry too much."

"Don't forget what another O'Connell did to me one night in East Aurora. Good night, Barbara."

Barbara had to admit Mary had a right to be suspicious. Peter O'Connell was the manager of a counterintelligence operation which had Mary serving as a double agent for years. In the end, she was brought in from the cold, but it wasn't easy and it wasn't fun. Barbara simply said, "Good night, Mary." As she hung up the phone, she hit send on the email message from a recently purchased, pay as you go smart phone. For additional security, Barbara used a separate proxy server for a new email address named MAGPIE. It said,

Landscape job not completed. Lawn still has weeds. Follow up required.

Contact me. MAGPIE

Now all she had to do was to get the East Aurora Police Department and the FBI in Buffalo to play along in a story that Andropovich survived the poison. Barbara was fairly certain Terry would agree but she wasn't sure about Benzinger. She just hoped he had a sense of humor and a commitment to seeing justice done in this case. As to Special Agent Ellen Jones, Barbara had no idea what would happen once Jones realized that Barbara O'Connell was the one running the operation.

>>>>>> DOWN BY THE RIVER

Sue was sitting in the back seat of an air conditioned black Russian-made ZIL limousine from the 1980s heading toward the Hairatan-Termez bridge. The vehicle fit the cover story of a meeting between a Russian oligarch and a local smuggler, and Sue was doing her best to fit the mold as well. She was dressed in a black pantsuit and white silk shirt recently delivered from Kabul along with a $10,000 Rolex Milgauss on her left wrist and a large gold bracelet on her right. The suit fit, more or less, though she had to modify the trousers so that her prosthetic didn't show when she sat in the car. She also had to let out a seam under her left armpit to allow for the shoulder holster and her Glock26 compact pistol. Next to her was Jamie, again dressed in black. Black suit, black shirt, black shoes and, clearly, black expression. Jamie's suit didn't fit him at all, but that meant that any passenger who joined them would see the large frame of a Russian Stechkin pistol peeking out of his suitcoat. Sue turned to him and said, "What exactly is your problem. This was your idea after all."

"It was my idea to arrange a meeting between an oligarch and the smuggler. I just didn't expect my role in the equation to be the oligarch's muscle."

"Do you speak Russian?"

"Nope."

"Well, I do. I learned Russian when I was a kid in Moscow. My folks did a tour in Moscow during the bad old days and I actually remember most of my language and can describe the city in detail if necessary. My Russian may be a bit rusty, but certainly good enough to fool the target. Besides, you make a scary bodyguard."

"She's got you there, mate." Dozer was in the front, driving the Zil. He was also dressed in black, though the suit from Kabul did not fit the very large, very fit, UKSF operator. Though not visible to either Sue or Jamie, next to Dozer was an MP5 submachine gun sitting in a recently added set of clips under the dashboard. This might be a simple meeting, but everyone was ready in case it went south.

Sue decided to change the subject for a moment. She tapped the butt of the pistol under Jamie's left armpit and said, "Where exactly did you get that piece of Russian hardware?"

"Found it. I heard the guy who owned it didn't need it anymore."

"Moved away?"

"Permanently. By the way, don't lose that Rolex or the bracelet. The watch belongs to the COS and I promised it was only going to be used as a prop in some quiet conversation over tea. The gold is from our stock of stuff used for various disguises. No funny business, eh?"

Sue rolled her eyes and said, "Do I look like someone who is going to do something funny?"

Before Jamie could come up with a response, Dozer said from the driver's seat, "OK, we are about a kilometer away. Two minutes out." He switched on his body microphone and said, "Micron."

George's voice came through their earbuds, "*Roger 5, MICRON. All, Zero. We are about to start the play.*" George was in one of the SBS Defenders. He had just dropped off one of Jamie's team on the street.

"*Zero, 3. Roger.*" Mitch, one of Jamie's team, was on the street walking toward the pickup site. He was their Russian, Uzbek and Dari speaker and was dressed as an Uzbek wool trader nominally headed to the small marketplace near the ferry terminal next to the Termez bridge. Under his long Uzbek coat was an AKMS assault rifle and inside the canvas bag filled with sheep's wool was a Russian GM-94 grenade launcher. As Jamie said when they did the final check before departing the compound, "You can never be too well armed."

"*Zero, 2. Roger.*" Dozer's partner Mac was in one of Jamie's Toyotas with his partner Brian, circling the area in the opposite direction of the Zil.

"Zero, this is Dune. Roger." Flash wanted to be on the street, but Jamie vetoed her demand. So, she was running the command post back at the compound, much to the chagrin of the rest of Jamie's team.

The Zil pulled up next to the ferry terminal where a small, hawk-faced man wearing a mix of Western and Afghan clothes, a camouflage coat and a rolled wool hat known as a pakol waited. Jamie got out of the car, offered him a jump seat facing the rear seats. Once the target was settled in the car, Jamie reentered, sitting directly across from the smuggler.

The Zil pulled away from the terminal and the smuggler took a moment to get used to the transition from bright sunlight to the darkened interior of the limousine. When he finally settled into the car, his eyes opened wide as he faced Jamie and then next to Jamie, a woman dressed in black.

Sue almost laughed out loud when she saw the smuggler's reaction. "Bug-eyed" was the only way to describe it. Instead, she maintained her stern look and addressed him in Russian. "You are Mohammed Zarif?"

The smuggler nodded.

"You can speak, no?"

The smuggler struggled with Russian. He finally said, "My Russian is poor. Do you speak Tajik?"

Sue waved her left hand in a dismissive manner. It was as they rehearsed. She turned to Jamie and said in her most crude Russian, "Handle this piece of shit."

Jamie leaned over and gently tapped the smuggler's cheek. He said in Dari, "You have not made a good impression with my boss."

"She is your boss?"

"She is everyone's boss on the other side of the river. She is the person that you have been cheating on for the last year. She is the one who will decide if you leave this car alive tonight. Do you understand me now, Mohammed Zarif?"

The smuggler nodded. This meeting was not going the way he expected. His contacts on the river had made it sound as if this would be a profitable meeting. Now, profit was the last thing on his mind. He was not used to dealing with women. He would have to convince these Russians that he was compliant even if it was only until he could get out of the car. He smiled and reached into his field jacket. When he looked up, he saw two pistols pointing at his head. One from the bald Russian and one from the Russian woman. At first, he could only focus on the barrels of the pistols. Eventually, he looked into their eyes. He tried to smile, but he could see nothing but death.

"I was just going to show you my recent deliveries. I wanted to show you how good I have been in our relationship. It is just paper. I will show you."

Jamie said, "Tajik, you need to be careful because you are walking on the edge of a cliff. A false step and you will fall off that edge."

The smuggler nodded and carefully pulled out his notebook. He started to read off details from a list.

Sue waved her left hand again and entered the conversation in her best and most formal Persian: "We do not care about the past, Mohammed Zarif. You will give us this book, but we only care about the present and the future. You will tell us about your distribution network for the next shipments. You will tell us who receives our goods and when. You will not cheat us in the future. You will tell us these things and, perhaps, we will agree that you are worth keeping alive. Or, perhaps not. But the choice will always be yours."

Sue nodded toward Jamie and continued, "Listen very carefully to Agha-e-Meshki, follow his instructions and tell no one, no one, that we had this conversation. Do you understand?" The smuggler nodded. He handed the notebook to Jamie and then began to list all of his contacts in Hairatan and in Mazar-e-Sharif. With a little prodding, he admitted that he was trading with both the Iranians and with the Taliban and that along with the money he received in the transfers, the Taliban gave him black tar opium that he shipped back into Uzbekistan.

Sue decided to reenter the conversation. "You are shipping poison to our country? Do you know what we do with drug smugglers in Russia?" The smuggler shook his head, so Sue continued, "We cut off their balls and then we shoot them. Mohammed Zarif, do you think it would be wise to continue to trade in this way?"

The smuggler shook his head and at this point, his whole body seemed to shake.

To end the shaking, Jamie grabbed the smuggler by putting his thumb and forefinger on one of the smuggler's cheeks and squeezed. He told the smuggler to listen carefully. Jamie outlined a meeting schedule that included where, when and how they would next meet. He warned the smuggler and said that he should pray to God Almighty that he never saw "the woman in black" again. Again, he asked if the smuggler understood. The smuggler nodded. Jamie did not accept the nod and told the smuggler to repeat all of his instructions. After two efforts with corrections, the smuggler finally got the story right.

On cue, Sue issued instructions in Russian to Dozer to stop the car. Jamie opened the car and said in his most polite Dari, "Thank you for your time, Mohammed Zarif. I hope to see you again soon." The smuggler left the car as quickly as he could. He fell as he cleared the car door. Jamie closed the door and the Zil pulled away.

Dozer keyed his microphone and said, "Zenith."

In six sets of earbuds and in the speakers at the compound, George's voice said, *"All, Zero. Zenith. I say again, Zenith. Return to Base."*

Dozer turned to the back of the car and said, "Did it work out?"

Sue said, "I think we got everything we needed." She keyed her microphone and said, "Dune, you capture all the names and details?"

"We are already processing the list. I will send the reporting to higher tonight. I do want to see the notebook first."

"Roger." Sue turned to Jamie and said, "Anything good in the notebook?"

"Looks to be just what he said, six months of guns, money and drugs."

Dozer nodded and then said, "What is that awful smell?"

Jamie shook his head and said, "He peed himself when Sue pulled her piece. And by the way, when did you decide to call me Mr. Black?"

Sue responded, "The name fits your disposition, so why not? As to the smell, blaming me is so unfair. Dozer, he peed himself when Jamie grabbed him by the cheek. Until then, it was all very cordial."

Dozer said, "I may not have understood the conversation, but it certainly didn't sound cordial."

Jamie shook his head and said, "It is a good thing we stole this car. I wouldn't want to have to clean it."

The ambush started with a poorly aimed RPG-7 round flying past the Zil and exploding in a storefront near the ferry terminal building. Rounds from automatic rifles started to hit the front of the vehicle. Two deflected off the front windshield turning the entire windshield into a spiderweb of broken glass. Just before rounds started to hit the tires, Dozer threw the Zil into reverse and completed a high-speed reverse 180-degree turn. The long limousine barely slid through the gap made by cars, carts, and merchandise. As soon as the car stabilized, he shifted to drive and tried to accelerate. Unfortunately, by that time the tires had been completely deflated from bullets and from the stress of the high speed turn. The Zil ground to a halt. Automatic fire was cascading down on them from the second story of a building, hitting the car, other parked vehicles, storefronts and merchandise. Afghans, used to nearly forty years of war, disappeared off the streets well before there were any civilian casualties. The good news is the reverse 180 meant that the attackers could no longer see their targets on the far side of the car. The bad news was it still left Dozer, Sue and Jamie alone as they bailed out of the left side of the car. Just before they did, Dozer sent a radio message: "DOWNDRAFT"

George's calm voice arrived in the earbuds of the three officers, *"Roger, DOWNDRAFT. We will be in place in 2. Hold on."*

Dozer was already sending 9mm rounds from his MP5 into the likely firing position across the street. Sue crawled out of the left rear door and looked down the street. There was only one body. Mohammed Zarif. She pulled out her Glock and joined the fight. Jamie was next out the door and as soon as he cleared it, he reached under his coat and pulled out a nylon shoulder stock and snapped it on his pistol. He flipped the selector switch on the pistol and a steady stream of 9mm rounds from the Russian weapon were added to the mix.

For over a minute, the back and forth between the two sides continued. Jamie said, "I hope we get out of this soon. I'm down to my last magazine."

Dozer nodded, "You and me both, mate."

As Dozer completed his comment, several small explosions occurred near their attackers' position on the roof of the building. The gunfight was over as the roof collapsed and a fire started inside. Jamie looked at Sue's puzzled face and said, "I told you it never hurts to have real firepower." At that point, George pulled up in the Defender. Mitch was standing in the Defender and peering out from the hatch that normally would be mounted with a general purpose machine gun. He was holding the Russian grenade launcher in his hands. Three of the barrels on the multi-barreled grenade launcher were still smoking. The AKMS rifle was across his chest.

George said, "I think the party is over. Any reason to hang about?"

Jamie gathered up Sue and Dozer and said, "Just a second. I have something I have to do." He reached into the Zil, grabbed something from the floor of the back seat and then tossed a thermite grenade into the car. As he climbed into the back seat of the Defender, he said, "I reckon we can leave now." As if on cue, the thermite grenade went off, illuminating the interior of the car with a silver white flash. By the time they were one hundred meters away, the gas tank on the Zil exploded. When that happened, Jamie said to Sue, "I told you I was glad the Zil was stolen. And, by the way, O'Connell, you left this in the car." He opened his hand and showed her a slightly scuffed Rolex Milgauss. "I told you it was the COS' property. I hope he has a sense of humor."

"It wasn't my fault. The Oyster bracelet was too large for my wrist. See," Sue showed her right wrist, "the gold is still on board."

"O'Connell, it is never your fault. But you have to admit, bad things seem to happen when you are around."

"Only to bad people."

Dozer looked over from the far side of the back seat, "So far."

George sent a message to the FOB. *"All good, we are RTB."*

Flash's voice came on, *"Dang. I was just about to dispatch the cavalry."*

F lash looked up from the pair of computer screens that linked her to both RLSU headquarters in Italy and SOF headquarters in Bagram. On the RLSU screen, she had a series of intelligence reports and on the SOF headquarters screen she had a live UAV feed. Using her best imitation of a parade ground voice, she said to the entire SCIF, "Listen up. We have the live feed on the smuggler headquarters in Termez. It looks like they are up-loading a convoy of five cargo trucks. Lots of crates, not much data."

Jamie and Sue walked across the SCIF to Flash's work-station. They leaned over her shoulder to watch the feed coming from a UAV orbiting over their heads. The mix of altitude and superior optics allowed the UAV to capture images on the north side of the Amu Darya. Jamie said, "This is your bird, right?"

"Yes, sir. That's why the intel is so good."

Jamie nodded and said, "Hey, let's not forget the last time we were together, it was our bird that saved our necks."

"Got it. From the Klingon perspective, killer bird is better than surveillance bird. Still, pretty slick images, no?"

They had been working for the past week on two separate lines of inquiry. First, they followed the leads that were offered by the now deceased smuggler. His records took some deciphering because of his poor written Persian, but between Jamie, Mitch, and Sue, they sorted out the details of names, places, and weapons passed. Meanwhile, George and Terry had focused on the ambush. Their initial check of the ambush site and the Tomahawks' engagement with the Shia community in Hairatan argued that the ambush might have had more to do with a rival smuggling network than any exposure of the US-UK effort in Hairatan. Zarif regularly bragged about his Russian connections and how profitable they were. According to the Tomahawk network, the ambush was the work of a rival smuggler, an Uzbek who went by the name Ahmet Bey. The reporting suggested Bey decided that if he eliminated Zarif and, if possible, some of his Russian connections, then that would make it easier for him.

The two data sets allowed Flash and her counterparts in Bagram to focus their attention on warehouses managed by Ahmet Bey. The coverage on Bey's company telephones and his personal mobiles displayed how quickly this smuggler decided to capture the market. Of course, Ahmet Bey didn't realize that now he was considered a high value target for both the US and UK forces in the area. The result was demonstrated visually on a white board behind Flash. Overlaid on a regional map, the result showed four networks linked to Ahmet Bey. In Uzbekistan, a network labeled "suppliers" tied military bases in Uzbekistan and Tajikistan with Ahmet Bey. In Afghanistan, one network labeled "IRGC" tied Ahmet Bey with legitimate truck companies that transshipped goods to Meshhad, Iran via Meymaneh and Herat. The second network, labeled simply "Taliban" tied Ahmet Bey with known Taliban commanders in Balkh, Konduz, and Samangan Provinces.

Sue asked Flash, "So, how is this going to play out?"

Jamie answered, "We turn the Taliban network over to RC North Special Forces units. Now that they know where the Taliban logistics bases are, they intend to use a finish piece using Afghan government commandos backed by SF teams and US fast movers."

George offered the next piece, "UKSF task force, with our team in the lead, will be closing on the Meymaneh and Herat networks. We intend to intercept the current deliveries in the next time they head west. There are plenty of remote locations out there and we will find one that fits our needs. The plan is to intercept the convoy by helo. If there is resistance, well, then there are always Apache gunships on standby."

Flash spun her chair around and pointed her finger at Sue, "And the REAL SUE representative here, working with Klingons, will do a cross-border operation to convince Ahmet Bey to give up his Russian network."

Sue said, "You know I hate it when your make RLSU into words."

Flash nodded, "Yup. That's why I do it."

Jamie jumped in before there was further back and forth between his SOF colleagues, "The objective is to get Ahmed Bey onboard as a source. He will be under pressure once the next set of shipments is disrupted. We will use that pressure as leverage. He will either cooperate or not. If he doesn't cooperate, well, then, the word might get out that he is the source anyway. Accidents like that happen in this fast-moving enterprise in the borderlands." He smiled his most innocent smile.

"We?"

"Hey, don't forget that I am your muscle, Mr. Black."

"Right. Agha Meshki. And, your station in Tashkent is OK with this?"

"Their life is complicated enough that they don't need to try operations hundreds of miles away. I have coordinated with them and Flash coordinated with Bagram."

Sue stuck her tongue out at Flash. Flash returned the favor. Sue said, "What's the plan to get across the border and, once across, to get up close to Ahmed Bey. Our last effort with a smuggler didn't work out so well."

"Sue, you know the old saying…if first you don't succeed…"

"Yup, but I would like to think we will succeed this time."

"Because we are going to try again. Brilliant, no?

B arbara O'Connell wasn't certain why everyone agreed to her plan. Perhaps it was due to the fact that the plan was already in motion when she briefed it to Benzinger and Reimer. Perhaps it was the only plan out there. One thing was certain, the police had a vested interest in bringing a murderer to justice and they wanted to do it on their turf. It wasn't like murder was a common crime in the little town. Jones, on the other hand, was more of a challenge. Her ego was more than a little bruised by her original confrontation with Barbara, but she got over that. The real problem was that Barbara's "plan" would be considered "off the books" from the FBI perspective and that was definitely not the FBI way. Still, since the local authorities were on board and it was their murder case and because there was already direct support from FBI headquarters, Jones finally relented. Barbara was too gracious and too good a case officer to point out that Jones never really had a choice.

Benzinger and Reimer did their part. They simply delayed the coroner's report and placed a story in the East Aurora Advertiser and the Buffalo News that was a classic tale of "completely true, just not truly complete." The tale of the body found in Major's Park was released, the fact that Polchak was already dead on arrival, was not released. The brief story ended with "investigations are ongoing."

Barbara hadn't expected an immediate response. Delaney would not have survived all of these years if he hadn't been cautious, but he did respond that evening when Barbara was making her dinner.

The email said: Not possible. Lawn service completed.

Barbara responded back: Do not argue if you want to continue.
MAGPIE

She left the note ambiguous. Continue working? Continue living?
She felt that might encourage further contact. Barbara had already
informed both Mary and Janice about her plan and she hoped that
even if she wasn't able to get Delaney out on the street, the power of
the US intelligence community would be able to identify his location
from his email.

Delaney responded almost immediately: What is the new requirement?

Barbara waited for two hours and then responded: Meet for a new
contract.

The speed that Delaney responded demonstrated to Barbara that
he was tentatively nibbling at the bait: Where, when?

This was where the case could go either way. She had to play this
carefully. Play it too heavy and Delaney might recognize it was a trap.
Play it too light and her email persona became less threatening and,
again, Delaney might recognize it was a trap. It wasn't the first time
Barbara had played this game. However, it was the first time she had
played it using an email dialogue. It was so much easier either face-to-
face or on the phone or even in written messages. It would be possible
to elicit information through tone, body language, even handwriting.
In this case, it was all keystrokes. She couldn't interpret them, and any
forensics on keystrokes would have to wait.

The answer she typed was where Barbara had been forced to
give in to her partnership with her law-enforcement allies. The East
Aurora Police insisted that the meeting take place inside the village
so that they could maintain their jurisdiction. The Buffalo Field
office of the FBI wanted the meeting to take place in Buffalo proper
where they were in charge. Barbara would not have held a meeting
in either of the areas. She would have chosen a location in Canada
or Europe. Then the meeting would have been a CIA operation with
a supportive liaison service in play. But, that wasn't going to work
for anyone. After some negotiation and a pair of calls to Mary and

Janice, Barbara arranged a compromise. The venue would be outside the village but in the township of Aurora. That meant it was still in the jurisdiction of the East Aurora Police. However, the FBI insisted it had to be someplace where they could deploy the full complement of their technical resources as well as the Buffalo FBI SWAT.

Barbara typed: Erie County Emery Park, 30.5.1600. Shelter 21. MAGPIE.

He responded: Agreed.

Barbara hadn't realized she was holding her breath. The plan was set. The target had agreed to arrive. Over the years, Barbara had worked terrorist cases in three continents and she knew that just because the target said yes didn't mean that she had any idea what yes meant. In this case, it remained to be seen if Delaney would come, would send a surrogate, or just make a run.

She made the first call on her personal mobile to Terry Reimer. She figured he deserved at least that. He answered "Reimer."

"Terry, the invitation was accepted. Wednesday at 1600 hours. I hope you can come."

"I wouldn't miss it for the world. Will you come visit before the party?"

"Of course, just let me know when you want to see me."

"I'll call you tomorrow to confirm, but I think Tuesday at 10 would be a good time to come visit."

"Then Tuesday it is. Can you get me someplace to stay?"

"Count on it. Tschuss."

Her next call was to Mary. This time, it was an encrypted call. Mary answered after three rings, "Don't you ever take time to eat?"

"Not when I am on your clock, dear."

"So, you have news?"

"He responded. He agreed to Wednesday at 1600hrs at the venue selected by the FBI. You going to come play?"

"Did you think I would miss this? Janice and I have our go-bags already packed. I will get you details tomorrow. I have a file as well. We have a number of pictures of Delaney that we can share. When is the pre-op briefing?"

"The EA side have asked for Tuesday at 10 at their place. I said yes. Do you think Janice can convince the FBI not to arrive in shiny, black Suburbans and Crown Vic sedans?"

Mary laughed, "Barb, you have an archaic view of the FBI. Janice said they will be deploying their best surveillance team, plus a section from the Field Office SWAT, so I suspect we will have everything from pickup trucks and motorcycles to an ice cream van serving soft ice cream. Good enough?"

"I do like soft ice cream."

"I need to know if you can keep this in perspective as you move forward."

Barbara knew that "keeping this in perspective" was a stock phrase that Mary had to say. She also knew the stock answer, "Yes, Mary. I can keep this professional."

"I knew that would be the case. Now, let me get back to making dinner. I will see you on Tuesday morning if not before. Ciao Bella."

"Ciao." Barbara hung up the phone and sat still for a few minutes as she thought through the story of BREAKDREAM. A decent man, family, and caught up in a Hizballah network that was not of his choosing. Delaney might be his killer. Regardless of what she might say to Mary this was the "perspective" that Barbara would have when they met.

27 May 2007, Camp Marmal, Balkh Province, Afghanistan

Sue O'Connell had been out of the larger network of SOF operations for some time and so she wasn't used to what could happen when the full SOF enterprise kicked into gear. When she was in Surveillance and Reconnaissance in Afghanistan, her work was small-unit tactics supporting small raid teams with everyone based either in a safe house in Jalalabad or a small airfield outside the city. Her earlier work with MACE had shown her what a SOF intelligence fusion center looked like. The multi-service, US and UK effort code named MACE focused on a Russian organized crime network that was threatening to sell radiologic waste to terrorists. The MACE team travelled in multiple C17 cargo aircraft.

That had been a small example of what she now saw at one end of the Mazar-e-Sharif airfield. In less than 48 hours, an abandoned part of the airfield that was little more than concrete revetments last used by Soviet fighter aircraft in the 1980s became a temporary multi-service home for a fusion center: SOF aviation support; a full section from George's SBS unit; two Special Forces A-teams; and a small, but completely capable field hospital. The inflatable structures were matched in size to the revetments so from a distance, little had changed except for the aircraft parked nearby. At the other end of Camp Marmal, in a separate isolation compound, a full company of Afghan commandos supported by a section from the Afghan secret service known as the National Directorate of Security now awaited orders.

Sue and Flash travelled together to meet up with the SOF command team and their tactical analysts. While the RLSU mission was focused on a more strategic part of the puzzle, success would be based on timing their approach to Ahmed Bey shortly after the takedown of the convoys of his smuggled equipment. Both Sue and Flash were wearing their only uniforms in-country: sage-green flight suits with their name and rank on them. They used their military IDs and a password that SOF headquarters in Bagram had sent them in Flash's encrypted communications. Once inside the compound, they were directed to a concrete revetment with a faded red alphanumeric, V7, painted on one side. The inflatable structure inside the revetment was the tactical operations center.

Waiting for them at the entrance was Command Sergeant Major Jim Massoni in a set of desert fatigues that looked to be last used at the beginning of the Afghan campaign in 2001. "Greetings, you two. I hope the flight over here was worth it. I had to ride in a C17 hauling this stuff. Nothing but sling seats and an Air Force box lunch."

Sue realized they were well and truly inside a formal US Army environment rather than the informal RLSU team environment, so she addressed Massoni with a greater degree of respect than normal. "Sergeant Major, what are you doing here? Our part of this mission is pretty tiny and isn't going to happen at Camp Marmal at all."

Flash didn't seem to worry about the environment. She said, "Jim, just another excuse to get out of the office?"

Massoni decided to ignore Flash and answer Sue. "The boss wanted to be sure you were going to be OK when you get ready to cross the Amu Darya with that pirate Schenk. I promised to double check his plan since we both know he has an interesting way of doing business."

He turned to Flash and said, "And, I just wanted to get out of the office. The Boss agreed I could come visit. Flash, don't forget that I can tell the boss that you aren't needed here anymore. You will be on the next plane heading west." Massoni smiled his sergeant major smile which might mean he was joking or it might mean he was serious. Ever since Massoni was promoted to sergeant major, no one was willing to test either hypothesis.

A slightly chastised Flash said, "Check, Sergeant Major."

Massoni turned back to Sue and said, "Is it true that you destroyed another of Jamie's vehicles?"

Sue nodded and said, "But it wasn't my fault."

Flash had recovered enough of her normal style to say, "She always says that."

Massoni nodded and said, "Yes, she does."

The briefing was short and to the point. Each of the elements of the operation had already received the background based on the intelligence feed from Flash, and each outlined their plan to the SOF command group. In this case, it meant the Deputy Commander of SOF, the UKSF Task Force Afghanistan commander, and the Commander of RC North. Sue had expected a secure video conference link to the SOF commander, but Massoni told her the CG was on his way back to DC for a briefing at the White House. "Don't worry, he already has approved the general plan and, after all, we are all in trouble if his deputy, a Navy admiral with years in SOF, a British Brigadier, and a US one-star can't manage a briefing."

Sue was certain that Massoni — as a member of one of the most exclusive clubs on the planet, the most senior non-commissioned officers of the special operations community — had also played some role in stage-managing the briefing.

As Sue expected, the individual combat pieces were relatively simple. Both assaults were based on tactics that every SOF unit in the world practiced over and over again until they reached perfection. The challenge was timing. In the west, they wanted to stop the convoy somewhere west of Mazar-e-Sharif in the desert between the cities of Sheberghan and Meymaneh. In the east, they wanted to stop the convoy between Mazar-e-Sharif and Konduz. The route from Termez to Konduz was less than half the distance from Termez to Meymaneh. The solution was to set up a spot checkpoint run by the NDS for the Konduz convoy. Another checkpoint between Mazar-e-

Sharif and Sheberghan would be in place in case they needed to slow down the west-bound convoy.

As the briefing concluded, Massoni whispered to Sue, "This is guaranteed to be a cluster. There are way too many moving parts. I asked them why they didn't just hit the convoys on the desert road just south of Hairatan. The SOF planners answer was they weren't sure they had enough space to do the job. Mostly, I think it is because if you do it too early and along that road, you only need one SOF unit. Either the Brits or the two ODAs. This way everyone gets to play. We even get to use the Afghan commandos. It seems pretty goofy to me. Let's get out of here before someone important asks us questions and I am forced to give my opinion." He stood up and Sue and Flash followed him.

Just as they were throwing Massoni's ruck into the Toyota, they heard, "Hey, Massoni. Stop what you are doing and come here." A short, broad-shouldered man in a similar set of desert fatigues and a brown t-shirt was delivering this order.

Massoni looked up and said to Flash and Sue, "That's Command Master Chief Gleason. He's the senior SOF NCO in country. Formerly command master chief for Naval Special Warfare. Keeps his Admiral, the SOF Deputy Commander, out of trouble. I better answer the call."

Turning on his heel, Massoni jogged over to the SOF senior NCO. Massoni was about six inches taller and twenty pounds heavier than the command master chief. To Sue and Flash's surprise, Massoni seemed to shrink in size as he addressed the senior SOF NCO. In short order, Massoni walked back to the truck and said, "We can go now." Flash took the wheel, Massoni took shotgun, and Sue climbed into the back seat of the four-door pickup.

Once they were in the truck and headed toward FOB Hairatan, Flash asked Massoni, "What did the Command Master Chief say?"

"He said, 'Don't fuck up.'"

"Seemed like more of a conversation than that, Jim."

"He said it a couple of different ways."

"Did you tell him the plan was too complicated?"

"Can't tell you, Flash."

Sue leaned forward from the back seat and said to Flash, "Secrets of the Sergeant Major guild, Flash. He isn't going to tell you secrets of the guild."

Massoni smiled and said, "Flash, someday when you have a Sergeant Major working for you, he may reveal some of the secrets."

Flash turned to Massoni as she downshifted, turned north and accelerated on the last stretch of road to the FOB. "Seems unlikely, Jim. Can you imagine Flash in command?"

"I'll admit it is terrifying."

Sue nodded as she was tossed around in the back as Flash dodged the dozens of potholes in the road, "No kidding."

30 May 2007, FOB Hairatan, Balkh Province, Afghanistan

Sue had never been a patient person. Especially after her injury in Jalalabad in 2004 and upon entering the espionage world, she had been forced to accept the fact that she could seldom control the actions of her allies or her adversaries. When she was working as a surveillance operator in S&R, it had been different. In S&R, she was part of a small team, really a family, who had worked together for so long and in so many different places that they seemed to act as one body, not as a set of six surveillants. Sue attributed this to the actions of her team leaders, CW5 Jameson and SGM Massoni. Even then, Sue hated standing watch in some creepy observation point waiting for the action to begin.

As she worked deeper and deeper in the world of espionage, Sue learned to accept that her instructors at the Farm were correct when they answered all questions with the phrase "it depends." That absolutely frustrated Sue. The level of ambiguity in the intelligence operations, coupled with the fact that often she couldn't take any action until a source triggered a meeting, was hell for Sue. Still, she had come to accept it as the nature of the beast. But that didn't mean she liked the idea of waiting for the chance to approach Ahmed Bey in Termez. As Massoni said after their departure from Camp Marmal, the coordination of the operation was complex. They would receive word from technical collection when Bey intended to make the next shipment. That collection would come from the sensors on the UAVs that SOF ran along the border. Often referred to as an "unblinking eye," in this case the UAVs were serving as focused eyes and ears. The UAVs were watching Bey's compound and listening for his cellphone messages to potential clients in Afghanistan and Iran. The two SOF teams waited at Camp Marmal and Sue waited at FOB Hairatan.

Sue walked up to Jamie for the second time that day and said, "Why can't we just go across the border now?"

Jamie looked at Massoni and Flash and said, "Will you please try to explain to Dr. Impatient why we can't rush this."

Massoni raised his hands in surrender and said, "Not me, cuz. I'm not fighting your fight."

Flash looked at Sue and said, "Do we really need to go over this AGAIN?"

Sue bowed her head and said, "I know, we don't want to spend extra time on target in Termez where we don't have a QRF, we don't have a ton of support capability, and until the takedowns happen, we don't have any leverage. I just want to do this job."

Massoni finally decided to add his two cents. "And, let's not forget that we have a set of orders that make it clear that the Deputy Commander of SOF wants this to be quick and low profile. I suspect, since it is going to be an O'Connell operation, the low-profile requirement may be too much to expect, but we do have our orders, O'Connell."

Sue's work in the past hadn't required quite this degree of coordination and, she had to admit, the success of the takedowns in Afghanistan was far more important to the SOF mission and the RC North mission than Sue and Jamie recruiting Ahmed Bey. As she turned and walked out of the room, she said, "I'm going to go work out."

Massoni gave Flash a nod. She nodded back and said to Sue, "Wait for me."

The "gym" in FOB Hairatan was nothing more than a StairMaster, a rowing machine, a pull-up bar, and a weight bench surrounded by dumbbells and kettlebells. Still, it was a place to blow off some steam by throwing iron around. Sue was well at it before Flash arrived wearing black shorts, a black tank top and black hightop sneakers. She walked over to Sue as she started a set of dumbbell presses. It was a good time to ask hard questions because Sue was tied up concentrating on the weights. "Hey, what makes you so grumpy these days?"

"I'm not grumpy. I just want to do my job and my job is over in Uzbekistan. Not here. You have your intelligence feeds, your analysts back home, and you have your analytic challenges right here." Sue paused to drop the two dumbbells onto the concrete floor. She sat up and said, "I haven't got shit to do here."

"I'll bet you were a real peach when you were in college. You ever play any sports or any games?"

"Field hockey, lacrosse and backgammon."

"And yours truly was a fencer and a chess master. I guess that says it all."

"A fencer?"

"Yup. Nearly made the Olympic team, but I got distracted. First by a man and then by 9/11."

"I can understand both distractions. I suppose the difference between backgammon and chess captures who we are, no?"

"Beats me? I'm not trying to play Sigmund Freud here. I'm just waiting for you to get off the bench so I can use it."

Sue smiled and said, "Well, go right ahead, D'Artagnan!"

By the time they had finished their workout and their showers, Sue felt better and Flash was pretty comfortable that she wouldn't see an O'Connell flameout for at least another hour or two. They walked back into the SCIF to find Jamie and Massoni standing behind Terry at a work station with three screens. With an exclamation from Massoni of "Hallelujah!" the three men stepped back from the workstation. A 3-foot–by-5-foot plasma screen against the wall lit up to show a UAV feed. The screen showed a series of trucks leaving a warehouse in Termez and heading toward the Amu Darya Bridge. The UAV feed was in black and white with a grey site reticle and a grey box focusing on the convoys. The screens had two time listings: local and GMT. Local time was 1945hrs.

Sue was always amazed that these remotely piloted vehicles — with pilots based sometimes in Bagram, sometimes at Ft. Bragg, and sometimes in an Air Force base at an "undisclosed location" — could focus in on specific targets even though the aircraft was orbiting at 10,000 feet.

Flash said, "The wonders of science. A mix of computer power, satellite feeds and really good pilots. There really is nowhere to hide if you have a UAV on your tail."

"And that is a mighty good thing!" Massoni was in a great mood, now that he could see the images on the big screen. He had never been one for technology, but this setup allowed him to view the events with maximum clarity.

Over the next hour, they watched as the UAV tracked the two convoys across the Amu Darya bridge, through Hairatan and then headed along the main highway. A total of seven trucks. Somewhere between Hairatan and the road junction with the Mazar-e-Sharif, three of the trucks turned off the road and headed on a dirt cutoff that would intersect with the Konduz Road. Between Jamie and Flash, they also had the communications feeds from the Joint Special Operations Task Force, the Special Forces team setting up the ambush the east bound convoy, and the SBS team preparing to ambush the trucks going west.

Jamie said to Sue, "As much as I know you want to watch the show, we need to mount up and get across the bridge so that we are in Termez when the convoys are intercepted. I've already used one of my assets to give us an audience with Mr. Big, sorry Bey. I want to be sure that audience takes place just as he is hearing the bad news."

Sue was disappointed that she wasn't going to watch the operations unfold, but she understood the reasoning. She said, "Can we get something resembling comms with Terry and Flash so that we know when the takedowns happen?"

Jamie looked a Massoni and said, "Will you explain to Dr. Obvious that we have already thought of that?"

Flash interceded and said, "Sue, really? You need to ask? The feed will be forwarded to the comms in the truck you are taking."

Sue realized she was overthinking the operation as Flash, Massoni and Jamie all stared at her. As she headed out of the SCIF, she said, "Got it. I will go upstairs and change."

Sue and Jamie left in one of the Ford Rangers. Jamie was wearing a turban and mix of local and military kit in what was often referred to as jihadi chic. Sue was dressed in a set of the long shirt and pajama trousers and a long Uzbek embroidered scarf. As they loaded into one of the Rangers, Jamie said, "I have our documents for the border crossing. You are my wife on the documents." He smiled and said, "My second wife, of course."

"Don't push it, Shenk."

"Hey, first you complain about my music, then you complain about my car, which you destroyed, and now you complain about my skills at cross-border operations. What's a mother to do?"

"The destruction of the Zil was not my fault."

"It gets less and less reasonable every time you say it." Jamie started the truck and they headed to the border. As soon as they got out of the compound, Jamie said, "We are taking the ferry instead of the bridge. Less hassles and consistent with day travelers. The Afghans at the ferry crossing are on the payroll, so we won't even stop there. The Uzbeks on the other side of the ferry have seen the truck and yours truly multiple times, so it should be without drama."

"And why do they know you?"

"Because, as a master spy as well as a refined special operator, I know that I need to establish a pattern in country well before I need to travel in country. I've been back and forth across the border about a dozen times. Each time, I provide the border guards with a little something, usually small pieces of jewelry for their wives and daughters or perhaps a bottle of some hard-to-get beverage. Their preference is whiskey. I'm a smuggler after all. By the way, the name on my documents is Mohammed Jowzjani. You, of course, are listed simply as wife."

"Got it, wise guy."

"Now for something interesting to listen to while we drive."

"Not more music from the 1970s?"

"Nope. It is the feed from the base." He turned on the radio, switched to a setting simply listed as SAT and turned up the volume. Digitized voices came through the speakers.

"*TURNKEY, this is BLAZER. We have the convoy in visual.*"

Jamie said to Sue, "That's the SF ODA. They intended to stop the convoy about 50 klicks west of Konduz.

A different digital voice, this time surrounded by additional vibration noise arguing the speaker was in a helicopter: "*TURNKEY, this is MANCHESTER. We are 5 mikes out from interception. Request approval to engage.*"

Jamie said, "That's the SBS guys. They decided to hit their target just outside the village of Balkh before it got to Sheberghan. I guess Massoni was wrong. The coordination worked out."

Sue nodded and said, "So far, so good."

A louder signal on the speakers pointed to a transmission from Camp Marmal. "*BLAZER and MANCHESTER, you have approval to engage.*"

Jamie said to Sue, "I wish I was in the FOB so I could watch."

"Me too."

"Well, instead, we are going to be crossing the Amu Darya in a very romantic way. The ferry is a Soviet landing craft. Really not much more than a barge with a lift gate, but then again the Amu Darya here is barely 200 meters across. I don't think we are at any risk." As he said that, he turned off the main road, headed west on a single, poorly paved street and ended up at the ferry point. As Jamie said, he simply waved at the Afghans and drove onto the barge.

ODA 134 commander Captain Gene Tambler sat in the ancient Toyota Land Cruiser that served as his low visibility command vehicle. Behind the wheel was his team sergeant, SFC Nate Mizkowicz. The team deputy commander, CWO Jason Markus, was in the back seat managing the internal team communications. They were on a ridgeline overlooking the highway. On the left and right sides of the highway were the rest of the ODA along with a company of Afghan commandos. This type of stop and search was pretty routine for the team. The only challenge was to prevent the Afghan commandos from transitioning between stop and search to stop and destroy. Markus said, "All good, Gene."

"Jason, let 'em loose."

"*Blazer 3, Blazer 4, this is 6. TINFOIL. GO, GO, GO.*" Tambler watched through a long-range night vision scope that would normally be attached to the ODA machine guns.

A flash on the road in front of the trucks told Tambler that the road-cratering charge had worked as planned. It forced the lead truck in the convoy to stop. The other three trucks stopped and tried to reverse to get out of what they perceived, correctly, as the kill zone of an ambush. Unfortunately for the drivers, just behind the last truck the Afghans had pulled a set of heavy-duty spike strips, designed to shred tires. In short order the first truck was stopped and the last truck could no longer run because its tires were completely destroyed. The Afghan commandos, dressed in desert camouflage, approached the convoy carefully. The company commander and the local National Directorate of Security paramilitary chief were in the lead. Tambler watched as the convoy drivers crawled out of their trucks with hands up. They fell to their knees as soon as they touched the ground. No shots were fired. The commandos used flex cuffs to control the drivers before putting hoods over their heads and leading them to a waiting NDS van. They would be in the joint SOF-Commando-NDS interrogation facility in Camp Marmal in less than an hour.

"*Blazer 6, 3. We have control of the vehicles. As advertised. A weapons shipment headed to some bad guy.*"

Markus said, "*Well done, gents. We will send for the Commando trucks to clear the cargo and move the trucks off the road.*" He turned to the ODA commander and said, "Gene, another good night's work, eh?"

Tambler said, "Let's hope our Brit colleagues have it this easy."

George looked down from the UK Joint Special Forces Aviation Wing Westland Gazelle that was carrying his team toward the target. His Gazelle was the first of three aircraft approaching the convoy at 90 degrees from the route of travel. Through his night vision goggles, he could see the three-vehicle convoy stretched out in front of him and about a mile ahead. The doors on the Gazelle were open and the four SBS operators were sitting on the floor of the aircraft with their feet on the skids. George and Mac were on one side, Dozer and Brian on the other. Dozer had an AW50 .50 caliber sniper rifle in a harness attached to the aircraft for a more stable shooting platform. The plan was to fly over the lead vehicle, turn the aircraft so that Dozer had a clear shot to disable the vehicle, and then land. The four SBS operators would then approach the lead vehicle and capture the driver and any other passengers. Just behind the Gazelle was a UKSF Chinook carrying another SBS section mounted in a light strike vehicle lovingly called a war buggy. Once the lead vehicle was stopped, the Chinook would land behind the convoy, and the SBS section would drive off the tailgate and secure the rear of the convoy. A second SBS section was following in a US SOF MH60 Blackhawk. Once the convoy was secured, they would land and assist in controlling the drivers and site exploitation. UKSF, including SAS and SBS, trained for these types of convoy operations and conducted them in Afghanistan, Iraq and the Horn of Africa for years. Not an easy job, but one that was completely within the normal range of the SBS skills.

George switched to the command net and said, *"MANCHESTER, this is 6. One minute out."*

The team leaders in the two other helicopters responded. The pilot of the Gazelle throttled up as they passed over the lead truck, banked right and placed the aircraft in a hover approximately 100 meters in front of the truck. As soon as the aircraft stabilized, Dozer fired his first shot. The round passed through the radiator of the truck and entered the engine block, damaging pistons along the way before exiting into the firewall of the truck. A second .50 caliber round followed, completely destroying the engine block. The truck ground to a halt as the mix of engine heat, moving parts and cracked block spun the driveshaft out of control. The Gazelle landed and the four SBS operators headed to the front of the convoy, their rifles at the ready.

The drivers in the second and third trucks only knew that the lead truck stopped. No brake lights signaled the halt, so the second truck crashed into the rear of first truck and the third truck barely avoided a collision with the second. The RAF Chinook landed and the war buggy drove off the ramp and toward the trail vehicle. The SBS vehicle stopped ten yards to the rear of the truck. The gunner with his general purpose machine gun in the war buggy covered the trucks while the two SBS troopers in the back started to move toward the convoy. As the Chinook took off, the MH60 Blackhawk landed and delivered another eight SBS operators.

The driver from the second truck got out to berate his partner. He saw one pair of the SBS lead section working carefully toward the first truck, M4 carbines at ready and night vision googles on their helmets making them look like creatures from another world. He turned toward the rear of the convoy and saw another set of alien creatures headed his way. Fear captured him and he started to run away from the convoy. He made it to the ditch on the south side of the road when a round hit him in the chest.

The gunshot from the ditch was the first sign that things were not going to go precisely as planned. The first round was followed by several more. Rifle fire started from a location to the south of the road and then intensified to the front of the convoy. George looked to the south and couldn't see any sign of the shooters, but it was clear they would have to secure the trucks and handle the shooters at the same time. He couldn't see the shooters in front of the convoy, but he could hear the rounds hitting the front of the truck. Those rounds were definitely not rifle rounds. Heavy machine gun to be sure. He keyed the boom microphone on his helmet and said, "*3, can you engage the shooters to our south?*"

"*Roger, 6. Standby.*" The sound of the GPMG fired from the war buggy settled more than a few nerves on the SBS team. "*My scope shows a half dozen of the villains 100m to our south. I can put suppressive fire on the target. The tracers should give you location and range.*"

"*Roger, 3. 2, your move.*"

"Roger, 6. We will flank."

"5, We have villains in front of us as well. I don't know whether they are allies of our smugglers or just everyday bandits. Either way, we need to set up fighting positions on the north side of the convoy."

"Roger, 6." George, Mac, Brian and Dozer moved to the north side of the vehicles to stay clear of any incoming from the ambushers to the south. As Brian and Dozer searched the road heading west to determine who was shooting at them from that direction, Mac and George worked their way along the vehicles. Green tracer rounds from the front continued to hit the truck. Rounds hit the road in front of the truck, ricocheted off the pavement and hit the tires. The truck tires deflated and suddenly the lead truck was resting on its front bumper.

Dozer said, *"6, 2. We can make out three trucks. HMGs mounted in the back of each truck. Movement to our front. Looks like there is a squad headed our way."*

"Roger, 2. As soon as you can engage, do so."

Dozer and Brian were in prone firing positions located slightly to the rear of the front tire of the front truck. Dozer still had the AW50 and was working with Brian to get the proper range so he could engage any target that came into view. Just as he sent the first shot toward the threat, two of his SBS mates arrived in the war wagon. Made of tubular aluminum, the war buggy looked like something that should be cruising a sand beach, except for the heavy machine gun attached to the top of the frame. As it arrived and the driver identified an appropriate position for the vehicle, the gunner turned to Dozer and said, "You need some help?"

"Might do."

"Excellent. I will start by sending some general delivery up the road. OK?"

"Sounds good." The roar of the GPMG machine gun ended any further conversation.

Meanwhile, George and Mac were working along the convoy, trying to determine who and what they had stopped. George immediately realized the shooting from the front had killed the first driver and his passenger. As they scrambled to the back of the truck, George moved the tarp as Mac ducked into the bed of the truck to check for other adversaries. What he saw surprised him. He shook his head, flipped up his night vision goggle and turned on the light mounted to his M4. He shouted over the gunfire to George, "This is not what we expected. We have just intercepted what looks like a drug convoy."

At the same time, George received a call from the end of the convoy, "*6, we have a bit of trouble back here. We have hospital supplies as well as a dozen young women chained to the floor.*"

George responded, "*5, check the boxes. I think we are looking at smuggled morphine. Now you are telling me we have smuggled women. We don't have any people up here but we have crates of hospital grade morphine.*" George had already run to the middle vehicle. In the chaos of the firefight the driver and passenger had disappeared. In the bed of this truck, he found weapons crates. The crate closest to him identified the weapons as the newest generation of AK74 rifles.

At that point, the headsets of all the SBS operators were filled with a much louder, much clearer voice. "*MANCHESTER, this is TURNKEY. The UAV has identified three technicals parked side-by-side firing at your position. The images show some additional fighters headed your way. This is no longer a simple ambush operation. I have called in air support.*"

George responded, "*Roger, TURNKEY. We have the full team on the ground, multiple dead or missing drivers and along with weapons, we have crates of hospital grade morphine and it looks like a dozen women prisoners.*"

"*MANCHESTER, say again. Women?*"

"*Roger. They were in the back of the last truck. I say again, there are weapons in this convoy but there are also smuggled crates of morphine and the dozen women chained together and chained to the floor. We are engaging a small ground force to the south. Once we have them under control, we will move to the rear of the convoy. Please tell air, anyone west of the lead truck will be enemy.*"

"*Roger, MANCHESTER. Do you need any additional manpower?*"

"*Not at this time. We have the ground situation handled. We will need air for the technicals and, eventually, helos for extraction.*"

A new, American voice came on the air, *"TURNKEY, this is REAPER. We are on station. I understand MANCHESTER is located around the three trucks we see stopped on the highway. Correct?"*

George responded, *"Roger, REAPER. We have our ID flashes on. Can you confirm?"*

The gunner in the AC130 used his IR sight to scan the convoy area. He counted the number of small flashes of IR tape attached to the SBS uniforms. He said, *"MANCHESTER, I count sixteen, one six, friendlies. Please confirm."*

"Roger, REAPER. One six friendlies."

"OK, you will hear from us shortly."

The one SBS team flanking the southern attackers arrived at the firing position to find two dead fighters and no sign of any other shooters. They did a quick search of the bodies for intelligence, grabbed the ancient Kalashnikov rifles left behind and headed back to the convoy. Just as they arrived, they heard coming from the sky what sounded like a giant piece of Velcro hook being torn from a giant piece of Velcro pile. Each time they heard the ripping sound, they saw a line of red tracers coming out of the sky and hitting some distance away. This sound was followed by the sound of multiple cannon rounds and then another Velcro tearing sound. More cannon fire, more ripping Velcro. The AC130 was engaging the targets with its mini-guns and the automatic cannon. The sophisticated guns and gunsights on the left side of the aircraft allowed the pilot to focus on simply orbiting around the target and allowing his onboard gunners to do the rest.

George was at the end of the convoy now, counting heads and looking at the terrified young women in the bed of the trailing truck.

Brian turned to Mac and said, "Mate, you hear that sound? That's the sound of freedom."

Mac nodded and said, "More like the wrath of Zeus."

Brian said, "Where did a Scottish heathen get a classical education?"

"My local school taught me to read. While you are sleeping on our flights, I read. *The Odyssey*, mate, is a cracking read. You should try it."

In his headset, George heard *"TURNKEY and MANCHESTER, this is REAPER. We have eliminated the vehicle and foot threat to your West. We will continue the orbit until you are clear of the area. Have a good evening and call if you need additional assistance."*

George smiled and turned to Dozer and said, "A gunner with a sense of humor."

Dozer said, "Fine by me. I love the gunships. They are life savers."

"Too true, mate."

Sue and Jamie had pulled the Ranger to the side of the road while they listened to the firefight. In the glow from the instruments, Jamie could see Sue fidgeting. He said, "They are going to be OK. As long as you have SPECTRE on your side, you have good fortune."

Sue nodded, "Yup. The gunship makes all the difference in the world. Especially in the dark. But what do we do now that we know half the convoy was going to drug smugglers and people smugglers? And, by the way, which drug smugglers? It's not like we have a shortage of those guys up here."

"Sue, I'm going to go for the big bluff. I'm hoping that our guy doesn't really know who the end user was going to be, so we are going to tell him that it was Mansour Baluchi. He is basically the super smuggler on the Afghan-Iran border. He runs convoys across the entire region. Armed technicals traveling at high speed deliver drugs to Iran, Syria, Lebanon and Europe. The fact that the shipment had hospital grade morphine argues that it had to be someone with a major distribution network. As to the people smuggling, probably sex slave smuggling, there is only one network that could do that: Mansour Baluchi. He might be shipping the women to a smuggling network in the Gulf, to Europe, or even to the USA. No matter what, he is the guy who could pull this off. His convoys regularly run up against the IRGC border guards and absolutely smash the poor kids because his guys have plenty of firepower and motivation to succeed."

"I have never thought of the IRGC as poor kids."

"These aren't the high-end creeps we usually face. Definitely not the al-Quds special forces who train the Shia militias in Iraq or the Hizballahis in Lebanon. The IRGC border troops are basically underpaid and understaffed recruits. They aren't given the arms necessary to fight in any firefight. And why should they be? After all, it's been a couple of centuries since the Afghans invaded Iran. Think about what George and his crew would have been facing if they didn't have SPECTRE on call? Bad juju."

"So, what do we gain by telling Ahmed Bey that we intercepted the convoy going to Baluchi?"

Jamie put the Ranger into gear and said, "We tell him that we are going to let Baluchi know that he gave us the details on his smuggling operation for a simple lump sum payment. That way, we get LEVERAGE over him. He either works with us, gives up the network and we put him on ice somewhere in Afghanistan, or we just let Baluchi come visit and they negotiate in an entirely…different sort of way." Jamie was smiling in his most personable way. Sue realized it could be a terrifying sort of smile. "Now, what I want to know is whether you want to play the good guy or the bad guy."

"I think maybe the good guy."

"Because you think I like playing the bad guy?"

"No, because you are a terrifying bad guy."

The same smile. "Thank you!"

>>>>>> A GRAVEYARD FOR SPIES

A ll across the United States, Memorial Day weekend is the opening of summer picnics. As one of the largest parks in Erie County, Emery Park was crowded over that weekend as families moved to the outdoor pavilions under hemlocks, maples and sycamore trees. They cooked on charcoal grills and children enjoyed the swings, slides and teeter-totters. Teens and 20-somethings used the Frisbee golf course, ran or biked along the trails on the park. The work week after Memorial Day was when the Park grounds crew used the time to clean the park and prepare for the regular summer visitors who would flood the park after the schools closed in June.

By 30 May in Emery Park, there were other, less common visitors. FBI teams converged on the park to set up surveillance cameras and audio equipment in the pavilion that would be used for the meeting between Barbara O'Connell and the Irish assassin Brian Delaney. The pavilion location at the far end of the park meant that SWAT would be able to set up their command vehicles outside the park grounds. The SWAT team would enter the park over the low fences that separated the grounds from private property. FBI surveillance teams were prepositioned in half the pavilions in the park as well as along the main roads in and out of the park. Benzinger approached the closest household just outside the park and received permission from the homeowners to use the garage as a tactical command post. It would be in the command post where Benzinger, Jones, her supervisor Nate Chason, and the FBI SWAT team leader, a young, Marine Recon veteran, would wait and watch. Reimer insisted he needed to be inside the park, so they gave him an Erie County Parks and

Recreation vest and let him drive one of the garbage trucks involved in the post Memorial Day cleanup. He was not amused.

The Buffalo FBI Special Agent in Charge, Don Peabody, was stationed along with Janice Macintosh and Mary Sanderson in the FBI field office mobile command post parked inside the South Wales Fire Station a mile from the park. Peabody had years as a field agent and he made it clear to Janice and Mary as he picked them up at the Buffalo airport that they were welcome guests but they were not going to mess with his operations. This wasn't the first time that Buffalo Field Office had been involved in a high-profile case. The arrest of a terrorist support network in Lackawanna in 2002 was just one of many cases where the field office was under scrutiny from FBI headquarters. However, it was the first time the field office had this type of case since Peabody took charge. He had spent a career working violent crime and, post 9/11, working Hizballah cases in the Detroit field office, so Peabody knew that it was always good to deploy extra resources just in case. This was the first time he had ever done so for a counterintelligence case, and he wanted to let his people do their job. The visitors from Washington could watch it all on the screens inside the command center.

After the briefing, and as the resources were deployed to the park, Barbara hoped that something would happen. If not, there were plenty of people involved who would be pissed at her since everyone acknowledged this was *her* plan. She drove her Range Rover to the empty pavilion five minutes before the meeting time, got out, and waited for the arrival of…who? Would Delaney show up himself? Would one of his teammates show up? Would a Russian agent show up? Barbara didn't know, but she hoped someone would show up. She had refused the offer of Second Chance lightweight body armor. At over 75 degrees Fahrenheit, she knew it would be a dead give-away if the target saw her wearing heavy clothes in this heat. What she didn't tell the FBI or Benzinger when they set up her communications was that she was carrying a pistol. Her Smith and Wesson revolver was in a deep, inside-the-waistband holster. She knew she was surrounded by shooters, but if there was shooting to be done, Barbara wanted to be the one who did it.

Summertime in western New York can be rainy, hot and humid, or cool and dry. As Barbara waited at one of the concrete picnic benches inside the pavilion, she said to no one in particular, "This is a perfect summer day."

Almost immediately, Mary's voice went off in her earbud, *"Is there someone there we can't see?"*

Barbara was more than a bit embarrassed. She answered, "Nope. Just an old lady talking to herself."

The next time the earbud sounded, it was a young man's voice. Clearly one of the FBI surveillants. *"Time check. It is 1606hrs and we have a guy in black leathers on a red Ducati motorcycle entering the park."*

A minute later, a second surveillant said, *"He's on the road toward the target. We didn't get the license plate. It has a black filter plate cover"*

Chason's voice came on the net, *"Standby, standby. We have a possible heading to the target. Black leathers, red Ducati bike. No plate identified. Barb, it looks like it is showtime."*

"*Roger.*" Barbara couldn't think of anything else to say. She didn't want to gripe to Chason that no one had called her Barb since she left high school. She took a couple of deep breaths in an effort to wash out some of the adrenaline. She stood up and placed herself in the pavilion in such a manner that the man on the bike would have to dismount to get to her. She assumed the persona of the angry client about to complain about a job half-done. First, she heard the Ducati engine echoing through the trees as it ran through the narrow roads toward her pavilion. She thought she heard the sound of a diesel heading her way as well. Terry in the garbage truck? Well, that might be an amusing chase. She hoped he kept his distance for a bit.

The motorcycle rider was in view as he cleared the tree-lined path and drove on the last 200 meters of pavement toward the pavilion.

At the time, Barbara just knew. She couldn't explain why she knew, but she just knew it wasn't going to go well. Barbara walked toward the Range Rover as the bike pulled up. In what seemed slow motion, she saw the rider raise his right hand in a greeting and then realized he was tossing a hand grenade towards her. She heard the ping as the spoon left the grenade and armed the green baseball shape. Barbara jumped in front of the Rover keeping the engine, transmission and front axle between her and the grenade. The grenade hit one of the picnic tables just as the rider accelerated at full throttle. For some reason, the uneven surface of the table resulted in the grenade rolling toward the center of the pavilion and away from the Range Rover and Barbara O'Connell. The explosion was deafening as the pavilion roof and concrete picnic tables contained both the explosion and the shrapnel.

Barbara completed a shoulder roll and was on the far side of the Rover standing up when the grenade exploded. She pulled out her revolver and fired two rounds at the retreating motorcycle. The two rounds hit in the center of the black leather jacket. The motorcyclist straightened up as if pulled from the handlebars by a large hand. He fell off the bike. The Ducati continued for several feet before it fell over. By the time Barbara had watched these events, she could see multiple vehicles with flashing red and blue lights arriving on scene. They probably had their sirens on, but the ringing from the grenade still filled Barbara's ears. First on site was the black FBI SWAT van. Two men in sage-green flight suits and armored vests jumped out carrying M4s and headed toward the motorcyclist.

Barbara felt two very strong hands grabbing her shoulders. At first she was scared the motorcyclist had an accomplice. She ducked and twisted in a way to break the grip. As she turned and came up to face her attacker, she saw the black vest with FBI emblazoned on it and then the black helmet and face shield. She saw the camouflage uniform and the M4 carbine. Four more men dressed in similar outfits were coming out of the woods. FBI SWAT had arrived in force.

"Ma'am, are you OK?"

Barbara could see he was talking to her, but she couldn't hear him. "What?" she shouted.

The SWAT officer spoke into the boom microphone on his helmet, "We've got her. She's suffered some hearing damage and there are at least four shrapnel wounds on her back and left shoulder. Nothing life threatening, but we will start first aid now. We need the medics and an ambulance." He gently reached out and put both hands on Barbara's right hand that was still holding the Smith and Wesson. "Ma'am, I need to take this now." Barbara complied.

Reimer ran up to Barbara. He was dressed in a county park jumpsuit. He looked at Barbara and then over at the Range Rover. He said with a smile, "You know grenade shrapnel is probably not covered in your auto insurance."

"What?"

Reimer said, "Never mind" as he tossed a space blanket over her shoulders and walked her to the ambulance.

31 May 2007. Termez, Uzbekistan

Jamie drove the Ranger into a run-down business district less than a mile from the river. They set up in the warehouse that he had rented shortly after his arrival in Hairatan. One of the first rules of cross-border operations in both the espionage and the special operations trades was to build infrastructure. This was part of Jamie's infrastructure. They pulled the Ranger into the warehouse, closed the steel doors and waited. The warehouse was empty except for broken and abandoned lathes, drill presses and power saws that were remnants of a tool-and-die shop from the last decade of the USSR. At the far end of the shop was an office with a metal desk, three metal chairs, and a small table set with tea, Russian glass tea cups, and a small plate of Uzbek cookies.

Sue looked around and said, "You are such a good host."

"At your service. The Tomahawks do all the work. I just give them the requirement and like magic, it appears."

"And they are delivering our guest?"

"Why yes. They are inviting him to come visit even as we speak. I told them I want him here by midnight. I hope they set their watches to Uzbek time because…" The exterior door opened and a small, former Soviet ambulance pulled into the warehouse. Jamie looked at his watch and said, "I guess they didn't sort out the time change. Afghanistan is 30 minutes behind Uzbekistan. Confusing, no?" Jamie looked up at the ceiling and said, "Terry, do we have good comms?"

In their two earbuds, Terry's voice came through, *"Absolutely fine. We are taping the session. We have audio and video."*

"Excellent."

As Sue looked out through the plate glass window in the office, she said, "Audio and video?"

"Audio because I can't remember shit. Video so that I can prove, yet again, that I am gentle when I have an offsite interrogation. I know this may seem silly, but Headquarters always wants to see the video to be sure."

Flash's voice came through the comms, "*I am shocked.*"

Sue watched as three of Jamie's Afghan hires, known as the Tomahawks, pulled a short, fat man from the ambulance. He was hooded and his hands were tied in front of him. The rope around his hands was tied to one of his legs. The very end of the rope was under the control of one of the Tomahawks. Another rope was tied around the hooded man's neck and controlled by a second Tomahawk.

Sue turned to Jamie and said, "Overkill?"

"I work for the department of redundancy department. If one set of ropes is good, a second set is even better. Plus, it emphasizes to our guest that we are serious."

"OK, so do I start or do you?"

"Good guy always gets to start."

"Perfect."

The Tomahawks brought Ahmed Bey into the office and sat him down in a chair in front of the desk. They tied the two sets of ropes to the chair legs. Ahmed Bey was going nowhere. The three Tomahawks sat on the floor next to the door. They were not about to miss the show. Jamie put his finger to his lips. They nodded. They would make no sound.

Sue used her most polite and formal Persian to address their prisoner. She said, "Agha Bey, thank you for coming to see us."

Bey responded with a croak.

Sue said, "Throat dry? Would you like some tea? If I give you some tea, will you promise to drink it without lifting your hood above your lips?"

Bey nodded.

"Excellent." Sue took her time filling a cup with tea and sugar. The smell of the black tea filled the room. She handed the cup to Bey and he raised it to his lips. He slurped his tea and finished it quickly.

"I hope you feel better now."

Bey nodded.

Jamie slammed the flat of his hand on the metal desk that was less than three feet away from their prisoner. The noise echoed in the room. He spoke in very slow Persian in the style used by senior clerics trained in Qom and Najaf. Jamie spoke in barely a whisper. "Do you want to live, Ahmed Bey?"

Bey nodded.

"Do you hope to profit from tonight?"

Another nod.

"Do you know why you are here?"

Bey shook his head.

"You are here because you have done a very bad thing, Ahmed Bey. You have been working with Mansour Baluchi. You have given him poison that he intends to distribute in the Islamic Republic. Do you know how we feel about this, Ahmed Bey? We are the Guardians of the Revolution. We have lost men to Baluchi. We are losing people to the venom of his drugs. We have captured your shipment, Ahmed Bey. The real question tonight is whether you will see the dawn."

Sue walked over to Bey and said, "Would you like more tea, Ahmed Bey?"

He nodded.

Jamie said, "Do you know why the Colonel is so nice to you, Ahmed Bey?"

Bey shook his head.

"Because she is certain that she will be the one to kill you tonight."

Bey started to shake. Sue arrived with the tea and said, "Here you are, Ahmed Bey."

As he drank his tea, Sue said "Please tell us what you know about your network, Ahmed Bey. We want to know how you get your guns, how you get your drugs and, most especially, how you get the women you were sending to Mansour Baluchi. My colleague, Colonel Meshki will be taking notes. We already know much about your operation, Ahmed Bey, so please do not waste our time."

Jamie and Sue crossed over to Afghanistan on the first ferry of the day. They were both in a good mood. Ahmed Bey had cracked like an egg and offered up everything he knew about his network. In two hours, they were able to build a network analysis that would allow for joint operations across three countries. Ahmed Bey described his network that stretched into both Uzbekistan and Kazakhstan and then extended as far south as Kabul.

Sue said, "Now what happens to Ahmed Bey?"

"The Tomahawks will drop him off just north of Termez. We told him that he would be watched and that we intended to destroy his network. If he doesn't believe us, then he will be resolved either through the Uzbek and Kazakh operations or through some operation we do here in Afghanistan. I suppose you saw the tag we put in his wallet."

"Small. Good range?"

"Good enough when you have the UAV network we have here. Let's just hope, for Ahmed Bey's sake, he decides to make a run for it and start some other criminal enterprise someplace else."

Sue nodded, "The best news is we got the Russian paramilitary contractors' link to Afghanistan. We can't do much if they stay in Uzbekistan or Tajikistan. If they come across the Amu Darya, we now have enough information to find, fix and finish them."

Jamie smiled his not so nice smile, "Sweet revenge for killing your pal, Nicolai."

"Hardly my pal. Remember, he locked me in a trunk."

Jamie smiled and said, "You say that like it is a bad thing."

Bill O'Connell was sitting at his desk working through the previous day's surveillance logs trying to match known offenders with his list of Hizballah activists and with suspect Iranian intelligence officers. It was like trying to piece together a jigsaw puzzle with some of the pieces missing and with no idea what the picture might be. He looked up to see his former teammate from the Gang Task Force, Molly Norton, walking up to his desk with two cups of coffee in cobalt-blue ceramic FBI mugs. Bill had been plotting to arrange a meeting with Norton for months. She was definitely the target of his affections.

"When exactly were you going to tell me you were from a family of superheroes?"

Bill smiled, took the coffee and said, "I have no idea what you are talking about."

Any opportunity to spend time with her was a good deal. When they were on the same squad, it was not close to a good idea to date. Now that they were on different squads, they would date but they couldn't find the time to do so. Office conversations seemed the only time they could get together.

"OK, so you don't know?"

"Trust me, I don't know. I've been here since 0700 this morning trying to make sense of the material in front of me. Is it something about my sister? Wounded warrior, special operator, savior of the free world?"

"Don't whine. I actually think your work is going to be part of saving our little part of the free world. No, I was talking about your mother."

"My mother?" All Bill could think to say next was, "Not again?"

"Hey, the word is she was involved in a case hunting an assassin. The assassin sends a man to kill her with a hand grenade…," she nodded, "Yes, a hand grenade. He tosses the grenade, she ducks, the grenade goes off, she stands up and puts two rounds into the villain before he can get away."

"She's ok?"

"The word is some temporary deafness from the grenade and a couple of stitches, but otherwise, fine. And, since she didn't kill the perpetrator, even the locals are pretty happy. I guess she runs with a revolver and the first round was bird shot followed by a regular .38. Dropped the guy with the second shot. Since he was wearing a modern biker's jacket with a Kevlar back, no real damage done. He is now being interrogated. Cool, eh?"

Bill looked up from his coffee cup. "Yeah, cool."

03 June 2007 Chautauqua House

Terry Reimer drove down from East Aurora to see how Barbara O'Connell was doing after the evening in Emery Park. He also wanted to pass on an update from the interrogation of her assailant. He would not have admitted he also just wanted to see Barbara O'Connell. On arrival, it was clear Barbara was doing fine. She greeted him at the door in a set of black sweats and some sort of karate shoes. It looked as if she had just finished a workout, so the few stitches she got from the shrapnel wounds hadn't slowed her down. One clue that she was still a little rattled was that as she opened the door, Reimer noticed that she was holding an ancient revolver in her right hand.

He asked, "Always greet guests this way?"

Barbara smiled and put the pistol down on a small table by the door. "For the last few years, yes. Well, at least unannounced guests. Come on in."

Once he walked into the house, she closed the door, locked it, bolted it and jammed a thin steel chock under the door. She invited him into the kitchen. The back side of the house overlooked Chautauqua Lake.

"I brought some cannelloni from the bakery in East Aurora."

"Well, for cannelloni, you get to sit at the table and get your choice of coffee or tea."

"Barbara, coffee will be great." There was a small table with two chairs at the window. On the table were a computer tablet and a cup of hot tea. Reimer looked into the coffee cup Barbara O'Connell just poured for him. It had been a while since he had a friendly conversation with a woman his own age and he was trying not to make it sound too awkward. He started as best he could, "You OK?"

He was surprised when Barbara replied with more than a simple "sure." She said, "I've still got some ringing in my ears, and the stitches on my left shoulder and the general bruising from the explosion meant some restless sleep. But, considering the alternatives, the fact that I am vertical and breathing is pretty darn good."

Reimer smiled and said, "Did you have any intention of telling us that you were armed?"

"No."

"Any reason?"

"No."

"I know you have a legal permit to carry in New York, but you were surrounded by about twenty armed lawmen."

"And you saw how much that made a difference at the time."

"You haven't changed much since Germany."

"More miles, more tears, and more than my share of bad times."

"During the debrief yesterday, Mary said you lost your husband to a Russian assassination. What happened?"

"Peter was running a case against the Soviets. The USSR falls apart, parts of the KGB become the Russian mafia, parts morph into the Russian secret services. We still don't know for sure who decided to kill Peter. They poisoned him."

Reimer hadn't expected the candor. He didn't know what to say. He just nodded.

Barbara realized she had crossed the line into "too much information" for this old colleague, so she switched to a subject that would take them well away from the past. She said, "What do we know about my pal on the motorcycle?"

"Who only survived because your round was a standard .38."

Barbara shook her head, smiled and said, "My bad, actually. I didn't change out my loads. When I carry my Smith in self-defense mode, the first round is bird shot, the second round is .38 and the last two are .38 hydroshock. The bird shot is designed to emphasize to any villain that I don't want trouble. The .38 round is just in case the bird shot doesn't do the trick. If that doesn't work, then two hydroshock rounds are designed to end the argument. I'm not in the business of killing folks. Even with a firearm, I want to have options. Think of it as a ladder of consequences. I prefer not to climb the ladder too quickly." Barbara paused to take a sip of her tea.

"I wasn't expecting a gunfight. If I had, I would have gone with full .357 loads or brought a bigger gun."

Reimer smiled and said, "A Smith and Wesson Model 60 is certainly a big enough gun. As to what loads you use, that explains the pellets the forensics dug out of his jacket. The forensics folks were going crazy trying to find the missing first round. The second round of .38 hit him just below the shoulder blades but he was wearing one of those new motorcycle jackets that has a Kevlar back designed to prevent a road rash if the rider falls off his bike. It shook him up, but didn't do much damage at all."

"Shame. I do hold a grudge."

"Yeah, well, I can't blame you. I never had someone throw a grenade at me."

"First time for me as well."

Reimer smiled. "According to Janice Macintosh, this wasn't the first gunfight you have lived through."

"True, but it is the first time the bad guys used explosives. More coffee?"

Reimer nodded and watched as Barbara walked over to the coffee pot and poured his second cup. He noticed that throughout, the ancient revolver stayed within reach. She added some hot water to her cup as well and returned to the table.

She said, "Who the heck is he anyhow?"

"Jason Macalvey. According to the Bureau, he's a local enforcer for the mob. Lawyered up right away, so we don't have a lot going for us. The forensics crew didn't find anything interesting on him. He wasn't even carrying a pistol."

"Figured the grenade was good enough."

"Guess so."

"How pissed is your boss? I ask because I already know how pissed the Agency and the FBI are at me."

"Benzinger is good people. He couldn't see any reason why you wouldn't try to cap the guy who threw a grenade at you. His only heartache is we don't seem to be any closer to catching Polchak's murderer."

Barbara took a sip from her tea and said, "I don't know about that. Take a look at this." She worked the small keyboard on the tablet and then turned the screen toward Reimer. The screen displayed an email that Barbara O'Connell had received earlier that morning. She said, "Note the address. This isn't the address we were using to contact our assassin. This is my personal email account."

Reimer read the email:

Magpie or should I say Barbara?

It appears I did not appreciate your skills. The good news is my messenger was just a local villain, so it really doesn't matter to me what happens to him. Now, what happens next? I can't believe you cared about the Russian traitor living in your midst. Perhaps it was something I did in the past?

It will be better for you and your family if we simply call this a draw. By the time you read this, I will be back in Europe enjoying my villa on the beach. You should do the same. There comes a time when cease fire is the only solution. There is a special graveyard for spies, but I would hate to think you would join your husband and his father there anytime soon.

Michael Patrick O'Connell

Reimer looked up from the screen. He said, "Is this some sort of game you Klingons play? And who the heck is Michael Patrick O'Connell? I mean, this guy seems to be enjoying the cat and mouse."

"I can't say what's going on, Terry. I thought I was brought into this whole thing because of the assassin's link to a case of mine in 1994. You remember that Mary told me that this creep may have killed an asset of mine in Germany back in the day."

Terry nodded and said, "When we were working together?"

"Yup."

"The case in Bad Homburg?"

"Yup."

"I hate this guy."

"Me too. But now it appears that there is some sort of link between my husband's family and this assassin, Michael O'Connell. What I haven't sorted out yet is how much Mary Sanderson, Janice Macintosh, or even our young Special Agent Jones knew about the case. I will be seriously pissed if I find out they all knew that Delaney was really O'Connell and there is some sort of link to who killed either my husband or his father. I spent a couple of years believing that it was a Russian mafia family. I don't know anymore. The only thing we can say for sure was Peter O'Connell Senior was killed in this house by a sniper."

"So what are you going to do next?"

"I am going to engage some assistance outside the system."

"Do you need someone inside the system?"

"As long as you understand this is going to get more confusing and, probably, more dangerous."

"I already know you, so how much more dangerous can it become?"

Barbara smiled, "You never know with the O'Connells."

>>>>>> OLD COLLEAGUES, NEW FRIENDS

S ue and Flash had packed their kit and walked it down to the main entrance of the FOB. Both were dressed in flight suits with just name and rank on the leather ID patch, drop holster on a black web belt, and red beret tucked into the zippered pocket on the right calf. They had their M4 rifles leaning against their kit bags. Assembled at the door were the Agency crew working with Jamie. They had stopped work long enough to say goodbye to their SOF counterparts.

Each of Jamie's team gave Flash a bear hug followed by, "See you on the other side, Flash."

Sue got a more formal handshake, but the same farewell. She could see why Flash had enjoyed her time in Jamie's newest spot. They were a war zone family working hard against an important target. The addition of drug smugglers and people traffickers made the work even more important. For now, the SOF mission would be more kinetic and less collection. Sue and Flash's time here was never supposed to be more than a TDY to expand the SOF target set, and their mission was complete. They had to return to Italy to work the next set of targets. They walked outside in the bright sunshine and 100-degree heat. Jamie was waiting in one of the Ranger pickup trucks. Even through the armored doors, Sue could hear the music from what she had come to recognize as "Jamie's playlist."

"More of Jamie's music?"

Flash shrugged and said, "His turf, I reckon we have to give him at least that much one more time."

Jamie opened the driver's door and said, "Hey, are we going to stand here all day? I know you feel sad about leaving this luxury hotel, but I would like to get you back to Mazar before you figure out a way to destroy either another of my vehicles or my new home."

Flash flipped a one fingered salute at Jamie as she threw her black duffle into the seat behind the driver. She grabbed Sue's bag, tossed it on top of hers and jumped into the open back seat. Sue got into the front seat and closed the armored door. She looked over to Jamie and said, "How about a quiet drive back to the airfield."

Jamie smiled and said, "Not a chance." He flipped on the CD player, and a mix of songs from the 1980s started to play as he barreled out of the compound and headed toward Mazar-e-Sharif.

B arbara was working as hard as she could to keep her temper in check. So far, she hadn't had much luck. She was talking on the encrypted phone to Mary Sanderson and at several points in the conversation she considered simply hanging up, driving down to Northern Virginia and choking her old friend.

"So, when did you know that this guy was Michael O'Connell?"

"Barbara, I know you are pissed, but it's not as if you needed to know that part of the equation to get the job done."

"And what part of the job are we talking about? The part where the creep threw a grenade at me? The part that the FBI is pissed that I had a pistol and resolved the case before SWAT could do the job? The part where I have now received a letter from an Irish assassin ON MY HOME EMAIL ADDRESS? Which part did I not need to know?"

"See, I knew you weren't going to be open-minded about this case."

"OPEN MINDED?!"

"That was a joke, sister. You have every right to be angry. I just don't have a lot of good answers for you. First, you may or may not believe me, but we didn't know that Delaney was O'Connell until yesterday when you got the email. In fact, we still don't actually know that Delaney is O'Connell. We only know for sure that the person who sent you the email claims to be an O'Connell and claims to have been part of the operation that killed Andropovich."

"So, you still don't know much about O'Connell?"

"I didn't say that."

"I noticed. So, spill."

"OK, but remember, this is still a pretty close-hold deal. Janice still wants to move forward on the case tracking O'Connell. Any action on your part might run up against our efforts, so I need you to tell me you are going to follow my lead on this."

Barbara knew enough about Washington to know that this was the moment when she needed to calm down and sound cooperative. That didn't mean she had to buy into any directives from the Agency or the FBI. But it did mean that if she wanted to know what they knew, she had to play the game by their rules, at least for a while. "OK, I get it that this is a bigger game than just me and my grudge against a guy who killed one of my agents and almost killed me. So, what do you know?"

Over the phone Barbara could hear Mary turning the pages on a file. She said, "Michael Patrick O'Connell. Born, 09 October 1956. New York City. Son of James O'Connell, born 12 December 1929, and Mary Anna Kelly, born 30 May 1933. James O'Connell was one of the more notorious captains of the Irish Republican Army and, perhaps, a Nazi support agent during World War II. Part of a famous family of IRA killers. Moved to New York in 1948 and returned to Ireland with his family in 1968. By the time the Troubles in Northern Ireland were seriously violent in the early 1970s, James O'Connell was already considered a senior leader in the IRA efforts in Armaugh. Based on recovered Stasi files, the father also served as a part time East German intelligence service asset from the early 1960s when he was living in New York. James O'Connell was killed in a British raid on an Armaugh safe house in 1974. In 1974, Michael O'Connell was a foot soldier in the IRA and we assume already linked to the Stasi and maybe the KGB. There was a question at the time on how the Brits knew of the safe house and why they knew to raid it at the time."

Mary Sanderson paused and then continued, "British Intelligence reporting shows Michael was convinced that someone in the Armaugh hierarchy of the IRA was the traitor who delivered his father to ambush. He became a rather brutal enforcer in the IRA counterintelligence arm as he explored the nature of the British penetrations of the Northern Ireland IRA." Mary stopped the story for a moment and said, "Barbara, did you know that your husband had Irish cousins?"

"I didn't know he had any cousins. His father was a pretty closed-mouth type who grew up in a tough Irish neighborhood in the First District of Buffalo. I don't know what was going on in Buffalo in the 1930s, and I'm not sure my father-in-law knew anything about Irish relatives in Ireland. In the 1940s, he was busy fighting the Nazis and in the 1950s, he was plenty busy fighting covert wars against the Soviets. By the mid-1950s, he was already in the Agency and living abroad. I can't imagine he crossed paths with the O'Connell family in New York. What makes you so sure we are even talking about a family member rather than just another alias?"

She took a deep breath and said, "After all, some guy living under the alias Michael O'Connell is a hit man for the KGB. We may assume he is still a hit man. O'Connell isn't exactly Smith in Ireland, but it is a pretty common name. How do we know there is any link to my family?"

Mary said, "The most recent evidence came from the Polchak crime scene. The assassin's sample from the teacup was matched against known DNA. The only close match in the database was pulled out of the Agency databases. It was Peter's DNA, Barb."

Barbara quietly said, "The Agency takes samples of our DNA in case there is a need to identify our remains."

Mary continued, "Of course, Peter's murder remains part of an active Bureau investigation, so they have his DNA as well."

"Where is this guy now?"

"The cyber folks are going after the point-of-presence server from the email. There are a couple of proxy servers involved. So far, all we know is it is somewhere in the Balkans."

"Once you get the geo-location, you are sending in the Reivers, correct?" Barbara used the in-house name for the Agency teams used to capture and manage the safe delivery of selected terrorist targets to appropriate authorities.

"Not as easy as it sounds, Barbara. The Reivers are pretty busy right now on al-Qaida targets. The good news is once we find him, we can definitely make sure we keep him on our targets list until the Reivers are available."

Barbara knew that the list would be long and a Russian contract killer was probably not someone people would go out of their way to capture when the entire force of the United States was hunting the perpetrators of mass terror attacks in New York, Madrid and London. Until they were captured or killed, those resources would be focused on the senior leaders of al Qaida. Barbara couldn't argue that point, so she said, "So long as he doesn't disappear again, it makes sense that we go after him."

"I told Janice you would see it that way."

"She thought I would understand?"

"No. Actually, she said that if someone threw a grenade at her, she would want to be the one to resolve the target."

"Have you sorted out how in the world he got my email address or, for that matter, my true name? In case you haven't noticed, someone has a leak somewhere."

Barbara could hear Mary take a breath. If she was face-to-face with an old colleague, she might have sorted out the truthfulness of the next sentence. Given the fact that this was on the phone, even an encrypted phone, Barbara just assumed she wasn't going to get anything resembling the complete story. Probably not a full-blown lie, but something in that espionage netherworld of half-truth, half lie. Except with officers directly in her chain of command and in field partners, Barbara knew every conversation was colored by the question of "need to know" as well as trust. Barbara just had to listen and then judge for herself where the truth ended and the lie began.

Mary said, "It could be something at your end."

Barbara grew more than a bit peeved, "You mean the end that you provided to me?"

"Hmmm, there is that."

"Do I need to be involved in this witch hunt? After my confrontation with Cyzneski, I know there are witches out there." The capture of a deep penetration of the CIA named Stan Cyzneski was something they both remembered from a previous misadventure.

"Suggestions?"

"Have you thought about asking the spy you have in prison about the leak? He was an arrogant shit, but a few months in solitary confinement might have made him more talkative."

"We did and he hasn't changed much. I'm not sure he is going to change anytime soon. He made it clear he expects to be traded for the next case officer caught in Moscow. In the meantime, he is quiet as the grave."

"Grave indeed, Mary. In the meantime, you can tell Janice that hunting O'Connell somewhere in the Balkans is not something I have any intention of doing. I am not in the globetrotting game anymore."

Mary said, "Except when you are, Barbara. I will let you know more when I know more. Now that you have said that you understand, I feel comfortable sharing the targeting data with you. You never know when we might need your help."

"You never know. Ciao bella."

"Ciao."

Barbara hung up and looked out over Chautauqua Lake. What had she just heard? Did Mary say she would help? Or, did Mary really believe Barbara was finished with this job? As her bosses had told her about difficult cases, it was too soon to tell.

The flights from Mazar-e-Sharif to Bagram and then from Bagram to Vincenza were completely uneventful. Sue put on her Bose headphones, stretched out on the red nylon web seats along the left side of the C17 aircraft and slept for almost the entire flight. Just forward of her position, Flash was working on her laptop. Massoni was stretched out on a pallet loaded with black PELICAN footlockers. He had an inflatable mattress and a camouflage poncho liner and, once airborne, he was out like a light. For once, Sue was not troubled by "the dream" which often haunted her. Perhaps she was too tired, or simply too satisfied with the results, to let her unconscious mind take her to a troubled place where she was unable to help friends on the battlefield.

On arrival in Italy, Flash and Massoni went back to work. The RLSU admin chief, known exclusively as Marconi, which may or may not have been his real name since Sue had never seen him in uniform, offered to help Sue move into her new quarters. They took two of the RLSU pickup trucks filled with her household effects from Ft. Bragg and drove across the base to the bachelor officers' quarters or BOQ. While Sue checked in, Marconi loaded her boxes into the freight elevator and they met at her room on the third floor. Once the boxes were in the room, Marconi left. As he closed the door, he said, "Boss wants to see you tomorrow at 0800hrs. Check?"

Sue answered to the already closed door, "Check."

The BOQ at Camp Ederle provided housing mostly for young, single Army lieutenants and Captains assigned to the 173rd Airborne Infantry Regiment or single officers assigned to the Southern

European Task Force (SETAF). Each set of quarters mimicked a condominium in the US, with a small bedroom, a kitchen and a living room. Each space had one closet with stackable washer and dryer, and a storeroom in the basement. Not as large as her place in Fayetteville and certainly not as luxurious as the Potomac River House that Sue now called home. Still, since Sue figured she would be on TDY more often than on post, the housing worked for her. It was certainly better than the shipping container she lived in on her first tour in Cyprus. She hooked up her laptop to the base internet server and immediately received a dozen emails from her brother and two from her mother.

Once she read them, she immediately called her mother. Sue said, "Mom, I go away for a couple of weeks and you can't stay out of trouble?"

"Good to hear from you, as well, dear. It isn't as bad a tale as Bill makes out."

"Anytime you have a conversation that includes the word 'grenade,' I reckon it is pretty serious."

"The story will have to wait until I see you again. It is complicated."

"Really? And I should be surprised?"

"More surprised than you think. I am glad you are back safe."

"Me too. Don't know how long I'll be here in Italy, but for now, I'm living in the BOQ and writing reports."

"Excellent. If I get a chance, I may come visit. I think I will be coming to Europe soon and a trip to northern Italy in the summer would be lovely."

"Family business?"

"Perhaps. I am still trying to sort it out."

"Mom, please be careful."

"Coming from a woman who regularly goes to war zones, it is amusing. After all, I am…"

"Yes, I know, a mere, wretched federal pensioner."

"Exactly."

"Ciao, mom"

"Ciao, Bella."

Sue hit the close button on her mobile phone and looked up at the boxes in the middle of her living room. So far, along with her laptop and printer, she had unpacked her electric kettle, French coffee press, a coffee cup and her microwave. Three sets of uniforms and two pair of jeans, two pair of 5.11 field pants, and four polo shirts were in the bedroom closet along with her spare prosthetic, running shoes, civilian hiking boots, and another pair of military issued jungle boots. She looked around and said, "Good enough." Sue was wearing a set of Army ABU trousers, boots, and a t-shirt. She put on her military field blouse over the t-shirt, grabbed her beret and the keys from the RLSU pickup that she had borrowed for the move, and headed out the door. She needed to find out what had actually happened with her mom and that was only going to happen if she was inside the SCIF at the RLSU warehouse. Flash would find out for her.

Barbara ended the telephone connection to her daughter and refocused her attention on what she was going to do next with regard to Michael O'Connell. She took her cup of tea from the kitchen counter and opened the French doors leading onto the small deck that overlooked the lake. It was late morning and summer had arrived in full force. The sun was warm and the slight breeze from the lake made the deck an inviting spot to consider her options.

First, she thought about the discussion she had the previous day with Mary Sanderson. If there was another penetration of the intelligence community, why in the world would the Russians use it to hunt down a retired spy? If there wasn't a penetration, how did O'Connell get her name and email address? Sue had made it clear that the rescue of Nicolai Beroslav and his subsequent assassination on the Afghan-Pakistan border was based on some ability on the part of a Russian private military contractor to track their activities.

What if the CIA and the FBI were looking in the wrong direction? They were, after all, used to working against the corresponding intelligence adversaries from Russia, China and other hostile governments. What if the penetration is not from a state-sponsored intelligence service, but a private intelligence service? If that was the case, Barbara could imagine a private contractor using technology and bribery to locate her through her personal cellphone or the GPS tracker in her Range Rover. If it was a commercial adversary and the client was Michael O'Connell or his real employer, then it would be easy to find her, fix her in place, and attempt to finish her.

With that thought, Barbara walked downstairs to the garage, switched on the Range Rover and disabled the internal GPS. Next, she shut down her smart phone and put it in a small Faraday sleeve that she carried with her during domestic and international travel to block thieves from stealing her personal data at airports, train stations and hotels. It might be too late for this effort, but Barbara figured it didn't hurt to try to do the right thing now, even if now was too late.

Barbara shook her head as she thought about how foolish she had been. The adversaries that killed Peter Senior, attacked Sue and her as they left Chicago in December 2005, and ambushed Max and her in the Potomac House in the spring of 2006 would obviously use all modern techniques to find their prey. Barbara had been lured into a false sense of security simply because she thought the death of the Beroslavs had ended the threat. Now, she knew that threat would probably never go away. How many other adversaries, how many other terrorists, could use the modern telecommunications infrastructure to track her down? As she walked up the stairs toward the study and another session of reading Peter's journals, Barbara said to herself, "Even paranoids sometimes have enemies." She felt better when she made it to the upstairs where she had prepositioned both her own shotgun and Peter Senior's Colt revolver. Reiterating the motto of "two is one and one is none," Barbara opened the closet concealment and pulled out the High Standard pistol. She thought about taking the Swedish K as well, but decided that would be giving in to terror. As she looked at the submachine gun, she said out loud, "Not yet" and closed the concealment.

What she did have control over was her own contacts outside the intelligence community. Barbara wrote a pair of letters to two of these contacts: Peter Longstreet and Beth Parsons. They had proven to be able and willing partners in the previous hunt for the Beroslav family that took them to Greece. If she needed help in this new effort, these two would be able to provide the intelligence, the surveillance capability, and if necessary, the muscle to do the job. Longstreet, a former US Army special operator, ran a small security firm, so it was entirely possible he would not have the time or the interest in another non-paid job. Beth was a senior partner in an international law firm that might not be interested in identifying an Irish gangster. Still, they were the ones she would choose if there was a way to take Michael O'Connell off the game board and, if necessary, send him to the graveyard for spies. She had a pair of notecards with Edward Gorey impressions on the front. Inside, she wrote:

Interested in another adventure? If so, call me at this number.

She included the telephone number of a throw-away phone she purchased some time ago in Illinois. She would post the letters tomorrow. For the rest of the day, she would focus on the life of Peter O'Connell, Sr. There was just a chance that it might reveal something about Michael O'Connell.

A t 0800hrs, CWO3 Sue O'Connell, in her duty uniform, knocked on the door of Colonel Jed Smith, commander, SOF HICU. Smith was seated behind a standard US Army metal desk. CSM Jim Massoni was seated in a dilapidated couch that probably was lifted from some barracks just before demolition. Very much like Smith's office at Ft. Bragg, the walls were covered with 1:250,000 maps of the regions where HICU collectors were at work. The only difference was the wall-mounted plasma screen and camera across from Smith's desk that allowed for secure video teleconferencing. At their headquarters in Ft. Bragg, Warehouse 171, those communications were run off Smith's laptop.

One other difference was that in Camp Ederle, they were strongly encouraged by the post Command Sergeant Major to work in military uniform. Massoni had put out the word and HICU quickly responded, except for Flash who translated duty uniform to mean regulation PT uniform, so she lived and worked in her authorized SOF black sweats and black trainers. Even Smith wasn't willing to push that requirement too far.

Smith waved Sue into the office and started without any preamble. "You did a good job on the last TDY. You didn't even get me into trouble this time."

"Thanks, boss."

"She did blow up one of Jamie's vehicles." Massoni wasn't going to let her forget that.

"It wasn't my fault."

"Right," was all Smith said.

"Are you ready for the next job?"

"Sir."

"So, we are continuing to exploit the Beroslav material and matching that data with the material that you and Jamie received in Termez. It appears the Eastern Med remains part of the equation because the Russian mafia are continuing to smuggle advanced weapons to Hizballah. The boss wants that to stop. I told him that we had our own neutron bomb designed for just this sort of mission. CWO3 Susan O'Connell. He agreed."

For the first time since she had been assigned to HICU, Sue noticed Smith was smiling.

"Boss, does this mean a return trip to Cyprus?"

"No dice, O'Connell. As much as you enjoyed your time on that island paradise, you have to share that with your pals. Especially with your pals who have served, just like you, in crappy places. Nope, no islands for you. But, according to our Command Sergeant Major, your next TDY isn't such a bad thing."

Massoni looked at Sue and said, "Lovely architecture, great food and wine, decent infrastructure, and dozens of war criminals on the run. Anyhow, what could be better? Can you guess?"

"Paris?"

Massoni laughed and said, "Nope."

"Vienna?"

"Close."

Smith decided to intervene before this guessing game tied up the rest of his morning. "O'Connell. Ignore the Sergeant Major for just a moment." Smith looked at Massoni as Massoni made a growl. "The wizards in DC have identified a number of different computer and telecom networks used to link Hizballah and a Serbian organized crime group that call themselves the Dragon Triad. Flash has the details. Basics are: the Russian Crime Syndicate Beroslav worked for buys material in Belarus and transfers it to Belgrade, where the Serbs take charge. Representatives from Hizballah and the Dragon Triad meet in Zagreb, they do the deal in Croatia and everyone returns with what they want. DC thinks the Serb network transports the equipment out of the port of Split, but Flash seems to think there is an alternative location where they load and transport the material to Lebanon. Your job is to travel to Zagreb, sort out what you can with station, use their sources or build your own, and end the Hizballah side of the equation. If we know where the Hizballah ships enter the Adriatic, then NATO can intercept the ships and, ideally, close the pipeline. You got it?"

"Check, boss."

Massoni interjected, "See, what did I tell you? Great food and wine, plus, easy access across the border to Serbia where this Russian network resides. Well, sort of easy access."

"I want you in Zagreb by the end of the month. Flash will get you up to speed. Meanwhile, we have to sort out your official job description for this TDY. We have already started the paperwork with SETAF for you to be on temporary duty with the military attaché in Zagreb. You will have follow-on orders, if needed, to serve temporarily in the US contingent in Kosovo. The multi-national force in Kosovo, KFOR, has lots of flexibility in patrolling the area so if you need the option of tracking into Serbia, you will already have the reasons to do so. The only hold-up right now is coordination with the Agency and the Embassy. I expect that coordination to happen in the next two weeks, so you have that time to get smart and unpack." Smith offered a rare smile, "Don't ever say I don't care about you, O'Connell. Now, go talk to Flash, get smart and then go unpack your kit."

Sue was on her way out the door when Smith said, "And, just a reminder. When you get to Zagreb, please no international incidents. Both Massoni and I were there in the 1990s and it can get ugly real fast. The Balkans are filled with ethnic feuds and folks who hate our role in the breakup of Yugoslavia. Friends can turn adversaries pretty quick. Sort of like Afghanistan or Iraq, but in Europe. So, just get the intel and let the Navy do its job. No gunfights, no explosions, right?"

Massoni added, "And bring back some of the great Croatian wine!"

Sue found Flash bathed in the green-blue glow of five different computer screens. Two appeared to Sue to be running lines of code at a breakneck speed, two had intelligence reports, and one was a feed from a UAV. At the bottom of the UAV feed was GPS data, but the data were not about to reveal anything to Sue, who was most definitely an old school map-and-compass navigator. Dressed in a t-shirt with a SOF insignia, black sweats and black high-top sneakers, and typing feverishly on two different keyboards, Flash looked like the evil genius that she claimed to be. The small camera on the top of her screen caught Sue as she approached. Flash spun around on her high-backed, black nylon chair and said, "It's about time. I've been waiting for hours."

"I just got the instructions from the boss."

"I'm talking about the tasking you gave me yesterday."

"You got that information as well?"

Flash rolled her eyes. "Like finding out the details of your mom's recent adventure was hard? I got that about ten minutes after you left yesterday."

"I was tired."

"So was I. Time-zone jumps like Afghanistan to Italy are not much fun. Still, they are less annoying than Afghanistan to North Carolina."

"Go to sleep on the time zone you are at. Force yourself."

"Or, drink coffee and keep working. It's all the same."

"Are you going to tell me something, or do I have to put you in a headlock until you tap out."

"Best not try that, sister. Among other skills, The Flash has a black belt in judo and a brown belt in Brazilian Jujitsu."

"Is that another one of those skills you learned while not sleeping?"

"It helps to have dated a guy who…"

Sue put up her hands in surrender. "Please, not another tale of your love life."

"Just sayin' you can learn a lot from guys."

"I was hoping to learn a lot from you."

Flash held up her coffee mug and said, "You deliver caffeine and I will deliver news."

Sue was sufficiently new to the RLSU spaces that it took her a little time to find the coffee and tea location. She poured coffee and sugar into Flash's mug. She found her new mug hanging on the mug shelf. It was a gift from Massoni and it had the image of Long John Silver on one side and a large alpha-numeric, M4, on the other side. Sue wasn't entirely sure it was funny, but he was the unit sergeant major and it was a gift. She made a cup of tea in her new mug and walked back to Flash.

"Caffeine and sugar as instructed."

"Who says you can't train military case officers?"

From the next cubicle, a small voice belonging to Blaster, another of the HICU analysts said, "I never said you couldn't train case officers. I said case officers couldn't be house broken." Blaster was responsible for the HICU collection from Dubai to Djibouti. He rarely said much unless it was involved in his area, which he titled "from dreamland to dreadful" or D&D.

Flash ignored the comment and pointed to the chair next to her desk: "Sit and be amazed." Sue did as she was told. Flash might be annoying at times, but she always delivered.

"First, let me say, I now know where you get your gumption. I pulled up a video from the FBI showing your mom in action. Its only about thirty seconds long, so just watch. After that, I will relate the rest of the story."

Sue watched in amazement as the footage from the FBI surveillance cameras showed a rider in black leathers riding toward a location on a red Ducati motorcycle. There was a series of voices from FBI surveillance team describing the rider and his approach to what they are calling the target location. A second surveillance camera picked up the rider reaching into his jacket pocket and tossing a grenade toward the camera. A third camera captured the flash of the grenade and in the corner of the screen Sue's mother doing a shoulder roll behind her Range Rover, coming up to a crouched shooting position with a revolver in both hands, and firing two rounds. The surveillance footage ended with the first camera showing the rider on the ground and the Ducati on its side.

"Holy shit."

"You know, that was precisely what Massoni said when I showed him the video."

"Massoni saw this?"

"Massoni and the boss."

"Why?"

"Because they caught me doing your bidding on company time."

"It's always company time here."

"Exactly."

"Anyhow, the short version of this story is your mom was part of a joint Klingon-FBI operation going after a Russian hit man. It didn't work out as planned."

"I saw that."

"Sadly, they didn't get the hit man. Only his minion."

"Not good."

"Oh, it gets better, Sue. The hit man is an Irish cat named O'Connell."

"A relation?"

"Distant, but definitely."

"Swell."

"And that's precisely what the boss said when I told him."

"Can we shift to our work for a bit? I'm not sure I'm ready for another O'Connell in Wonderland misadventure."

Flash smiled and said, "It's all good, Sue. We can come back to this anytime you like, because working with you is always a trip to Wonderland."

B
arbara thought about holding the meeting with Jake Longstreet and Beth Parsons in the Chautauqua house, but the
house on the Potomac was closer for both of her guests. It
was also far enough away from her residence in western New York
that she felt it offered some additional security from potential adversaries. It also prevented interference from a known intrusive, Special
Agent Ellen Jones of the Buffalo FBI Field Office. Jones had become
a regular visitor, dropping in odd times and pushing for additional
details on Michael O'Connell. Since Barbara had no further details,
Jones left each time progressively more disappointed. She had decided
that Barbara wasn't going to stop hunting the target and intended to
be sure that she and her FBI colleagues knew whatever Barbara knew.
Barbara smiled at the thought of Special Agent Jones. The Special
Agent's instincts were right about one thing: Barbara did not intend
to stop hunting Michael O'Connell, at least until he was "resolved"
either through arrest or "resolved kinetically" as the Agency politely
called some of their counterterrorism operations.

Barbara arrived at the house a day early to open up, put basic
groceries in the fridge and check the grounds. It all looked perfect.
The husband and wife team of housekeepers and watchers visited to
be sure Barbara had everything. They were very pleased to know that
they were doing precisely what family O'Connell needed. Once they
disappeared, Barbara decided to focus her attention on a brief meal,
some red wine and some reading. She had to review her notes based
on the file on Michael O'Connell and she brought along another
of Peter O'Connell's journals. This one was set in Cold War Berlin.

After washing up the dinner dishes, checking all the locks and confirming the surveillance cameras were operating, she took the journal and a cup of tea upstairs to the guest bedroom where Peter Senior had hosted his grandchildren. This would be Barbara's room for the next two days.

She walked into a room with a single bed, a small writing desk and chair next to the bed. Across the room was another ancient leather chair with a reading lamp next to it, exactly like the ones in the Chautauqua house. Her open suitcase was sitting on an antique suitcase rack and her shoulder bag was hung on the chair. The FBI was still holding her beloved Smith and Wesson as evidence. They had promised to return it soon, but Barbara knew that soon could easily translate into never in the federal bureaucracy. She reached into her bag. First, she pulled out the 2-inch Colt Commando Peter Senior had left in the Chautauqua house concealment in a very worn leather holster that she found in the house. She checked again to make sure it was loaded and put it on the writing desk. Next, she pulled out the High Standard .22 and put it in the central drawer in the desk where writing paper and two old fountain pens resided. Finally, she looked at Peter's old Bulova watch that was on her wrist. It was 2030hrs and she hoped to get through a few pages of the journal before sleep. Tomorrow, she would go to the basement and recover the Colt Python that Sue had left behind in what they all called the "wine cellar," which had been an arms locker and secure ops center for Peter Senior. At that point, she would secure the High Standard for another day.

She opened the journal titled *Hungary and Berlin – 1956-1962*. As with her previous deep dive into Peter O'Connell's life, this journal was not something compiled every day. The handwriting and the ink pointed to the journal as a summary of events and his thoughts about them sometime after the fact. Barbara assumed this journal was written sometime well after Peter was back from Laos simply because once he returned from Laos, Peter spent years in Headquarters and at the Farm. Plenty of time to write. Of course, it could have been a retirement project as well, but the handwriting seemed more like that of a man in his 50s rather than a man in his 70s. She opened the first page.

Hungary 1956

I arrived In Budapest just before the Soviet tanks rolled in. Wisner sent me to sort out the level of resistance and how we might help. Judith and I were living In Munich. I was working with Frank Wisner on a number of projects designed to give the Soviets headaches across the entire Warsaw Pact. Radio Free Europe and our balloon leaflet campaigns were telling the true story of the puppet governments. We were collecting Information from couriers crossing the border with East Germany. Life was ugly In the East while life improved In the West due to the Marshall Plan. Even the socialists In the West could see that their Instructions from Moscow were stupid. The entire US government was working In synch to undermine the Soviet propaganda of the socialist paradise In the East.

I drove my ancient Mercedes from Munich to Graz. From Graz, we used a Brit network to get me across the line Into Hungary. A half day in a trunk concealment and I was In Budapest. A night in the safe house, a change of clothes and I was out on the street. The political protests were non-violent at first. There was almost a carnival atmosphere as the Hungarians believed they were finished with their communist leaders. It wasn't that they were hostile to some Ideology. They were hostile to the corruption, the overbearing secret police and, more than anything else, they were tired of the Russians In their country.

I don't speak a word of Hungarian . My documents said I was an Irish businessman from Dublin trying to ship Irish agricultural goods. That would explain my mediocre German , poor French and even worse Italian. When Wisner briefed the mission to our team, Judith started working with the forgers to build the document package. She thought it would be a reasonable cover simply because everyone knew Ireland shipped mutton and milk products anywhere it could. She gave me some basic notes and then told me to simply act like the ruffian that she knew I was.

Barbara stopped reading. Her husband had talked about his mother, Judith, and that she died in Berlin the early 1960s. In this return to the early Cold War, Barbara wondered if her husband ever knew that his mother worked for the Agency as well. From the note-book, it appeared that Judith was part of the tech shop in Munich. If so, she certainly must have known that the documents she was preparing for her husband would have to be good or he would never be seen again. The early Cold War was a time when US and UK agents went across the border and were never heard from again. Did they die in a minefield? Shot by border guards? Tortured in prison? No one ever knew.

Now that she knew Judith and Peter were part of the CIA team in Germany, she decided to flip through the pages to see when Judith was mentioned again. One of the sections made her stop reading for the night. It had started simple enough.

Berlin, March 1961

I had been up most of the night working in the Soviet sector. I was dressed in a long, well used grey wool overcoat, black wool trousers and a wool roll neck sweater. My documents said I was Jakob Fleis, a local laborer. Judith and her team had created a full document package Including my ration cards, a card saying I had served In the Soviet Army of the occupation In the 1950s and even a card saying I had a head wound while on the lines which effected my speech. I was always safe so long as Judith and her team were on my side. In a concealment on the left side of my coat, I had my real US mission documents identifying me as a civilian member of the military mission at the US consulate. In the concealment on the right side of my coat, I had two rolls of film taken by one of our best military sources inside the East.

It had been a long twenty-four hours. The previous midnight I crossed the border and hid in a concealment space in the station safe house in East Berlin. I waited in the concealment, ate the meal provided by the safe house keeper, and worked through in my head the meeting plan for the brief encounter with my GDR police source, the walking route taking me to the dead drop site and then my final route back to the safe house. Two meetings in one night violated all of our security protocols, but it was getting harder and harder to work in East Berlin. The normal handler for the source ser-vicing the dead drop had been identified by the KGB and was under nearly 24hour surveillance in West Berlin. He simply couldn't get clear. I already had a meeting scheduled within the time window for servicing the drop, so I offered to pick it up on my return run back to the safe house. Everyone in the office agreed it was that or terrify the source when he kept going back to the signal site over and over again waiting for some proof that his message had been picked up.

The face to face meeting was little more than an exchange of words with my guy outside a bar in the Red Light District of the city. Of course, in the German Democratic Republic there were no acknowledged brothels. The Red Light District was a small street of German bars offering beer, wurst, and duckpin bowling. Each of the owners paid a hefty bribe to insure the police and the Stasi turned a blind eye. Men took their beers outside to wait for an opportunity to "bowl" with a hostess. Men loitering outside a bar door was a clear sign of a successful brothel. We stood for ten minutes nursing our beers in the cold ostensibly waiting for our turn inside. Ten minutes was just enough time for a debriefing and a plan for the next meeting – if you were organized and good in German.

The dead drop site was near the Pergamon museum. The museum still had bullet holes from Russian forces occupying Berlin in 1945. The Russians didn't want any German to forget they were an occupied country and the GDR wasn't willing to fight a battle over masonry. I approached the museum at midnight. There was no one on the side street and the street lights did little more than reflect the light sideways above the fog. I noticed the tell tale chalk mark was there signaling the package was in place. I walked along the wall of the building, taking on the gait of a German worker who had one too many beers – bumping occasionally into the wall. On one of those bumps, I stumbled slightly and had to put a hand up against the wall to steady myself. As I did so, I reached into one of the crevices left by a Russian or German machine gun bullet from 1945 and palmed the concealment designed to look like a piece of trash stuffed into the wall. In fact, it was two film canisters from a Minox camera with 25 exposures of documents from the GDR army.

I continued the drunken stumble for no one in particular until I came to one of the lamp posts in front of the museum. To anyone looking, the drunk steadied himself against the lamp post. With my left hand, I placed another chalk mark on the post signaling "package recovered." Now all I had to do was cross a guarded border with secrets both in my pocket and in my head.

It was the best time of an operation. You knew that there were secrets stolen and all you had was your plan and your skill to get them back safe and sound.

As I turned a corner into another side street, I changed my gait, my manner, and turned my coat inside out to reveal a more stylish wool coat. I replaced my worker's cap with a more formal wool dress hat. Instead of a drunk on his way home, I was now a shopkeeper returning home after an evening meal at a respectable restaurant. I worked my way back through the streets in hopes of avoiding any of the German or Russian military police patrolling the streets. I realized that I may have the clothes of a German shopkeeper, but I looked like a German black marketeer trying to avoid the police. That meant that there was no good cover story if I was seen by anyone associated with the GDR police or the Russian KGB.

It was cold and there was freezing fog filling the streets and alleyways. The Spree River was not very deep or very wide, but the drains and sewers of East Berlin emptied directly into the river and raised the temperature enough that at the current air temperature well below freezing, the river created a wall of fog. Good for smugglers and spies, bad for policemen. Through the fog they could just see the lights on both sides of the border checkpoints — Soviet and US at Checkpoint Charlie. None of the streets this close to the US zone were marked, but I knew that I needed to stair step down the streets keeping the lights to my right. I reached into my coat and touched the concealment holding the two film cannisters. If approached by GDR security, I figured I could get far enough away at a sprint to use the small dump zipper in my wool coat that would dump the concealment from the pocket onto the street and I could kick it into one of the storm drains without appearing to throw anything away. I was feeling very good about myself.

The station safe house in East Berlin and tunnel under the house that connected it with a corresponding house in the West was about a quarter mile from the checkpoints. All I had to do was keep calm and walk along the side streets until I reached the safe house. My rubber soled work boots made little noise as I disappeared into the shadows. Now, my biggest challenge was to keep adrenaline in check and walk at a normal pace while my brain kept saying "Hurry up, hurry up, HURRY UP!"

I made the safe house on time and through the tunnel before dawn. The safe house at the other end of the tunnel had my support team including a tech to help opening the concealment and an analyst who would review my notes immediately to determine if the material needed to be sent back to DC the same day. I poured a cup of strong black coffee and started the debrief. The German source was a member of the GDR border security force and he had reported a supply depot just outside Berlin which was filled with concrete barricades, barb wire, and the makings of a dozen watch towers. He didn't know what was going up, but he said a colleague had seen delivery of a thousand anti-personnel mines to the laager. AP mines were common along the East-West German border but didn't belong in a storage site near Berlin. He also saw an invoice for further deliveries of the same volume of material in early April as well as several bulldozers. None of this was critical reporting, but it was curious.

The analyst took notes and left. The tech officer hadn't developed the film yet, so I went upstairs to wash up and get out of my East German clothing and into my U.S. consulate suit and tie. We would all go back to the Consulate together in a Volkswagen with Berlin plates. We would transfer back to a consulate vehicle in a separate garage in the city. All told, the trip would take about an hour.

I was in the bedroom pulling on my trousers when the analyst came in. He looked white and shaken. I made a joke. It was probably the last joke I have ever made. "What is it, Bill? Have the Commies decided to invade West Berlin?"

"Peter, I'm sorry. We just got a burst commo message from the station. Your wife…she was killed in a traffic accident yesterday evening. They want you to go directly home. The station is watching over your son while this gets sorted out with the Berlin police. You need to go home. We have the car ready and need to get you to the consulate now."'

The next few days were a jumble. I had to tell Peter his mom was not coming home. I had to arrange Judith's return to the USA. The station and the consulate were great, but some of the things that needed to be done had to be done by me. Judith had no family left after the war, so It was just us. We had agreed years ago that we didn't want a funeral, a wake or anything resembling a formal burial. Just a cremation and Internment. But where? We were both raised Catholics and I wanted Peter to have one last chance to say goodbye. It turned out that our service in the war meant we were authorized a military funeral and Internment In a military cemetery. So, Judith is in a plot at Arlington, waiting for me.

June 1961

When I read the after-action report, It stated Judith was taking a pouch from the Consulate to a joint base we share with Army CIC. They still haven't told me what was in the pouch, but the report makes it clear it was taken before the police got to the site. Given her tech work, it could have been anything or nothing. The strangest part of the story is the German police accident report identified the truck and the driver. The driver was an Irishman and he has disappeared. All we have is an abandoned notebook for deliveries. What the hell is an Irishman doing In Berlin? Why did he kill Judith? What did he want with the pouch?

Barbara closed the book. She hadn't yet accepted that the Beroslav threat was finished and now she faced another Cold War tale where it was entirely possible that one part of the O'Connell family had attacked and killed another part of the family. The date meant that Michael O'Connell could not have been the attacker. Would it have been possible that his father, James did the attack? If so, why? The file said he was a part timer for the Soviets. An Irish passport would have been an easy travel document in and out of Tempelhof Airport in 1961. But, as Peter wrote, why? The pouch? Barbara realized this was not going to be a night for sound sleep.

Barbara was driving through the rubble of a decaying industrial park in the former Soviet Union. It was mid-winter and it was sleeting. People were standing beside fire barrels trying to stay warm in the freezing temperatures. They would step out in front of her car at the last minute. Barbara was lost. She was going to a meeting, but she couldn't remember the route she was to take. When she finally got on the right route, she couldn't remember her cover name, the name of her asset or the debriefing questions. As she approached the car pickup site, she could see her asset being arrested by Nazis and shoved into a 1930s Mercedes. Her last image was of the asset looking directly at her as she drove by him. He looked terrified.

She woke from the dream covered in sweat. It was 4 a.m. and it hardly made sense to try to get back to sleep. Barbara hadn't had that sort of dream in years. At one level, she understood it was just her subconscious trying to make sense of everything that had happened in the last six weeks. It hardly mattered about the intellectual answers to why the dream had returned. It had caused an adrenaline surge and that was really all that mattered. No more sleep tonight. She put on her sweats and sneakers, took her phone and the pistol from the desk next to the bed and headed downstairs. Perhaps some yoga and a walk along the Potomac at dawn would help. Before she left, she checked the outdoor surveillance system. It never hurt to be careful.

Just after she returned from her walk, her phone rang. It was 6 a.m. and it was her daughter calling from Europe. Sue's digitized voice along with the satellite bounce and Barbara's hearing loss made for a difficult conversation.

"Mom, did I wake you?"

"Sue, do I need to buy you a GMT watch so you can track two time zones?"

"So I did wake you."

"Nope, I have been up for a bit."

"The dream?"

"How did you guess?"

"How many times have I told you about my dream? Since I heard about your little discussion with a hand-grenade-bearing creep, I figured it was probably a nightmare. By the way, I did lose the thread on what time it is on the East Coast. Isn't it 7 a.m.?"

"6, daughter mine."

"Ugh. Maybe I do need a GMT watch."

"Or you could do the subtraction in your head. It is European summer time. That means you are five hours ahead. Eleven a.m. your time, right?"

"Oops."

"Well, that's OK because I am awake and about to make myself tea. I have plenty of time to talk."

"Are you ok?"

"A couple of stitches but my hearing is about back to normal. That was the most annoying part."

"Grenades will do that."

"So it seems. I haven't been near an exploding grenade since… well, I suspect it is 1992 or 1993."

"When you were…?"

"Might have been a little unrest in Dushanbe when I was there. At least that time they weren't throwing the grenades at me."

"Another story."

"For another time."

"Are you going to let go on this recent attack?"

"What do you think?"

"Probably not."

"It remains to be seen. Right now, I don't have any way to make any forward progress."

"Good news."

"On a different subject, I am going to see Beth Parsons today."

"Just a chance meeting, right?"

"Sure."

"Mom, please take care of yourself. If I had a vote, I would say, let it go."

"Thanks, dear. I will take that into consideration. If you asked Mary Sanderson, she would tell you she said the same thing."

"I'm not the only one."

"Bill as well."

"Lots of votes against further action."

"Exactly."

"Not going to listen are you?"

"You ever have someone throw a grenade at you?"

"Not so far."

"When it happens, let me know what you think."

"Fair enough. Have you made your tea?"

"Just finished."

"I'll let you go now. It was a lovely mother-to-daughter conversation."

"Just like a normal family."

"Right. Ciao, mama."

"Ciao Bella."

Jake Longstreet was the first to arrive that morning. He was driving the ancient Land Rover Defender that Max Creeter left to him in his will. Barbara hadn't expected the Land Rover nor the flood of emotion that it brought as she thought about Max and how his life ended in this same Potomac River House. He died fighting to keep her alive. Longstreet got out of the Defender and headed to the house looking more like a gentleman farmer than a retired commando. He was wearing a canvas sport coat over a polo shirt and jeans. He had ankle high Australian boots on his feet and a baseball cap with a stitched logo: *Free Pineland*.

Barbara met him at the door and brought him into the kitchen. While waiting for her arrivals, she had made a half dozen blueberry muffins and chopped up a pineapple she picked up at the local grocery. Along with yogurt and black coffee, she figured it was about as close to a late breakfast as she could provide for her visitors.

"Jake, thanks for coming up to the O'Connell safe house on the Potomac."

"And, the scene of the last crime, I believe."

Barbara winced and said, "Well, perhaps not the last crime, but certainly the place where Max was killed."

"A more recent crime?"

"I just had a small meeting with a live grenade."

"Never a good thing. Was it something you said?"

"Apparently."

"And now you want to find the man who delivered the grenade and convince him of the error of his ways?"

"Not exactly. The actual delivery boy is in federal custody after I put a couple of rounds in his back. Sadly, he was wearing a Kevlar motorcycle jacket and I was only using .38 Special rounds."

"I recommend Plus P rounds."

"Those were the next ones in the cylinder, but the .38 did drop him off his motorcycle so it was all good."

"So...?"

"I hope to find the guy who paid for the delivery service."

"And have a chat."

"Something like that."

"Care to share what is exactly going on?"

"Let's wait for Beth Parsons if we could. It's a long story and honestly, I'm not sure I am up for telling it twice."

"OK. How about you pour me a cup of coffee and tell me about your life and how your children are doing in their jobs keeping us safe."

Barbara obliged in both cases. She told Longstreet about her move to the Chautauqua house, her discovery of her father-in-law's journals, as much of her daughter's adventures as she knew and of her son's work with the FBI. It took about a pot of coffee and two cups of Earl Grey tea and two of the muffins. Jake was a good listener and the stories were completed just as the house security system alarmed to tell them Beth Parsons was in-bound.

They watched as a series of cameras along the driveway showed a royal blue Maserati Gran Turisimo convertible pulling up to the door. Barbara was at the door as Beth got out of the sports car. She was dressed in what could only be described as sports car high fashion: cropped trousers, a silk top, a red leather jacket that matched her red Hermès scarf and Ray Ban Wayfarers.

Barbara said, "Welcome back to the O'Connell Potomac River

House." She laughed and said, "Beth, you certainly know how to make an entrance!"

"Hey, I'm off duty today and the Maserati needed to stretch its legs. It was a great drive along Highway One and then on two-lane blacktop that doesn't seem to have a name at all. The GPS had no trouble finding the spot and I just enjoyed the ride."

"Jake is here already, so come in. Coffee or tea?"

"Whatever is hot."

"Both, dear. Jake is working coffee and I'm working on my second cup of Earl Grey."

"Coffee will be great."

After they settled in, Longstreet offered some amusing tales of his most recent commercial work doing what he called pen-testing. Barbara wasn't familiar with the term, so he explained, "Basically, a firm hires my team to determine their security status. We go after them. Physical, electronic and computer security. Not very different from what we used to do for the USG, but the pay is better. It turns out most companies think that a set of locks, a wire fence, and maybe an armed patrol is enough. In today's world, that isn't even a good start."

Beth looked up over her coffee cup and said, "I don't suppose you would be interested in going on retainer for my firm?"

"Beth, the team would be very interested in working for you. After all, Mutt remains your most devoted fan."

Barbara laughed and said, "That approached too much information, Jake."

Beth smiled her perfect Medici smile and said, "We do need to work together in the future. After we finish whatever Barbara wants us to do, we can sort this out together."

"My pleasure."

Once the pleasantries were over, Barbara relayed the entire tale of the murder of the double agent, her involvement, the confrontation at Emery Park, and the revelations from Mary Sanderson that the assassin was Michael O'Connell, a cousin of her husband Peter. Added to the story, she offered the fact that O'Connell probably killed one of Barbara's assets back in the 90s. Barbara concluded by saying, "I have to admit, I thought the Beroslav tale was bizarre, but this new story of the O'Connells is just as strange. What I need from you at this point is an attempt to identify where in Europe this guy is hiding and whether it would be possible to bring him to justice, meaning bringing him into a country that would comply with the Interpol Red Notice."

Longstreet was the first to speak. "I think this has some real possibilities, but also some real challenges. First off, do we know what name he is using in whatever place he is staying?"

Barbara shook her head. "We don't know much and I'm not saying there is anything other than a dead end ahead. What we have are a couple of things. First, the email server is somewhere in the Balkans. Second, we know he said he was living on the beach. A lie, perhaps, but possibly just an arrogant mistake. We know several of his aliases. Finally, we know that Serbia doesn't have an extradition treaty with the US."

Beth shook her head and said, "And Serbia doesn't have a coastline."

Jake said, "Montenegro does and it only recently broke away from Serbia after years of working together in their military and police. If O'Connell bought the property in the late 1990s, he probably figured he was safe since at that point Montenegro, like Serbia, had no extradition treaties with the US. Now, all of that changes. But the geography hasn't changed and there are likely a fair number of senior police in Montenegro who would be susceptible to financial opportunities or, possibly, pressure from Russian criminal organizations. We could try some property searches in Montengro and see what happens. This is precisely the sort of thing that Mark takes as a challenge. My vote is we see if we can find the guy. If not, then we are done. If so, then we have to think about what we do next."

Beth was listening carefully to Jake's comments and said, "My firm has some very interesting clients in Croatia and Bosnia. We are looking at both international reparations for some of the ethnic cleansing as well as looking at business development. I have wanted to go there for a while, but honestly, didn't want to do so until we sorted out the security environment. Stearns and Mandeville don't pay me enough to go back to war zones. If we found a lead in Montenegro, I am sure I could get funding to get us to Zagreb. You would both have to do some work for the firm…" Beth smiled and continued, "properly compensated of course, and then we could take a vacation on the beaches of the Adriatic."

Barbara smiled and said, "Well, let's just hope Mark finds a lead."

Beth said, "Even if he doesn't find a lead, I still need help in Sarajevo."

Jake was eating some of the pineapple Barbara had cut earlier, so he simply nodded as Barbara said, "I am definitely interested in a paid vacation or, if possible, an opportunity to help Interpol find a murderer."

Jake had finally finished his pineapple. He said, "Or maybe both."

Sue enjoyed her flight on Lufthansa from Marco Polo International to Zagreb. Marconi had searched the US Government and US Military regulations and determined that for any operational mission, HICU personnel were authorized a full-fare economy ticket. That fare allowed them to change flight reservations without penalty. It also meant that the HICU travelers were almost always bumped up to business class on short haul flights. A little more room and much better food in the front of the cabin meant Sue didn't have to suffer the challenge of fitting her prosthetic in the cramped, standard airline seat. She stayed clear of the free prosecco but indulged in the German meat and cheeses offered as they cruised over the Adriatic toward Croatia. She also enjoyed two cups of German coffee and chocolate before they landed.

Marconi told Sue that a driver would meet her and take her to the Embassy before she checked into her hotel. What she hadn't expected when she arrived at 1300hrs was a face she recognized.

Nancy Garrison walked up as Sue waited in line for passport control and said, "You don't wait in line in my town. You are a VIP."

Sue laughed and as she hugged her classmate from the Farm, she said, "Nancy, who knew you were such a player in this town?"

"The answer is no one. But, my boss is a player and I borrowed her airport pass and her Audi so we better get going before she misses it."

They passed through the Diplomat/VIP passport control line, picked up Sue's suitcase and headed out the door. Waiting at the curb was a black Audi A6 with diplomatic plates with its four-way flashers going strong. Sue said, "No driver?"

"You think I was going to give up the chance to drive this engineering dream? Nope. Since I did leave it out here, we will have to go through the formal check at the Marine Gate, but otherwise, we are on our own."

They drove through the airport checkpoints and headed into the city. They considered adding a few miles to the short drive to the Embassy, but Nancy remained nervous about the fact that she said she "boosted" the boss's ride. So, there was only enough time for Sue to find out what Nancy had been doing since they were classmates at the CIA training facility known as "the Farm." Nancy said she had just arrived in Zagreb after a tour in Afghanistan in the Agency base in Jalalabad. They shared brief tales of kebab stands in Jalalabad, and before the conversation could get more serious, they were at the Embassy.

"Sue, I know you need to check in with the MILATT first. The Gunney will make sure you get processed into the Embassy and then he will take you upstairs. We are right down the hall from his office. Feel free to wander down once he lets you go. I know Stacey is going to want to say hello."

"Stacey? As in Stacey Mackenzie, one of our instructors at the Farm?"

"Just the same. I will let her tell you what's up with her. Now, I only need to ask one question before we get started. Would you be willing to bunk with me while you are here? I have a four-bedroom apartment and according to Stacey we are going to be working together. It just seems easier if we also live together. I know the MILATT booked you in the Palace Hotel, but…"

Sue smiled and said, "A chance to hang out all night with my pal? One continuous pajama party? Who could ask for more? Still, will it cramp your style?"

"Given the fact that we are going to be working at night, I suspect it won't."

"OK, then I will tell my boss I'm spoken for."

"You might want to word that a little differently. The MILATT is a pretty serious guy."

"Check."

As with her introduction to the Embassy in Nicosia, her military ID and her official red passport resulted in substantial support from the Marines at Post One, including the detachment gunnery sergeant. He was expecting Sue and he took her to the Regional Security Office, arranged her embassy ID card, walked her through the security measures in the Embassy and then took her up into the secure spaces that housed the military attaché and the station spaces. Sue dropped her briefcase holding her phone and her laptop and her military suitcase and roller bag in one of the bins just outside the cipher locked door that was called the hard line – meaning the secure area of the Embassy. He left her with the NCO in charge of the office and returned to his job of managing the entire security detachment. Before he left he said, "Chief, as you suspect, we are going to be busy on Independence Day. However, on 06 July, I expect to see you at the Marine House at 1800hrs. Your first beverage of choice is on me."

"Thanks, Gunney. If I am here, I will be there."

"Check, Chief. I heard you are on a work trip. Still, the invitation is open."

"Roger, that."

Sue walked into the MILATT's office at 1430hrs. The NCOIC for the MILATT office was a US Air Force Chief Master Sergeant named Rollins. His Air Force rank identified him as a senior NCO of the same rank as Jim Massoni. Rollins was in his class B uniform of Air Force Blue trousers and pale blue shirt. He had a combat medic badge and a master parachutist badge above his row of ribbons which included campaign ribbons for Afghanistan and Iraq. He came around his desk and shook hands with Sue. He said, "Chief, welcome to Zagreb. I know you guys are in Italy, so the flight was sure to be an easy one."

"Chief Master Sergeant, I honestly haven't ever had a better one. Most of my flights have been in the back of a C17 or a C130. No offense, but an Air Force box lunch doesn't compare. Just curious, are you a PJ?" Sue used the acronym for members of the US Air Force pararescue teams involved in combat search and rescue. While the Air Force didn't designate them as part of the special operations community, everyone in the Army and Marine Special Operations community certainly thought they were part of the family.

Rollins laughed and said, "Good catch, chief. I was a PJ for most of my career. Hurt my back in a CSAR operation in Western Iraq. I will return to my unit once I am 100 percent, but for the time being, the Air Force decided to assign me here. Wife and kids are happy to see me for dinner every night and it isn't a bad gig. By the way, you can dispense with the formalities with me. I'm Gino."

Sue said, "I'm Sue. Hardly anyone who knows me would call me chief."

Rollins said, "Just to be clear, the boss is a pretty formal guy."

"I have my uniform in my bag just outside the hard line. Should I change?"

"It couldn't hurt. The ladies is down the hall to the right."

Sue nodded and headed down the hall to retrieve her bag. Her suit roll inside the duffle worked fairly well and her uniform came out with very few creases. Sue had packed both her summer uniform and her formal dress blues because she expected to attend the formal Independence Day ceremony. For now, she simply put on her green trousers and pale green shirt with her ribbons and master jump wings. She pulled out her jump boots, shined up the toes, bloused her boots, did a quick check the mirror, and was back in the MILATT office in less than ten minutes.

Rollins was waiting. As with all senior non-commissioned officers in the armed forces, he did a quick scan of Sue's ribbons to see where she had been and what she had done. The Purple Heart and the bronze star ribbon with two V devices were over the campaign ribbons and the various awards from her time in the 18th Airborne Corps. Just under the right pocket was the US Army Special Operations Command insignia identifying her affiliation with SOF. Only two sets of soldiers wore that identifying badge. One set were seniors assigned to the USASOC command and staff. Most members of the subordinate units of the Army Special Operations community would be wearing either a Special Forces or a Ranger Regimental insignia in this position. Only SOF operators who needed some sort of identifier on their uniform would use the USASOC badge as unit designator. In a few seconds, Rollins knew he was talking to the real deal. He decided to be square with the new arrival.

He said, "Chief, the boss is Navy Captain Robert Truckee. This is his first assignment outside of either the fleet or the Pentagon. He arrived two weeks ago replacing a Marine during the summer rotations. Colonel Dan Macey was a Marine grunt wounded in the Gulf War in 1991. He got out, finished his degree, went to OCS and then worked in both positive collection and counterintelligence for most of his career. Macey was popular with the Embassy and, no surprise, especially with the Marine House. Captain Truckee is still trying to find his way. I'm working on that, but he can be a little conscious of protocol. I'm just saying, first impressions matter. Check?"

Sue smiled and said, "Gino, I got the picture and will work hard to meet his...and your...expectations." She walked up to the closed door, gave it three hard raps and waited until she heard the voice inside say, "Enter."

Sue came into the room, stopped precisely three feet from the front of the desk and rendered her best salute. Across the desk was a 40-something-year-old Navy officer in his full uniform including his uniform jacket. He had a very severe haircut and his lean face argued the captain was in marathon runner condition. She said, "Sir, Chief Warrant Officer Susan O'Connell reporting."

Once Truckee returned the salute, Sue moved to the position of parade rest and waited. While she waited, she did a quick scan of the office. It was filled with pictures from Truckee's career. What surprised Sue was he had service pictures from two Navy carriers and an Amphibious Platform Dock known in the Navy as an LPD. As a Navy intelligence officer, that meant he would be familiar with both strategic intelligence designed to protect a carrier battle group and operational and tactical intelligence to be used by a joint Navy-Marine task force. She noticed a series of pictures from the Army-Navy games in the past. She looked down at his left hand and saw his Naval Academy ring. Sue had never served with any Navy personnel other than SEALS and had never served on a Navy ship, so she wasn't sure what to expect.

Truckee was working over some pages on his desk. Finally, he looked up and said, "Chief, why are you in my city?"

"Sir, I have just arrived. I will be on TDY working for you and with station for the next few weeks until my mission is completed. SOF HUMINT has a lead to a smuggling operation run by a Russian crime syndicate delivering high tech weapons to Hizballah. My job is to find the coastal departure point so the US Navy can intercept the Hizballah ship and close down the pipeline."

Truckee nodded and said, "And why precisely are you the one doing this?"

"Sir, I have been running agents and tracking the pipeline for the past year, starting first with one of the nodes in Cyprus, then into the Black Sea. The network runs through both Afghanistan and Iraq. I have been involved in disrupting that part of the pipeline. Once we received information that Croatia was part of the network, the SOF commander and, specifically, my Colonel, Jedidiah Smith, decided I was the one to come."

"I don't like visitors on my patch."

Sue wasn't sure what to say about this, so she didn't say anything. She figured there was more to come. What she knew was that Smith had obtained approval from the MILATT, the Station and the Embassy before her travel.

Truckee continued, "The mission of this military attaché in this country," emphasizing the word this, "is to build a positive working relationship with the Croatian military. Our goal is to fully integrate them from the partnership for peace into full NATO membership. I will not tolerate any activity that will disrupt that mission. If I had been in country when this request arrived, I would not have approved the mission or your TDY."

This wasn't the first time that Sue had run into a senior military officer who had his mind made up well before she arrived. While serving in 18th Airborne Corps and especially while serving during the early days of the Kosovo campaign, she met more than one senior who decided that he knew what he knew, and no one from the unit intelligence shop was going to tell him otherwise. The secret to success was to make sure the senior realized two things: first, that Sue understood who was in charge and, second, that what she had in hand was precisely what would make the officer look good.

Sue started her opening gambit by saying, "Sir, while I am here, I am under your command and control. That said, my boss and his boss, the commanding general of SOF, want to be sure this operation works. What better way to encourage the Croatian military, especially the Croatian Navy, than to work together to find and demolish a Serbian and Hizballah smuggling network?" Sue knew from her days in the 18th Airborne Corps that the two biggest Croatian hot buttons were Serbian and Islamic intrusions into their state. If Truckee knew anything about his host nation, that should be enough to pull him on side. She waited while Truckee gave her what she learned years ago was the commander stare. Sue assumed that somewhere in the senior command and general staff schools, the instructors taught their charges how to stare down subordinates. Sue had been through too many commands and too many schools as well as Surveillance and Reconnaissance Selection to be bothered by "the stare." Still, it never hurt to appear to be affected, so she offered her most obsequious face.

"So, you intend to work on this with the Croatians?"

"Sir, I have every intention of working with anyone who can disrupt this network that in the past has delivered weapons to the Shia militias in Iraq. I have yet to meet with station so I don't know for sure at what level they want to work with the Croatians. If you have any suggestions on Croatian partners, I'm ready to act on your plan." Based on the recent in-brief from Rollins, Sue knew that Truckee was new in country and might not have any Croatian contacts that would be defined by the term partners. That said, Sue was willing to say anything that would get her out of this office and avoid the risk of being sent home immediately by this Navy officer.

"O'Connell, let me think this over. In the meantime, I will introduce you to the COS. After that, I will work with the COS to craft a plan that will match the needs of the SOF Commanding General and the diplomatic requirements of the Embassy. It may or may not include you, so don't get too comfortable in Zagreb." Truckee stood up and walked around the desk. Until this moment, Sue had not realized that Truckee was a good three inches shorter than Rollins and two inches shorter than herself. She assumed the proper subordinate position, one step to the left and one step to the rear, following Truckee out of his office. As they walked past Rollins, Truckee said, "Rollins, we are going down the hall to station. I'll be back shortly."

"Yes, sir." Sue was certain that Rollins gave her a clandestine thumbs-up as she followed the MILATT.

Truckee arrived at the Station and rapped hard on the door. After he did, he said, "I don't know why these spooks think their work is so secret that they can't keep their doors open, after all..." The rest of his sentence was interrupted as a familiar face opened the door.

Sue couldn't help herself. She said, "Debbie?"

After years of serving in the field, including nearly a decade as a rover, Debbie Henshaw was not about to be surprised by anything. She was also not about to mess with protocol. She greeted the MILATT with a formal, "Captain, it is good to see you. The chief is waiting for you." As Truckee walked past her toward the COS's office, Debbie smiled at Sue and said in German, "*Shtum*." Sue knew from her days with her grandfather, the word meant a conspiratorial "Be silent." Sue nodded and followed Truckee into the office.

Before she saw the COS, she heard a familiar voice from the Farm say, "Robert, good to see you. Please have a seat." Stacey Mackenzie hadn't changed a bit from her days as an instructor at the Farm. Still lean, still blond, and still wearing clothes tailored to absolutely complement her. Today, she was wearing a cream-colored suit and a sapphire silk top. She looked like she should be in the corner office of some large law firm in corporate America. Instead, she had the corner office in the US Embassy in Zagreb running espionage operations in the Balkans. Truckee complied and even seemed to become more human inside "Stacey's world." The COS turned to Sue and said, "Chief O'Connell, welcome to Zagreb station. Please join us."

By the time they were settled, Debbie had delivered a tray of coffee and biscuits in white china with a floral design. The setting looked like something out of the 1950s and, most probably, it was. Sue watched for the next half hour as Stacey Mackenzie charmed, cajoled and explained to the MILATT that it was in the interest of the Embassy to support Sue's mission. She pointed out that the mission was sufficiently important that the Ambassador already had received notification of the mission from Main State and approved Sue's trip. Stacey said she was assigning two of her officers to the job. Her deputy, Harry Needham, would be in charge of introducing Sue to the Croatian service representatives and another officer, Nancy Garrison, would be working directly with Sue so that there were no flaps caused by his visitor. Stacey also offered to introduce Truckee to a number of different senior officials in the Croatian government. Stacey said that, since he was the newest member of the senior staff, she felt it was important to give him the best possible access to the complement of Croatian military and civilian leadership. Stacey closed by saying, "Of course, our contacts are not as senior as the Ambassador's but it is a start and, I think once we get this new mission up and running, you will find the Croatians will be ready to help you in the future."

Truckee didn't have much to say during the discussion other than ensuring Mackenzie and O'Connell both understood that he was the senior military officer in country and would be both responsible for and directly controlling Sue's operations. Mackenzie nodded and said, "Absolutely. Of course, we can offer some advice based on our relationship with both the civilian and military intelligence services, but you will always be the one who gives the go-ahead during the country team meetings with the Ambassador. I think tomorrow's meeting will be a good time to start that discussion, don't you?"

Mackenzie paused and then said, "Robert, if you don't mind, I would like to have Chief O'Connell stay for a bit so we can socialize her on the Croatian security environment. You are welcome to stay, but you have already sat through our briefing when you arrived. I suspect you have better things to do than hear us say the same things over again."

As Truckee stood up, Sue followed protocol and stood up as well. He said, "O'Connell, you stay put and listen to the briefings. Our relationship is too important for you to make a false step in the next few days. I have meetings outside the embassy tomorrow. Meet me in the office at 1000hrs after the country team meeting. Clear?"

"Check, sir. I will be there." Truckee turned and left. Both Stacey and Sue let out a deep breath. They had both been holding their breath to see how he would respond. It appeared he was going to cooperate. At least for now.

Mackenzie stood up and leaned out the door. "Debbie, do we have any more coffee left?"

"Chief, on the way. Need anything stronger?"

Mackenzie smiled and said, "Not for now, thanks. Its only 4 p.m."

"Just sayin,' Chief."

Stacey sat back down and said to Sue, "She is dangerous."

"Don't I know it. She was the rover in Cyprus on my arrival. She and Patty Dentmann were scary together."

A voice from the next room said, "I heard that."

Sue raised her voice and said, "I meant that as a compliment."

"OK, then."

Stacey Mackenzie poured the last bit of coffee into her cup and said to Debbie, "And when you bring the coffee, please bring real mugs."

"Chief, I'm just trying to teach you how to impress the locals."

"And starve me of caffeine."

Debbie brought a new tray with a four cup French press and four white ceramic mugs. "OK, Chief? By the away, Harry and Nancy are on the way."

The next two hours were spent with the COS and her deputy debriefing Sue and reviewing what they all knew about the overall target set. Nancy served as the notetaker and periodically inserted data points from her own operations against the Serbian target in

Zagreb. They all agreed that the operation was compatible with their current relations with the Croatian services. This made Sue's life easier. The COS said she would brief Truckee before the morning country team meeting with the Ambassador. That would let him be the one to tell the Ambassador this was a joint operation with the Croatians. "The Ambassador is good people and willing to take measured risks, but he will be in his happy place when we tell him that everything we do in this case will be with the Croatians."

Harry said, "And the MILATT might turn it down a notch."

Stacey said, "Fingers crossed on that one."

At the end of the meeting, Nancy summed up, "Here's what I got from the session. Sue and I meet with my Croatian service contact and, ideally, his Serbian assets as soon as I can arrange the meeting. Our job is to identify a lead to this Serbian criminal enterprise known as Dragon Triad. Chief, you and Hank will give us top cover by meeting with the chief of the service and by brokering a meeting between the MILATT and the chief of the military intelligence service. Those meetings will be focused on the Hizballah side of the equation and the hunt for where on the Dalmatian Coast the smugglers are running their operations. With some luck, we get traction on the operation this month and are ready the next time the route is opened up."

The COS said, "Sue, we are doing all the work so far. I need you to figure out how we can get access to the SOF analysts and their databases. As this moves forward, we will need all the analytic horsepower we can get to close the pipeline. At the very least, we need to have reporting that we can share with liaison. I've already worked that out with our headquarters, your job is to work it out with yours."

"Check, Chief."

"One more thing before you call it a day: I hope you understand that on Independence Day, you are going to be the MILATT's minion. That means doing whatever he wants during set up on the 3rd and mingling with the crowd on the 4th. Before that happens, I will encourage Robert to introduce you to the Ambassador, the Deputy Chief of Mission, and the head of the Political and Economic Section. I suspect you already met the Regional Security Officer or his deputy when you got your Embassy ID. Independence Day is a big deal here and, no matter what you and Nancy have cooking in operations, you have to be on your best protocol behavior so the MILATT doesn't decide you are more trouble than you're worth."

Harry smiled and said, "Based on what we have heard from Cyprus, you are lots of trouble. I mean, thrown into a trunk? Gunfights on the docks? Really?"

Sue said, "All exaggerated."

The voice from the other room said, "I didn't even tell them the bad stuff."

Longstreet was the first to report a lead in their effort. He called Barbara's throw-away mobile at 1930hrs and said, "Mark has identified a house, on the beach. It looks good."

Barbara said, "Thanks! I will contact our realtor and tell her we need to meet. What is good for you?"

"I can be there tomorrow by dinner time. Do you want me to bring the moving company?"

By this, Barbara assumed she meant the rest of Longstreet's team. She answered, "Jake, for now, just come yourself. I have to check with Beth."

"Roger. See you tomorrow around 5."

Barbara made a quick call to Beth to see if she could break free from work and join them for dinner. Beth said she had her normal set of Monday morning meetings, but could leave in time for a 5pm session, especially if Barbara was cooking.

Barbara put down the phone and looked at the volume of Peter Senior's journal that she had been reading. Her time travels with her father-in-law had taken her through the 1960s and into the 1970s, with Peter serving as a paramilitary officer in Laos and then deputy and finally Chief of Station in Bangkok. She was nearly through the journal that ended in 1973 when she found the story she had been searching for over the past week.

May 1973

My assignment in Headquarters was not as bleak as I expected. I was assigned to the Near East Division and specifically to the part of the Divi-

sion focused on Palestinian terrorism. After years of fighting commies of one sort or another, I was working on a new enemy: Terrorists who chose civilians as targets and chose the most extreme violence as a method to gain political advantage.

At first, it was hard to keep track of the various parts of the Palestinian target. There was the Palestine Liberation Organization also known as FATAH, a splinter PLO surrogate terrorist force, Black September, the Popular Front for the Liberation of Palestine (PFLP), the Popular Front for the Liberation of Palestine – General Command (PFLP-GC), and the Democratic Front for the Liberation of Palestine (DFLP). I had trouble keeping them straight since they worked as much against each other as for some political or military gain against Israel and the West. If there was anything in my favor, it was that most of these outfits were socialists and getting training from some intel service in the East Bloc. That meant there was something I could contribute almost immediately because most of my NE colleagues hadn't served in the Bloc and they found the Commie services just as confusing as I found the various Palestinian groups.

Barbara remembered the first time she started working for Near East Division and eventually for the Counterterrorism Center in 1985. The wall charts that the analysts made for the competing parties and their code names were a wash of color that looked like something put together by the abstract artist Piet Mondrian. The curved, straight, and dashed lines connecting the boxes offered some degree of logic to the relationships among the groups. As she began to handle and then recruit cases, she realized that some of these relationships were not logical at all. They were based on personal and professional jealousies that preceded even the creation of Israel. Some of the relationships didn't exist, except on paper. The deeper she dove into the terrorist world, the more she realized terrorists often just searched for some organization to justify their personal hatreds. The politics of their organizations often made no more sense to them than it did to Barbara.

After a brief pause, Barbara jumped ahead in the piece when she saw the link to Ireland.

August 1973

I met with my counterpart from the British Security Service to determine how we could work together on the PFLP. He was an old hand from the SOE and we got along pretty well. However, he mentioned to me that my name might cause some heartache in London. When I joked that there were plenty of British soldiers with the name O'Connell, he said, "True enough, but there is also an Irish terrorist named O'Connell who just moved back to Ireland from living in the USA since the war." While he knew I was not "that bloke," there would be some in his office who might be hesitant to work with me.

I figured the only way to get this resolved was to sort out what, if anything, we could do to help on this terrorist case first. Luckily the O'Connell we were talking about appeared to be on the list of known trainers for the PFLP. He periodically traveled to East Germany and would work with the Stasi and the KGB to train the Palestinian terrorists in tactics used in Northern Ireland. We had a Stasi source from my Berlin days who might have contact with this guy. I cabled Berlin to see if his handler could get anything about O'Connell. We did get some contact information in Ireland and in Northern Ireland. I passed it to the BSS. Whether it solved the problem or not, I never knew, but the BSS never again accused me of being an IRA sympathizer.

Later, I realized that this was one of the reasons I had so much trouble with Angleton. He assumed that all O'Connells on the planet were related. I tried several times to explain that it was as if all Smiths or Jones or Coopers were related, but he didn't buy it.

After we provided the material, I worked pretty well with the Brits on two cases that resulted in arrests by the Brits as the Palestinians transited London after training in East Germany. We also made some progress in recruiting Palestinians. In part, I think that was because we focused on recruiting the Palestinians while the Israelis and, for that matter, competing Palestinian organizations, were only interested in killing them. Now, after what the Palestinians did in Munich, I can't blame the Israelis, but sometimes you have to get your revenge by destroying an organization rather than killing an individual.

That night, Barbara thought hard about Peter Senior's comments. Had she been too focused on her efforts at revenge, whether the target was the Beroslavs or Michael O'Connell? Had she lost sight of the potential long-term success by destroying the networks they represented? More importantly, had she thought about the damage she might do in pursuit of a personal vendetta. Was she becoming as monomaniacal about these cases as she accused Peter Senior of being in his last days? As she assumed the Beroslav family had been against the O'Connells? Was this what happened to spies as they grew old?

Barbara had never been one to spend time focused on self-analysis. In the past, she always had her husband Peter or Max Creeter or one of her mentors in the building at CIA to serve as a sounding board. Now, she wasn't sure who would believe her ramblings if she told her story. It was one of the challenges of her life in the clandestine service. After you leave service, who would you trust even if they do have a need to know?

Barbara went downstairs, made herself a mug of cocoa and headed back to the bedroom. No more journal reading tonight. Peter's writings were not going to help her relax. Instead, she pulled a well-worn copy of John Buchan's *Greenmantle* off the shelf. Most probably a copy from Peter's library that stayed in the Potomac house rather than moving to Chautauqua. Buchan's writing was just the right amount of adventure coupled with predictability that would help her go to sleep. She took the cocoa, the book, and Peter's Colt to the guest bedroom and called it good enough.

Barbara woke just before dawn, put on sweats and running shoes, strapped on a small waist pack with her phone and the Colt, and headed out to the river. After a brief push through some brambles, Barbara found the remnants of the Potomac River tow path created in the 18th century to link the far reaches of Virginia to the Atlantic Ocean. A creation of far-sighted developers including George Washington, it supported barge traffic until the arrival of the railroads. The path was still there and used by intrepid runners and walkers who were willing to take the risk of a turned ankle in exchange for some time on a rarely used trail along the river. Barbara took no risks and kept her time on the path at a reasonably fast walk. She was not about to create a risk of further injury while recuperating from a grenade attack. As dawn arrived, the forest exploded in sound as thousands of birds woke and started to sing. The heavy forest along the tow path meant that the mix of light and shadow was dramatic. Barbara used the walk as a period of meditation, letting her mind free for that hour on the path. When she returned to the house, she felt better. After some yoga and a cup of very strong coffee, she almost felt human. She spent the rest of the day focusing on simple household tasks including preparing the evening meal.

Longstreet once again arrived on time. Barbara greeted him at the door and they settled in for a quick chat before Beth Parsons arrived.

Barbara started the conversation, "Jake, do you think we are doing the right thing hunting this guy?" She could see the question took Longstreet by surprise.

He said, "As opposed to doing nothing?"

"No. Nothing would not be a good solution. I'm just worried that I'm taking this too personally and going too far out of the box."

"Well, the last time someone threw a grenade at me, I took it personally."

"Do tell."

"Here's the short version. Max, Mutt and I were doing a raid in Bosnia. SOF had identified one of the Bosnian Serb war criminals…"

"Right. PIFWCs, right? Persons indicted for war crimes."

"I guess that's what you Klingons called them. Anyhow, the op was relatively straightforward. S&R had surveillance on the creep's bed-down location. We were to do a forced entry, throw a hood and flex cuffs on the guy and then drive like mad to the UNPROFOR compound."

"Sue may have been part of S&R at the time. I don't know if she was associated with the UN Protection Force or not."

"Before Sue's time, I reckon. This was early days of SOF involvement. As we used to say, we were never there, and if we were, you never saw us. Anyhow, we do a clandestine entry into the house and walk right into an ambush. The Bosnian Serbs knew the house was under surveillance, brought in individuals through a basement tunnel, and were waiting for us. I knew we were in trouble when one of the mugs throws a grenade at us. Max jumps on me and shields me with his body. Luckily, it was an old grenade. It exploded but didn't throw much shrapnel. Our body armor, helmets, and luck saved us. At that point, we decided it was going to be a full-up firefight and we ended the threat. I made sure the guy who threw the grenade at me received the necessary amount of lead in the head."

"Jake, that's war and I already did the lead delivery routine on my attacker. I'm just trying to decide if I should extend this to O'Connell."

"OK, so you are wondering…what? If we should manufacture some way to bring him to justice as opposed to capping this cat?"

"Do you think that's possible? I honestly have been in enough firefights."

"Anything is possible. I suspect we won't know if it can be done unless we invest some time in sorting out where, when and how."

"If we decided to keep it…non-kinetic…can we muster the necessary resources without breaking Beth's bank account?"

"Given this guy's pedigree, I think I can find the necessary resources from some British colleagues to grab the guy. That's assuming, of course, he doesn't have some private army guarding his house."

"Which means we have to go there to find out."

"Which means we have to go there to find out. Based on what we already know, I have asked a colleague, retired SBS pal, if he would be willing to help capture an IRA goon. He keeps a sailboat docked in Bari. Good place to sail, so he says. He said he would help if he and one of his mates can come along to make sure we have enough muscle. He also said he would do it for free, just to throw a member of the IRA into the hold of his boat for a day or two. A visit by boat might be just the thing."

"So, theoretically…"

"Theoretically, we could start from Bari, go up the Adriatic coast to the target location, do a quick entry op, throw a sandbag and some flex cuffs on the guy, put him in a sailboat and deliver him to authorities who would extradite him to the US. Of course, it might not hurt to have someone who wasn't a pensioner on board to make sure we have something resembling top cover."

"My daughter?"

"Well, maybe. I suspect she has more than enough to do as an SOF operator. What about that cop you knew back in the day? Would he take leave for a bit of piracy on the high seas?"

"Terry Reimer? Well, as they say in spy school, you never know until you ask."

"Sort of like the sniper's saying: 'you definitely miss every shot you don't take.'"

"Exactly." Just as Barbara said this, a small alarm sounded in the kitchen.

"Cake in the oven?"

"Nope. It's the motion sensor on the driveway. I suspect Beth has arrived. Jake, thanks for the talk. I feel better now."

"Justice instead of revenge is always a better choice."

"Even when the target uses grenades?"

"I didn't say that."

Barbara smiled as she walked to the front door. This time, Beth arrived in a Jaguar limousine with a driver and a body guard. She got out of the car wearing a Washington power suit. As Beth walked to the door, she said, "You have someplace where the guys can hang out? I need to get back to the city tonight and I figured I might have at least one glass of wine before we are through."

Barbara said, "We have plenty of room in Castle Despair and I made a ton of Chicken Marbella so they can hang out and eat with us as well. Sound good?"

"Chicken Marbella. The State Department classic for serving four, six, eight or a dozen." Beth turned to her driver and bodyguard and said, "Gentlemen, we are having a feast tonight. Come on in."

After dinner, Beth's driver and bodyguard went out to inspect the grounds and make themselves invisible. Jake Longstreet was the first to say anything as they lingered over their coffee. "Your guys are pretty good. I hope you pay them well because, if not, I'm going to ask them to contact me."

Beth laughed, "We pay them very well. Over twice what they would get from anyone else. We grab them from SOF, send them to our own training programs in the US and the UK and, after that, integrate them completely into the Stearns and Mandeville company team. We don't do a lot of high-risk accounts, but when we do, we know we have a team that can accomplish the mission."

Barbara said, "What sort of high-risk accounts do you have, Beth?" She had assumed Beth's team was focused on business development in the former Soviet Union, or FSU as it was known. Some risk due to the various organized crime families but hardly requiring a private army.

"We work primarily on linking US firms with firms in the FSU. High-end capital transfer accounts. Sometimes, we work on other accounts that are not as conservative. Sometimes the clients are victims of kidnapping, sometimes piracy, sometimes war-zone theft of international antiquities. Sometimes we do what is called lawfare which is legal warfare to make the front companies of terrorist and criminal organizations pay for their crimes. You never know who you might piss off."

Jake interjected, "Hence why Condottieri makes a nice living conducting pen testing."

Beth said, "More on that later, Jake. I have talked to the firm and they want to put Condottieri Malatesta on a retainer. In the meantime, what did Mark find out?"

"I am very glad that Mark is on the side of the angels, my friends. I now have a reasonable understanding of why he is such a paranoid bugger. He worked back into the records of land deals before the breakup of Yugoslavia and followed through on government tax records to today. What he found was the sale of a villa on the

Adriatic for an M. O'Connell. He then worked through the Serbian and Montenegro customs and immigration databases and found a scanned copy of Michael O'Connell's Irish passport along with his permanent resident alien papers." Longstreet pulled out an iPad and logged into a virtual private network that his company managed. He turned the screen around to show Barbara and Beth. "This look like the photos in the FBI or Agency files you have seen?"

Barbara nodded. It was a much clearer picture than the grainy surveillance photos that the Agency had in O'Connell's file, but it was definitely him. Now that she had a good look at his face, she would also see the family resemblance between the target and her long dead husband. It was definitely creepy.

Beth said, "OK, so where is this place? If it's in Albania, I will tell you up front that I'm not going there."

Jake laughed, "You have to remember that O'Connell bought this place, or had it given to him, back in the days of the Cold War. His villa is on the Croatian-Montenegrin border. The closest Montenegrin town is called Herceg Novi, but the closest real city is Dubrovnik in Croatia." He pulled up an electronic map of the Adriatic on his iPad. As he zoomed in, eventually they saw a satellite image of a two-story building with a small dock on the inlet. "This is why I think it might be worth our while to engage my pal from the SBS. He makes regular visits in the summer between Bari in Italy and Croatian harbors including Dubrovnik and Split. The harbor masters at both Croatian ports are his pals. I'm not entirely certain how we would conduct the operation, but we could start and finish at a Croatian harbor. If we thought the Croatians would follow through on an Interpol Red Notice, we could leave our passenger there. If not, we could take him over to Bari. As NATO allies, the Italians would definitely do the needful. The only difficulty at that point is whether the US murder case would be superseded by a British indictment. That I do not know. It is one of the reasons why I recommended that Barbara engage her law enforcement pal. If we had a lawman on board, no matter whether he had jurisdiction or not, we might have a good chance of convincing authorities that we are serious about the Red Notice."

Beth looked at Jake and said, "You think the locals would accept the credentials of a small-town cop from the US?"

Jake said, "No. I think the locals will accept the credentials of a big wig international lawyer, former US Ambassador who has on board a small-town cop. Depending on where we end up, we might just visit the US Embassy or the closest US consulate and get them to help."

"So, I'm not just a pretty face."

Jake smiled, "Not just."

Barbara interjected, "Now, I want to raise a question. I'm the one who initiated this project. Honestly, I've had second thoughts about whether we should do this or whether we deliver the entire package to the FBI and let them arrange the deal."

Beth said, "And by the time the official channels have been used, every lawman and every member of organized crime in Montenegro and Croatia will know and that means O'Connell will disappear. Barbara, what is the matter?"

"I just want to be sure I'm not getting too crazy in my old age and losing my perspective."

"Sorry, girl. I can't help on the crazy part. Here's what we can say for sure. O'Connell is a dangerous man. He recently killed an elderly man on contract from heaven only knows who. It's not as if he thought Andropovich was a traitor. He just did it because he was hired to make the kill. Then he tries to kill you using a local mobster. Apparently, there is some evidence that he killed one of your assets back in the day," Beth paused to drink her coffee. "So, I'm OK with trying to bring him to justice. If we can grab him and deliver him to authorities who will try and convict him, then I think we should try to do so.

"It is not so different from a recent case I had where we designed a program to bankrupt a Nigerian organized crime front company. All legal, well mostly, and everything stood up in court. The family harmed by the organized crime enterprise lived in Lagos but their distant relatives were successful tech entrepreneurs in the States. The goons tried to extort money from the family. Instead, they lost money and one of their front companies was destroyed. No lives lost, but it certainly was a satisfying way of doing business. The USG wasn't involved with the case, but Treasury and the Justice Department were all over the leads we uncovered. Don't get me wrong. I don't want to see us kill the guy. I want us to capture him and turn him over to authorities who will try him. So, I'm in if that can happen."

Barbara, listening to her friends, felt the excitement rising in the room. It was as though her ruminations about the meaning of it all had somehow sparked a surge of adrenalin: adetermination to do the right thing. Suddenly, the only question seemed to be, how would they go about the attempt?

Longstreet said, "I think we have a better than 50/50 chance to capture the guy. If it works, it works. If it doesn't work, we simply sail away on an Adriatic adventure after we help Beth do whatever she needs done in Zagreb. Mutt is in as well. My SBS pal, Theodore, and his SBS sailing partner, Neville, will definitely play. They know the guy is formerly IRA and that was all it took to close the deal. The sailboat can easily sleep eight, so that means we have the room to take everyone including, assuming he agrees, your lawman from East Aurora."

Barbara looked at her two friends and said, "OK, you've convinced me that this is about more than the fact that I am pissed off someone threw a grenade at me."

She turned to Beth and said, "Since we are working on your schedule, we will defer to you on when we get started."

Beth said, "I already told the senior partners that I would go ahead with the Croatia project so long as they funded expenses. They gave me carte blanche this afternoon. We can get started as soon as you guys want to launch."

"I will call Terry Reimer tonight and see what he says" said Barbara. "If he can't make the run, I say we make the run. I hope we can engage someone at the Embassy in Zagreb."

Beth said, "Agreed. Now, I'm going back to the city and will get my paralegal to start arranging flights. Stearns and Mandeville have a shared lease on a corporate jet. Do you think it makes sense for us to use that?"

"I certainly won't turn down a comfy ride to Europe," Jake said. "I recommend the flight plan take us to Vienna. From Vienna, you can easily take commercial air to Zagreb and I can catch a train down to Bari in Italy. Just breaks up the breadcrumbs we leave behind. If this all goes well, we will likely have to go our separate ways after the fact anyhow."

Beth agreed. "If we do go to a major city, we will probably ride share on the corporate jet. That might even look better, no?"

Barbara laughed, "Beth, before we are through, you will be more spy than diplomat."

Beth said, "I'm just a corporate lawyer who understands how the world works."

20 July 2007, US Embassy, Zagreb

Sue was the first to admit that working at the Embassy had both its positives and negatives. The positives included working with her colleague Nancy Garrison and Nancy's partners in the Croatian service at the civilian Security and Intelligence Agency known by the Croatian language abbreviation, SOA. After some hard work keeping the MILATT happy before, during, and after the Independence Day ceremonies, Captain Truckee introduced Sue to his contact in the Croatian Military Security and Intelligence Agency or SVOA. While the two services barely spoke, their representatives were charmed by their US female counterparts and agreed to work on the project. After all, it meant disrupting a Serbian criminal enterprise and an Islamic terrorist organization: Likely the two most important issues in the Croatian security and intelligence world. Meanwhile, back at the Embassy, the fact that the two services were talking to US representatives made the Ambassador, the MILATT, the COS and even Washington happy. Sue wasn't entirely sure about Smith's views until the first secure video teleconference where Smith told her that the work was satisfactory…so far.

The negatives were Sue's impatience with regular intelligence work. She was used to the SOF version of intelligence operations: Make a decision; hold the agent meeting; debrief; report; act on the intelligence; repeat. Even in her first tour in Cyprus, she had been an independent, operating in and around the port of Limassol and living in the safety of an RAF military complex. There were no cover concerns, because everyone on the RAF base knew she was an SOF operator. In Zagreb, she was exposed to an environment where operational security measures were at least as important as operational tempo. Stacey and Nancy spent time after Independence Day teaching Sue the nature of intelligence operations in Croatia and Zagreb in particular.

At one point, the COS said to Sue, "We live in a risky operational environment. There isn't a significant personal threat, but there is a significant operational threat. The Croatians want to know what we are doing in their country. Our adversaries, including the Russians, the Chinese, the Iranians, the Serbs, and a myriad of other countries with embassies here are convinced we must be doing something hostile to their interests. If that isn't enough, organized crime organizations work the same cracks and seams of society that we use for our recruitment operations. So, our world has to be based on making sure that any operation we run is prudent and has the best possible security measures. Do not forget that less than twenty years ago, this was a communist country with a communist security infrastructure. Yugoslavia may not have been close pals with the Soviets, but their service was trained by the Soviets and other members of the East Bloc. We have to assume that they have physical and technical surveillance on us. This isn't a denied area, Sue, and we aren't going to be operating like our colleagues in Moscow or Beijing. But we are going to conduct operations at a pace that allows us to be certain that we have done everything we can to keep our assets alive. Clear?"

That meant operations focusing on Sue's target were integrated into the station plan, and Sue and Nancy worked every case together. Even liaison meetings were conducted in a manner closer to the tradecraft taught at the Farm. Every liaison meeting was planned down to the second. Every agent meeting involved a two-hour cleansing route plus at least one change of vehicles. Even something as simple as obtaining a temporary safe house — really just renting a holiday villa on the coast — involved checking and double-checking security measures. Sue was a guest in Zagreb. She was under pressure from the MILATT to avoid trouble as well as to produce intelligence, so she followed the rules set by the COS. That didn't mean she liked it. Sue acknowledged to anyone who would listen that she was an impatient person.

When it was time to report to HICU on her recent progress, Sue had to use a secure conference room that was another remnant of the Cold War. The station had a room about twice the size of a phone booth serving as the secure video teleconference or SVTC location. The multiple layers of security meant that no one could stand the heat and the lack of fresh air for long. It gave the Zagreb end of the conversation an excuse to keep the discussion short. Sue was already cranky by the time the SVTC link was established. Massoni's head appeared on the screen. "Sue, you look hot. Not enjoying the Balkans?"

"Jim, I'm in a closet, it's about 90F inside here, and there is no fresh air. I am working at an operational pace that is driving me crazy, and I am living with a station officer so I never get away from the program. I'm definitely hot."

Smith's face and voice appeared, "O'Connell, I hope you are getting hot on making progress down there. I didn't send you there on a Balkan holiday."

Sue knew full well that Smith had been reading her traffic on developments, so this was just Smith being Smith. He always wanted to cut to the chase. She said, "Boss, I'm calling to ask if I can set up a direct SOF intel feed. The intel we just collected suggests that we have an exchange going to take place the last three days of the month. We are ready to pull the trigger on the surveillance, shutting down the Serbian end of the pipeline and turning the delivery of Hizballah maritime information to the US Navy. Once this starts, I am going to need real time support to make sure all the moving parts keep moving at our pace of operations."

"Are you asking if Flash can come visit?"

"Boss, if that is what it takes to get the live feed here, yes. We established a joint safe house with the Croatians near Dubrovnik. The Croatian military service is confident that Dubrovnik is the port facility where the transfer is going to happen. The station's resources suggest the same thing. The port is smaller, less well managed from a security standpoint and closer to areas of greater Serbian influence. At least that's what liaison thinks. I've been with both a Croatian agent handler and with a station handler and met with their sources. We expanded their requirements and now the intelligence feed is starting to come in. It all points to Dubrovnik or somewhere on the nearby coast.

"My problem now is I don't know what sort of real-time feed we can share with liaison. They are going to be the ones doing the surveillance, so I would like to give them as much support as possible, but I don't know the SOF protocol on working with a non-NATO partner."

Smith said, "If anyone knows, it is going to be our Flash. When do you need her in country?"

"I haven't worked the clearances here yet, I just wanted to know if you would support it."

"I do and I will. Here's what you need to do. You need to get the MILATT, the COS, and the Ambassador ready to receive a call from the CG. He has been waiting for an opportunity to push the accelerator on this one. Now is the time. Please tell them to expect a call or a cable or both from the CG by your COB tomorrow. I will send the country clearance request as soon as I know he has made the call. Check?"

"Roger, Boss. Tell Flash to pack light. We are going to move to the Croatian safe house as soon as she gets here, so no need for uniforms. Flash as Flash will work just fine. I will do the needful to prep the MILATT that she isn't going to be working in uniform."

"Has the MILATT been trouble? Do I need to let the CG know something about this guy?"

"Boss, he was a bit of a challenge at first, but after I worked on Independence Day to get him direct contact with his Afghan and Iraqi counterparts and then allowed him to take full credit for getting the VSOA to cooperate with us on a joint project, he has been fair. He isn't Massoni…"

A voice from the monitor said, "But who is?"

"Exactly. He is a fleet Navy guy so he is pretty challenged with the speed that we work. Also, he has trouble with our willingness to put mission before doctrine. Since he is getting more face time with the Ambassador and with the Chief Of Staff of the Croatian Navy than he has ever had before, my guess is it will work out OK. So long as I can close some sort of deal here before the end of the month, I will be fine."

Again Massoni's voice added, "And avoid blowing anything up..."

"That too."

Smith looked into the screen and said, "I got it. You will get Flash soonest. Out here."

Sue shut down the SVTC and walked out of the box. Given that her activities after the SVTCs would focus on meetings with SVOA, she was in slacks and a polo shirt. Both were sticking to her skin. She needed some fresh air before proceeding. After that and before she did anything with the Croatians she would have to tell the MILATT and the COS the news. The CG of SOF would be in touch and then HICU would request approval to send an analyst to work with Garrison, Sue and the Croatians. Mostly good news, though she knew the MILATT would have a cow and then a thousand questions. She hoped Rollins had some coffee ready.

>>>>>> BUILDING A BETTER MOUSETRAP

25 July 2007 Zagreb and the Dalmatian Coast

Zagreb Airport was busy when Flash arrived. A number of low-budget flights arrived at the same time, delivering tourists from Northern Europe ready to enjoy an Adriatic holiday during the August vacation season. Despite the crowds, it took no time at all for Nancy Garrison to find Flash. Holiday visitors, both men and women, came dressed in light pastels and white cotton outfits. Sleeveless dresses were the outfit of choice for women as they stepped into the air-conditioned arrivals hall and prepared for the warmth of the Balkan sun. In the same Immigration line was a woman dressed in black jeans, a black t-shirt, holding a black duffle with a black backpack over one shoulder.

Nancy walked up and said quietly, "Going with that spy black ensemble that is so popular this year among evil geniuses and world dominators?"

Flash looked at the tall brunette dressed in khaki trousers and a sky-blue polo shirt. She smiled and said, "Do I know you?"

"Not yet. Get your passport out and follow me."

Flash did as instructed, following Garrison through the VIP passport control line. Minutes later, she was in the back seat of an old Mercedes sedan with Sue and Nancy in the front seats.

Nancy started talking as soon as she pulled away from the airport. "Welcome to your Adriatic holiday. We will be driving for a few hours, so please relax and enjoy the view of the lovely Croatian countryside. We have made a picnic lunch and we will be stopping in two hours on a hillside overlooking the Sea. In the meantime, if you have any questions, please feel free to ask your tour guides." Nancy looked into the rear view mirror to see if Flash appreciated her humor.

"Hilarious. Now, what exactly is going on?"

Sue said, "Hey, I get you a few days on the beach and all you want to do is work?"

"I was planning on a holiday, so I guess this counts."

"Not really. We are going to set up in a safe house with the Croatian service, meet agents, run physical surveillance on a couple of beaches and generally work our tails off."

Nancy said, "Sue is just such a poop. The safe house overlooks the Adriatic, the beach surveillance really means spending time hanging out with some wild Croatian special forces guys. Then there is the grilled foods and chilled white wine. What's not to like?"

Flash nodded and said, "Sue has always been a spoil sport. I was just getting the hang of living with a dozen men in a safe house in Afghanistan and suddenly she decides we have to leave."

"It wasn't my fault you completed the mission."

Nancy cocked her head to one side and said, "You two sound like a married couple. You sure you want to hang out together? I could arrange for the Croatian Special Forces to take one of you down to a beach overlook and…"

Flash raised her hand and said, "Oh, take me, take me…"

Sue turned to Nancy, "Don't encourage her."

The relatively slow day at the American Citizens' Service desk at the US Embassy, Zagreb became more complicated with the arrival of Ambassador Beth Parsons and East Aurora detective Terry Reimer. James Turlock was a first-tour officer used to individuals with lost passports, young world-travelers whose money had run out and needed to contact their parents, and even Americans facing some sort of criminal proceedings in Zagreb. He had not handled the visit of a retired Ambassador or a US police officer before. Especially when the Ambassador looked like a movie star and the police officer looked like a character out of a 1970s television police series.

Beth Parsons looked at the young officer through the bullet-proof glass, checked his name tag on his Embassy ID and said, actually shouted to be sure he heard her: "Mr. Turlock, I would like to see Ambassador Josephson. If he is available, I believe he will be willing to take the time to see me." Beth smiled her Medici smile which implied to Turlock that not only might she kill him, but she might eat him afterwards. She passed him her State Department badge that identified her as a retired Ambassador. Turlock complied and called up to the Ambassador's office. He was surprised at the speed of the response from the Ambassador's secretary.

The secretary said, "Turlock, make sure the Ambassador is comfortable and I will be downstairs immediately." Since his arrival in country in October 2006, Turlock had little contact with his Ambassador. His boss was the senior consular officer who worked for the deputy chief of mission who, more or less, ran the mission. The Ambassador was someone you saw at American diplomatic functions and the rare times that you served as the duty officer over the weekend. Turlock knew one thing for sure: if the Ambassador wanted these two Americans treated well, he would do the best he could.

Turlock came through the armored, hardline door that separated the consular waiting room from the consular offices. He had two bottles of water in his hand and he said, "Ambassador Parsons, the Ambassador will see you immediately. We need to wait for his secretary. I apologize, but all we have to offer you is bottled water. Please have a seat."

Reimer was about to sit down when Beth touched him on the arm and shook her head. She turned to Turlock and said, "Mr. Turlock, thank you. You may not know it, but I've served in a number of posts including my first one as a consular officer. We do appreciate the offer of the water. It has been a long day."

Beth took the water and passed one of the bottles to Reimer. They had barely opened the bottles when the US Ambassador's secretary walked through the hardline door and said, "Ambassador Parsons. It is very good to see you. I don't suppose you remember me…"

Beth interrupted and said, "Jean, it is great to see you. I think we last met in…"

"Kuwait City, Madame Ambassador. You came out from Main State. I was your Embassy control officer."

"You took the words right out of my mouth." Beth smiled a sincere smile this time. She turned to Reimer and said, "Terry, we need to follow Jean upstairs." She then turned back to Turlock, shook his hand, and said, "Mr. Turlock, thank you. And good luck on your first tour."

"Thank you, ma'am."

As they headed up the stairs, Terry asked Beth, "Why didn't you want me to sit down?"

"Except for third-world bus depots, consular waiting rooms are probably the nastiest places in the world. Embassy personnel clean them every day and then the next day they are filled with people who are nervous about applying for a visa, nervous about the lies they are going to tell, nervous about the fact that they are abandoning their family, or nervous about the criminal act they are about to commit. By 10 a.m., the place is dangerously filthy. It is 2 p.m. and there is no way that I was about to sit down. I suspect you have experienced a place like that in the past."

"Waiting rooms at police stations can be pretty ugly. Hey, pretty amazing that you remembered Jean's name."

Beth smiled and whispered, "Her name is on her Embassy ID. It is important for us that she likes us. I remembered her face, but thankfully, she filled in the rest."

"Diplomacy."

"Exactly. Terry, when we get upstairs there doubtless is going to be a bit of State Department camaraderie. Just go with the flow, OK?"

"You are the boss."

"Well, for now."

And, indeed there was quite a bit of camaraderie as Terry Reimer found out that Beth Parsons was the officer who made John Josephson's career in State Department. There were precious few ambassadorial appointments that went to career diplomats and Zagreb was not usually one of them. It was, after all, a small posting in a very beautiful country that was working hard to become part of the

NATO alliance. It was the sort of post that could easily be filled by a political appointee who would cut ribbons, host dinners, and let the Deputy Chief of Mission handle everything else. Yet, Josephson captured that posting.

During the conversation, Reimer found out that Josephson's career was advanced by Beth Parsons as she took him from post to Main State and back to larger posts as she became more senior in State. He was a Serbo-Croat linguist who worked with Beth when they supported Ambassador Richard Holbrooke in negotiations in Belgrade. They were part of the process that resulted in the Dayton Accords to end the Balkan wars of the 1990s. Just before Beth retired, she made sure his DCM posting was in a NATO ally, in his case Poland. She was long retired by the time he was offered the Ambassador position in Zagreb, but Josephson knew that the review committees would have asked Beth's opinion about his skills. In short, Josephson owed Beth.

After what seemed an endless stream of tedious discussions of where this person or that person was posted and expressions of sadness over deaths of colleagues and expressions of joy over births of grandchildren, Ambassador Josephson decided to cut to the chase. "Beth, I heard that your firm, Stearns and Mandeville, was interested in some work on Croatian war reparations at The Hague, but I didn't expect to see you here to take charge."

Beth laughed. "Hardly take charge. I'm here more than anything else as the firm's advance party to hold a few meetings, check a few facts and report home. That said, if this trip goes well, you may see me again."

"That would be excellent. Joan and I would very much like to host you at the residence."

"John, for now, I am staying in the Palace and it would be probably in both of our interests for that to remain my headquarters. We don't want to put you in the crosshairs of the Croatian political establishment when Stearns and Mandeville investigators uncover war crimes."

"Thanks for that. Is Mr. Reimer also part of your team?"

"John, I brought Terry here because we have another…issue we want to discuss with you. It is a sensitive issue and I know it might not be…exactly within the bailiwick of an Ambassador."

"I know there is a but coming, so, Beth, just tell me. If I can help, you know I will do what I can."

The former Ambassador and the East Aurora detective spent the next hour outlining the main points of their plan. They started with the murder of Andropovich and ended with the fact that they had used open-source material to track their murderer to just over the border in Montenegro. They didn't mention that part of their team already was headed to Montenegro via a private sailboat. It might have caused the Ambassador to reject their request. After all, he might think it was some sort of pirate adventure. Josephson followed the discussion carefully and then stated, "I think we can make this happen. We share our FBI Legal Attaché with Lubljana. If I knew when he might be needed here, I could make sure he was here. He would work with Detective Reimer, correct?"

Reimer responded, "Mr. Ambassador, I am simply the courier of the legal material. I have the material necessary to confirm that we have both an indictment from the US attorney in Buffalo, the INTERPOL Red Notice issued by the FBI, and my department's interest in bringing a murderer to justice. I don't have any jurisdiction here. However, if we were to find that our fugitive arrived in your country under his own power, I would like to be there with your Legal Attaché and the Croatian authorities to ensure he is extradited to the US. I believe he is also a suspect in a number of crimes in Northern Ireland and in Germany." Reimer paused and then said, "While I think it would be a good thing bringing this man to justice, I can't be sure that it could be done without some publicity."

"It sounds like it would be good publicity and good for the US/Croatian relationship."

Beth entered the conversation and said, "John, once I heard about this, that was precisely what I thought. I've been out of the game for awhile, but bringing an international assassin to justice and doing it as a partnership with the Croatians seemed to me to be a perfect diplomatic coup. Not without some risks, but a coup nonetheless."

Reimer said, "Risks on the ground."

Josephson said, "And risks if Washington heard about it beforehand. They would probably muck it up."

Beth looked at Josephson and said, "Will you trust me on this one?"

"Yes, Beth, I will. I suspect you have a deeper role in this than you have revealed, but I do trust you. However, I need to bring my DCM, our LEGATT, and the COS into the circle of trust. The DCM because I might be hit by a truck the day you want to make this happen and we don't want any failure to communicate. The LEGATT and COS because they are the ones who have the necessary links to the security service that will help us make this happen."

Beth said, "Do we do that now?"

"How soon do you intend to do this?"

"With your approval, we would start working on this today with the goal of accomplishing it over the weekend. It will either work or it will not work, and that won't change the longer we wait."

"It would appear you had this already planned. What if I said no?"

"Then we would take our fugitive from justice someplace else. I really do have work to do here in Zagreb and, if you said no, then it would have been no. If we had to go someplace else, our fugitive might not have been transported willingly, and the delivery to a legitimate legal authority might have been more, shall we say, complicated."

"I really miss working with you, Beth."

"Well, let's just say that if this works you probably will see me more often than you wish as I work on the reparations program."

"Working on a righteous target is always a good thing. And the good news is, I am eligible to retire, so this is likely to be my last chance to make a difference." Josephson stood up and said, "Let's get my DCM and COS in the room and work through some details. I will have the DCM get our LEGATT back in country."

After the briefing, Stacy Mackenzie pulled Terry Reimer aside as Beth, the Ambassador and his DCM continued to share stories about each other and about known colleagues. Stacey said, "O'Connell? I don't suppose this guy is related to Barbara or Sue O'Connell."

"Chief, lots of O'Connells in Ireland. Just like there are lots of Reimers in Germany and Mackenzies in Scotland."

"Detective Reimer, are you always this glib?"

"Most days." Reimer smiled what he hoped to be a warm smile, but given the long ago results of broken nose, he doubted it. "My chief thinks it is one of my most endearing qualities."

Stacy laughed and then turned serious. "I have Sue O'Connell headed to Dubrovnik working on a counterterrorism project that has the interest of my headquarters, the SOF headquarters and the headquarters of two different Croatian services. Can you guarantee this is not going to dick up that operation?"

"Chief, I have no idea who Sue O'Connell is or who she works for. I suspect she must work for you if she is on some counterterrorism project. As to our small effort, I can't see how it could have any impact on what Ms. O'Connell is doing in your country. As you heard, our goal is to capture a criminal on the border. I know just enough about Croatian geography to know that Dubrovnik is close, but certainly not on the border. I don't see how any of this is associated with a counterterrorism operation. This guy is a murderer. He has multiple aliases and one of his names is Michael O'Connell. If what the FBI and your headquarters says is true, he has worked almost exclusively for the Russians for nearly two decades. We are involved, admittedly off the books, because your headquarters said they were too busy with counterterrorism operations to do anything about this guy. The FBI response was they didn't see the murder of a guy in my town as worth the effort. I want to see the guy tried in Buffalo, New York for a crime he committed on my turf. Nothing more than that. I'm just a cop trying to catch a murderer, but I understand I am not on my turf. I need your concurrence to do what I want to do. If your outfit had been willing to send a team, I wouldn't be here. I would be waiting at Buffalo airport for his arrival."

"Detective Reimer, you are a long ways away from home. You have any idea how complicated this is?"

"Chief, long before I was a police officer, I worked as an Army CID Special Agent, hunting Soviet and East Bloc spies in the 1980s. I get how complicated this is. The problem is no one in the USG seems to have an interest in doing something about this RIGHT NOW and right now is when we know where this guy is located. A week, a month, a year from now and this guy disappears again. If he disappears, it means he is out there killing other folks, perhaps one of your agents or one of your officers. I'm willing to risk breaking some bureaucratic china to get this guy arrested. The folks I am working with could just as easily have kidnapped him outside your country and thrown him in the Adriatic. Hard to swim with weights on your ankles. There are plenty of old scores that would be settled that way, but I don't want that to happen. I want this guy in court. My court."

"OK," Mackenzie said, after the slightest pause to give her words effect. "I'm willing to take you and Ambassador Parsons to my Croatian counterpart who is involved in organized crime. He is not in any way associated or even aware of the counterterrorism operation going on in Dubrovnik. He is the guy who has the authority to make that arrest if you can get O'Connell to walk, run, drive or swim into Croatia. That's as much as I can or will do. As it is going down, I will make sure my headquarters knows what's happening. If I don't do that, I am fired and I really want my pension."

"Check, Chief. Trust me, being a pensioner is a very fine thing."

Barbara, Jake, Mutt and their two British colleagues had left Bari two days earlier on a sailboat named *Marie's Bane*. Barbara asked Theodore about the name. All he would say is that his wife, Marie, was convinced that he loved the boat as much as she loved him. At that point, Neville said, "Mate, you know she is right."

"Hush, you Cornish bumpkin."

Neville looked at Barbara and said, "You know, in life you have to pick your friends carefully. I guess I made some errors along the way."

Now, after two days of gentle sailing on the Adriatic, Jake, Mutt and Neville were on deck conducting a final check of the kit that they would use when they got near the Dalmatian coast. Barbara was sitting at the helm. Theodore was close by to ensure she did no harm to his boat. While the plan seemed clear enough when they were in the US working through the details, now it was time to be sure they had all the necessary equipment. The three commandos laid out the three jumpsuits they would wear, three radios, three sets of night vision goggles, three pistols, and six flashbang grenades. They had already checked the small Zodiac rigid inflatable boat that they would use to arrive on site. When Barbara asked Terry where the weaponry came from, all he would say is "Theodore offered, I accepted, Beth paid." Barbara nodded. She understood there were aspects of the retired special operations community that she would never know.

That evening, as they sat at the galley table and talked through the operation, Jake took the lead. "We just got word on the satellite phone from Beth and Terry that the Embassy in Zagreb will help. Terry is going to be working with Croatian law enforcement and they should be waiting at the border. We just have to coax the Irish bastard to run for Dubrovnik by car or by boat. The Croatians will do the rest."

Theodore said, "We can certainly put a scare into him when we show up in his villa in the proper kit, green eyes on, using a few pyrotechnics. If he has a car, he might just drive to the border to get clear of us and if he has a boat, we can use the RIB to make sure he heads up the coast and not down."

Barbara added, "I would like to emphasize that we really want this guy in custody, not dead. I promised Reimer that we would do everything we could to take him alive."

Neville said, "What makes you think we wouldn't want the same?"

"Perhaps the fact that he was an IRA enforcer well before he was a Russian assassin for hire."

Theodore nodded, "There's that."

Mutt added, "Accidents happen, Barbara. I suspect you know that."

Jake said, "Right. Like teaching O'Connell to swim with his hands tied and weights on his feet."

Theodore smiled, "The SBS taught us that skill. We could give him some of the same training for free."

Jake finally said, "Look, mates. We all want is to get this guy off the pitch. If we can do this and turn him over to the Croatians, who likely won't be gentle souls, then I say we do what we can to do so. No one is saying we risk our lives. If he shoots at us, we shoot back. OK?"

The other three men nodded agreement and Barbara said, "I'm the only one here who he tried to kill, but I'm still interested in a capture, not a kill, operation. So, let's go through the plan one more time."

One hour later, they were confident that they would be able to get O'Connell to voluntarily travel to Croatia, either by car or boat. It would be up to their target to cooperate.

F lash was surrounded by several commercial computers, two Croatian service telephone monitoring modules, and a modified iPad that was cleared to receive all SOF intelligence to be shared with her liaison partners. Looking over her shoulder was Milo Navotnik, a young man in a black t-shirt, black running tights and black trainers. He was the counterpart to Flash in the Croatian Special Operations Battalion. Milo had been a member of the Third Special Operations Company, responsible for sea borne commando operations, but his skills in technical and computer operations resulted in an unwilling transfer to the Battalion command group. This was his first deployment in the new role. He was determined to succeed. It didn't hurt that his American mentor was a woman.

Flash said, "Milo, if you continue to pant over my shoulder, I am going to have to hurt you."

"Pant?"

"Like a wild animal…"

"I am that."

"Later, Milo. What I meant was you should pull up a chair and watch what is going on next to me instead of looking over my shoulder."

"Yes, Flash."

Flash turned the iPad screen slightly to the right so that Milo could follow the SOF drone feed as it tracked a trawler heading from the sea buoys toward the port of Dubrovnik. She said, "We are watching this end of the operation because I don't think they are actually going to dock in Dubrovnik. I think at the last minute they are going to divert to some cove north or south of the city. Someplace where they can take up their cargo unnoticed."

"You think this…because?"

"I think this because I don't trust anyone. I always assume terrorists are smart, don't want to get caught, and think we are too stupid to consider alternative solutions. They are used to working against policemen who are easy to bribe, generally overworked, and, even when they are good, have tunnel vision."

"Tunnel vision. I like that phrase. I will use that phrase."

"Feel free. Now, what I need you to do is to inform your surveillance team following the convoy to be prepared for the convoy to take some side road before they get to Dubrovnik. If I'm right, the convoy of weapons will not go to the port, it will go to some fishing village."

"I know one north of Dubrovnik that would work well. It is called Zaton Bey. Easy for a small trawler. Just a fishing village and someplace where sailboats anchor for tourists."

"Then what are we waiting for? Do you know someplace close where we could set up to confirm transfer of the equipment? A hillside? Someplace to set up the technical surveillance coverage?"

"Yes, I do. We can go there?"

"That is what I recommend. Of course, you need to get someone to agree, but we need to leave soon if this is going to work. All I need is my satellite phone and this iPad. You bring the long-range surveillance gear and we go. Now, go get someone to agree." Flash waved her hands at him as if she was trying to shoo a cat away.

Sue walked up to Flash. She had been watching this exchange as she leaned against the door frame. "You don't like the view here?"

"It would be better to have a view of the actual exchange."

"Betting that Milo is right?"

"Better than betting that I'm right. He's the local after all."

"You want some company?"

"You are bored too?"

"Waiting patiently has never been my strongest skill."

"What about your keeper, Ms. Nancy?"

"So, we bring her as well."

"And her keeper, Jan?"

"So, we use a van. It wouldn't hurt to have a gunfighter along with us, right?"

"These Croatians look pretty tough, so I'm saying yes."

"Excellent, I'll get Nancy on board."

Ten minutes later, they were in an old Volkswagen minibus headed along a coastal road. Rolling green hills were to their right and the azure blue Adriatic to their left. They were monitoring the Croatian surveillance team following the Serbian smugglers headed to Dubrovnik. Sue had a map on her lap, tracking the reporting using a yellow marker. She said, "We have about five more minutes and then the moment of truth. Either they turn off the main road and run down the same road we are using or we look like dopes."

Nancy was in the front passenger seat riding next to Jan Pivoch, another member of the Croatian Special Forces naval company. He was in his forest camouflage uniform, Navy blue beret and mirrored sunglasses. Nancy turned to Flash and said, "I'm hoping for the drive down this road."

Flash said, "The last feed I got from our UAV showed the trawler moving north from Dubrovnik. At the very least, we are headed in the same direction as the trawler. That much we know."

Milo was sitting in the last row of seats in the minibus surrounded by radio gear and three plastic cases carrying his video and audio technical gear. He was also in his full uniform now. Crushing the beret on his head were a pair of large headphones. He looked up and said, "They have made the turn. They are about thirty kilometers behind us."

Pivoch nodded. "The Commander will be pleased. We are both in front of them and behind them. It is an excellent surveillance operation."

Nancy said, "Well done, Jan."

He said, "It is all because of Milo and...Flash. Milo told me where we need to pull off the road and set up. This should work well for us."

Milo's voice from the rear of the minibus said, "The Coast Guard aircraft reported that the trawler is headed toward Zaton Bey. The

Coast Guard have pulled off and headed out to sea. They do not want to make the Hizballahis nervous."

Sue nodded. "Excellent. Once we get set up, we should be able to coordinate all the different parts from our overwatch position." Just as she spoke, Jan took a hard right onto a trail barely wide enough for the minibus. They bounced along the track for two hundred meters when the track turned north and ended at a cliff face. Jan kept the minibus in the shadows of the trees and the team moved forward on foot to their position.

Jan said something in Croatian to Milo and Milo beamed.

Sue said to Nancy, "What did he say?"

Nancy said, "He simply said 'excellent choice.'"

Flash set up her small satellite antenna and radio rig, plugged the iPad into the rig and began to download the live images from the UAV. The grey screen showed the trawler in the white cross hairs with a geolocation on the lower right of the screen. Sue noticed that the screen was missing all of the other data that usually came with a UAV transmission. Flash looked up and said, "They did a pretty good job of stripping the data that we don't need or want and leaving the best parts. I am impressed with whatever software jockey did the needful."

Nancy came over to Flash and Sue and said, "OK, kids. I have presents from the chief. Please tell me you will only use them as necessary." She handed Sue and Flash a pair of Glock pistols nestled in nylon paddle style-holsters and a second paddle holster holding a pair of magazines.

Sue smiled and said, "Nancy, it's not even my birthday!"

Flash was busy doing a quick functions check on her Glock and said, "It's always my birthday. Tell the chief we love her."

"You can tell her yourself soon enough. She is with the surveillance team trailing the Serbs. She said she didn't want to miss the party."

"Party?"

Nancy rolled her eyes. "Flash, do you really think the Croatians are going to let the Serbs go back home once they make the weapons transfer?"

Flash said, "And here I am without my sniper rifle."

"Sometimes a girl just has to make sacrifices. Right now, what we need to do is make sure Milo gets a digital video of the transfer. One way or the other, we want to make sure the Croatians have a solid case."

"Rats," was all Flash said.

The Serbian convoy arrived at the small village just before sundown. The three cargo trucks pulled up to a concrete pier and parked. Each of the trucks had a driver and passenger in the front and one or two men in the canvas-covered back. They all got out, gathered, and started to smoke and pass around a bottle of Balkan liquor. They were a rough-looking lot and the locals who walked along the streets steered well clear of the new arrivals. The rich European tourists who had anchored their sailboats in the cove walked along the pier in their white trousers and brightly colored shirts, oblivious to the Serbs.

Sue watched them. The digital screen on Flash's computer was now capturing a mirror of the feed from the two Croatian long-range cameras Milo had set up along the cliff face. At present, the sunset made it hard to distinguish what was going on, but Milo promised that, as soon as the sun went down, his night vision lenses would allow full coverage of the transfer. Flash said to Sue, "He has an IR lens as well as a standard night vision lens for the two cameras. The guy knows what he is doing. And did you see the directional boom mike that he has set up? I am very impressed. He said he made it himself in a shop that Special Forces command created just for him. How come I don't have my own shop?"

Sue shook her head. "Ask Marconi. He's the tech guy."

Flash offered a pout. "I know. I am just an analyst."

"But a mighty good one." Nancy intruded. "Thanks to you, we got in ahead of the game rather than following them. All the Agency analysts were expecting a Dubrovnik transfer. They even identified the slip they were convinced the Hizballahis were going to use."

"They were expecting the Hizballah and Serbian teams to be predictable," Flash said. "If there is one thing we learned in Afghanistan and Iraq, it's that the enemy is hardly ever predictable. So, Ms. Nancy, what happens after the transfer?"

"The plan is to let the trawler depart and between your UAV coverage and the Croatian Coast Guard, the US Navy should have no trouble with the intercept. Once intercepted, they will take the trawler back to Dubrovnik and we get to do a joint sensitive-site exploitation of the boat. It just might have intelligence on the entire network."

"And the Serbs?"

Another voice from out of the dark answered the question, "We work hard to convince our Croatian counterparts not to conduct an ambush, killing them all."

"Chief, when did you arrive?"

"A couple of minutes ago. I walked around the site with the Special Forces Battalion commander. He didn't want to miss the action. He is heaping praise on Jan and Milo right now for taking the initiative. In turn, they said Flash was the brains of the plan."

"Chief, I'm always the brains."

"Good to see you have a reasonably sized ego for a Special Operator."

Sue decided this exchange could go sideways quickly, so she interjected, "Chief, you said we needed to work hard to prevent an ambush?"

"Actually, what I said was we want to make sure our Croatian colleagues don't succeed in killing all of the Serbs when they do ambush the convoy on its return. I would like to see them capture as many of these guys as they could so we can get the maximum intelligence value."

"How can we help?"

"Sue, if you and Flash are willing, I recommend we split up and each of us joins a section of the Croatian Special Forces team. Just having Americans around might prevent…excesses."

"Your wish is my command, chief." Flash always knew how to craft a diplomatic end to a conversation.

They watched the transfer take place and listened to the Serbs and the Hizballahis argue over whether the Serbs were going to get a bonus for the delivery. In the end, the argument was solved when three of the Hizballahis on the deck of the trawler pulled out Kalashnikovs and threatened to use them if the Serbs didn't stop arguing. That ended the discussion, the Hizballahis on the pier cast off the hawsers and the trawler backed out of the pier with two of the Hizballahis still standing watch with their Kalashnikovs. The Serbs split up again to their various trucks and headed out of town.

The COS's voice called out from the darkness. "We are mounting up. Flash, you stick with Milo and Jan. Nancy, you are riding with Zoltan. Sue, you jump in with me in the large van. Let's go."

They split up and headed to their respective vehicles. Sue joined Stacey in a large Mercedes Sprinter van with twelve commandos. As she entered, Stacey said, "I am going to take the first six led by the battalion commander. You are working with Dietrich. I understand you speak Russian and some German. Dietrich speaks a little English but he is fluent in German. OK?"

"Check, chief. What's the plan exactly?"

"We should be able to get in front of the cargo vans pretty easily. Nancy and Zoltan are in another minibus like Flash and Jan. They will pull in behind the cargo trucks. The colonel calls the shots. There is plenty of empty road between here and Dubrovnik. We stop them. They surrender. We take them to Zagreb and everyone wins. If they resist or, as I should probably say, when they resist, our job is to try to keep at least one of the creeps alive for interrogation. The colonel understands the requirement and agrees. He just needs some additional assistance in limiting his troops'…enthusiasm."

"Check, Boss."

They roared down the dirt track and hit the highway just as the glow of the convoy's headlights were visible to their rear. The driver of the Sprinter accelerated as much as possible given the road conditions and the diesel engine. In a few minutes they were well ahead of the trucks. They blocked the road near an especially sharp turn that limited any driver's choice. Either stop or drive off the cliff into the Adriatic.

The Croatian Special Forces commandos deployed in two groups. The lead group, with the colonel and Stacey, set up next to the Mercedes, controlling highway access in both directions. Sue followed her team led by the major, who she only knew by the first name, Dietrich, as they climbed up the road cut overlooking the Adriatic. They set up above and slightly forward of the roadblock. Sue was one of the last to arrive as they set up. Scrambling over rocks was never a good idea when you had a below-the-knee prosthetic. She had to take her time to be sure she didn't twist the prosthetic, lose her balance, and end up in the middle of the road. She arrived late but without too much pain or drama.

She looked at the luminous hands on her dive watch. It was 2120hrs. Just dark enough to make sure the Serbs wouldn't be able to see the full team, but light enough that the team could distinguish friend from foe.

Sue remembered her early training at Ft. Huachuca. Basic infantry skills were taught to the military intelligence troops so that they would know what it was like to conduct an ambush or an attack. The instructors wanted their students to know how important intelligence was to a foot soldier. Later, in SOF she was spoiled by the SOF kit that included lightweight night vision goggles, small team radios that linked everyone on a team through voice communications, and sophisticated weapons with both infrared and night-vision optics. Here, she was sitting in an ambush position with six commandos wearing their camouflage uniforms, carrying AK74 assault rifles, and communicating with hand and arm signals. Not that much different from her training at Ft. Huachuca in the 1990s. She wasn't worried about their skills, but she did wonder how in the world Dietrich would prevent a violent and conclusive result in the ambush. She watched and waited. Dietrich moved quietly to her position and spoke in his accented German.

"I may need you to physically touch the three men to your left when I shout for a cease fire. They may not hear it or, more likely, may not want to hear it. Most of these men lost family to the Serbs in the early 1990s."

"I can do that, but what does cease fire sound like in Croatian?"

"Not to worry, you will know when I am shouting that."

Sue suspected Dietrich didn't intend to shout as much as man-handle his men. She planned to do the same, though more gently.

The approaching lights of the convoy stopped all further conversation as they prepared for battle. The last few seconds before an ambush were always the most important. Every soldier had to be prepared to act as a team member if an ambush was to be conducted properly. In her training, Sue had been taught that the team along the flank of an ambush would need to sweep across the objective. She looked down the incline to the road. It was a good ten feet below. No need to worry about them sweeping across the objective.

The convoy trucks turned the corner and faced the roadblock. The Croatian Special Forces colonel was standing in the highway with his left hand stretched out in the worldwide symbol to stop and an MP5 machine pistol in his right hand aimed at the truck driver just in case he didn't stop. The driver hit the brakes, worked the old transmission into reverse and tried to back away. At the same time, the second truck was accelerating uphill and around the curve attempting to avoid downshifting. He hit the first truck in the tailgate and drove the trailer hitch of the truck into his radiator. The two trucks were now headed back down the hill under the momentum of the first truck's power.

The third truck driver was working his clutch and stick shift in an attempt to climb the hill and make it around the curve just as he saw the two trucks coming back down on him. He knew he had no place to go to his left, so he turned hard into the cliff face to his right. The hood of his truck buried into the dirt on the cliff face and the shock of the crash dislodged the cliff where two of the Croatian commandos sat next to Sue. Sue was amazed to see them fall off the cliff and land on their feet on the hood of the truck ten feet below. As soon as they landed, they pointed their weapons at the driver and his passenger. The Serbs immediately raised their hands.

The two lead trucks, racing backwards down the hill, hit the third truck just behind the dual tires of the rear axle, bounced slightly and then shot off the cliff toward the Adriatic. Nothing could be done by any of the Croatians except watch as the two trucks and the six men inside tumbled to their deaths. Even the Croatians who had hoped for some degree of revenge for sins committed in the 1990s were shocked by the deaths of the Serbs. Dietrich slid down the edge of the cliff and landed on the hood of the truck. He ordered his two men off the hood and instructed them to take control of the two men in the front of the truck. The last two commandos next to Sue slid down, landing behind the truck. They were killed by gunfire from the two men riding in the bed of the truck.

The gunfire changed the entire scenario. The Croatians who were securing the captives in the cab of the truck started to abandon their job. Dietrich made it clear that they had one job and that was to secure their captives. He started down the right side of the truck, pistol at the ready. The two Serbs from the truck-bed were already out and spraying Kalashnikov rounds at Dietrich. As they heard the high-pitched sound of the trailing Croatian service van with Nancy and Zoltan rounding the curve, one of the Serbs turned toward the van and started firing.

Sue realized there was only one thing to do. Ego defeated prudence as she leapt off the edge of the embankment and landed heavily on her good leg, spraining her ankle in the bargain. She was able to come up in a shooting stance on her prosthetic leg and shouted in her best Russian, "Halt!" Both Serbs turned to her and raised their rifles. Sue put two rounds in the chest of one gunman as Dietrich came around the side of the truck and put two rounds in the chest of the other. They both dropped like puppets whose strings had been cut. Dietrich walked over to the two Serbs and kicked the rifles away from their dead hands. He turned to Sue and said, "Danke."

Sue acknowledged with a nod. She was left on the edge of the cliff nursing a quickly swelling ankle as she watched Dietrich and his men process their prisoners and all available evidence from inside the truck. The Croatians might not have the best kit, but Sue was convinced that if there was any information available in the truck when they arrived, it was now in a set of evidence bags that appeared from the cargo pockets of these commandos.

Stacey walked up to Sue. "You ok?"

"Sure, chief. Well, sorta. I think I sprained my ankle. The real question is whether Nancy and Zoltan are OK. The Serbs shot up their van."

At that point, Nancy walked up and said, "Well done, Superwoman. We saw you flying off the cliff and shooting at the same time. Pretty snazzy. Zoltan wants to marry you."

Flash appeared from behind the truck and walked past the two dead Serbs and over to the edge of the cliff. At the bottom of the cliff, the two trucks were battered by the waves. "We were supposed to take these guys alive. Sue, what were you thinking?"

"It wasn't my fault!"

Flash turned to Stacey and Nancy and said, "She always says that."

B arbara watched as Neville, Jake and Mutt loaded into the black Zodiac, the RIB as they called it, and paddled to shore. There was a sliver of moon rising over the coast and she could see two small security lights on the outside of O'Connell's villa. There were no lights on in the house. The three men and the zodiac disappeared into the darkness as *Marie's Bane* rocked gently on its sea anchor as the tide pushed toward shore. Barbara checked Peter Senior's old watch. The radium paint on the hands of the watch still emitted a faint golden glow. It was just after 3 a.m. They had been waiting at anchor for nearly an hour.

Jake had said, "The goal is to arrive between 0330hrs and 0400hrs. This is when people are the most vulnerable. In case you are interested, it is also when most geezers die of heart attacks. No matter how fit, the body just wants to be asleep at this time of night. With a little luck, we can get into his house, scare the shit out of him, and force him north. We won't use the RIB's outboard unless he makes a run by boat. If he makes a run by car, we will do our best to convince him we are following. The rest, honestly, is up to Beth."

Barbara dialed the Iridium satellite phone, calling Beth's corresponding phone. She simply said, "MAGPIE."

Beth was sitting inside the Croatian border patrol headquarters sharing a cup of very strong, very sweet Croatian coffee. She answered the phone and said, "Nest egg." She turned to the lieutenant colonel in the Croatian Security Service and said to him in unaccented Serbo-Croatian, "The operation has begun." Beth smiled at the FBI legal attaché and Terry Reimer and said to them, "Countdown has begun."

The lieutenant colonel keyed the hand-held radio on the desk and said, "Venom." In response, two majors in the Croatian service began their final preparations. One team was set up approximately a mile inside Croatia on highway 8 heading to Dubrovnik. The second major was sitting in a Croatian Coast Guard patrol boat almost exactly one kilometer inside Croatian waters.

Jake Longstreet had conducted more than his share of night raids over his time, first in the 101st Airborne, then in the 10th Special Forces Group and finally in the SOF raid units. Each time, the approach offered the challenge of controlling the adrenaline flow. Too much, and you lost your ability to shoot straight. Too little and you might not be able to move fast enough to stay alive. This was the first time he had ever conducted a raid where his goal was to force the target to run away. Usually, you planned on containing squirters, as they were called in SOF. In this case he wanted O'Connell to be a squirter. At least, so long as he headed north to Croatia. He had promised Mutt and Neville that if O'Connell didn't run, he was not going to allow the target to do them harm. They would resolve the target on site. There would be consequences, but none as severe as losing a comrade in arms.

They beached the Zodiac fifty yards from the villa. They silently crept up to the observation point that they identified previously during their map reconnaissance. The three men pulled out night vision scopes designed to be mounted on sniper rifles. The optics gave them both light and image amplification. Mutt was checking for surveillance cameras or alarm systems. Neville checked for dogs and obstacles that would not show up on a map recce. Jake focused his attention on the garage and the small boat dock next to the villa. After twenty minutes they conferred in a whisper.

"No cameras on the house. It looks like anyone's beach property."

"No obstacles and no dogs visible on the property. No neighbors at all. Very isolated."

"He has two vehicles in the carport. One is a late model Range

Rover and the other is a pretty beat up Land Rover Defender. The boat tied up to the dock is a simple Boston Whaler with an outboard motor. It should be able to outrun us, but just barely. It definitely won't outrun the Croatians."

"Do we give him the choice or try to drive him to a land or sea option?"

Mutt answered Neville. "I think a road option is best. The Croatian border is only a few miles away on the only road past the villa. If he takes his boat, we can work it, but we could lose him in some cove that we don't know about."

Neville said, "I can hot wire the Defender pretty quickly if he takes the Range Rover."

Jake nodded. "Sounds like a plan. Shall we dance?" They moved out silently. Just before they left, Jake turned back towards the sea and used his surefire flashlight with its red filter to send a single Morse letter. G for go.

Theodore watched with binoculars from the bow of the boat. He turned to Barbara and said, "It's a go."

Barbara dialed Beth. She said, "Omelette."

Beth turned to her counterparts and said, "We are cooking."

The three men crept up to the far corner of the villa. Along with their jumpsuits, they were wearing black balaclavas, safety googles, black gloves and black high top trainers. They approached on the oblique as silently as ghosts. Even if they didn't see a surveillance camera, they figured any camera would be facing directly out from the house or focused on the main door. They reached the side of the house without incident and found a French door on the mainland side of the house. They had previously observed another door on the coast side of the house. They hoped that their target would leave either by that door or the front door.

Mutt pulled a rubber coated sledgehammer from his shoulder bag. He looked at Jake and Neville. Jake had his recently acquired Sig Sauer in low ready. Neville had a flash bang out. Jake used the fingers on his left hand to count down. Three, two, one. As he made a fist, Mutt hit the plate glass window and it collapsed in a crash. Neville released the spoon on the flash bang and all three turned away from door as the flash bang exploded.

As expected, in a matter of seconds, O'Connell came down the stairs. He was wearing a track suit and beach shoes and firing some type of machine pistol. He was not aiming in any direction. Pistol cartridge rounds crashed around the walls and ceiling and the brass shell casings rang as they hit the tile floor. The three-man team were crouched on the outside waiting for this response. As soon as O'Connell stopped to reload, Jake put three rounds into the darkened room: close enough to make sure O'Connell knew they meant business, but not close enough to hit him either accidentally or on purpose. Neville threw another flash bang into the room. The explosion rocked the room and Mutt peered around the door frame from his prone position. The furniture was on fire and the parts of the two grenades were glowing. O'Connell was nowhere to be seen.

Jake and Neville had moved to the front of the house. Their goal was to goad O'Connell into his vehicle. Mutt moved to the opposite side of the house to make sure that if O'Connell did take his vehicle, he didn't try to drive back into Montenegro proper. His flash bangs and his pistol fire would make that a bad choice. They heard the Range Rover start and pull out of the carport. O'Connell had his vehicles combat parked: facing out toward the street. Even so, he pulled away so quickly that he hit one of the posts of the carport and nearly removed the passenger side mirror. Mutt watched as the Range Rover with its dangling side mirror headed north.

As promised, Neville had the Land Rover hot wired as soon as the Range Rover was out of sight. He pulled to the front of the house. Mutt came down from the road and jumped in the passenger seat. Jake came out of the house with a duffle bag and jumped in the rear seat. He turned on a short-range ship–to-shore hand-held radio and said, "Graveyard" as they pulled away.

Barbara dialed Beth's number. She said, "One light."

Beth smiled. She turned to the lieutenant colonel and said in Croatian, "He is coming by land." She turned to Special Agent Danny

Mayer and Terry Reimer and said, "It's just like the story of Paul Revere. One by land, two by sea. We got one light."

Mayer already had twenty years of service in the FBI. He was a street agent at heart and had not been thrilled with the assignment to Zagreb. He rubbed his large, calloused hands and said to Reimer, "It looks like we have a fugitive to catch."

"It's all yours, Danny. I just want to be waiting when we get him home."

"Deal." He turned to the Croatian lieutenant colonel and, in his best Croatian, said, "We would like to be there when your men detain the fugitive. Can we do that?"

The officer smiled. These were the reasons why he wanted to work with the Americans. To bring fugitives to justice and to tell stories of his days and nights working with the best law enforcement agency on earth, the American FBI. He said in his best and only English. "Why not?"

Mayer put on his raid vest with its armor plates and the luminous tape with the initials FBI and followed the Croatian security service officer out the door.

Neville chased O'Connell for several miles, as Mutt served as the navigator. It wasn't a difficult follow. At 4 a.m. there were no other vehicles on the highway. He could see the bright glow of the Range Rover headlights as the vehicle pulled slowly away from them. No matter what they did, the Defender's ancient diesel was not about to accelerate fast enough. Jake said, "Keep on him, but don't blow a piston. We still have to get back to the zodiac."

Mutt commented, "He is already in Croatia. That last curve we passed was the border. I think we can leave it to our colleagues. Either they have him or they don't. Let's get back."

Neville stopped the Defender. He carefully did a three-point turn on the narrow highway and headed back down to the villa. A quarter mile from the villa, he parked the Defender in a layby designed for tourists to watch the sunset over the Adriatic. They walked down to the surf line and then in the surf until they reached the Zodiac. They launched the boat and headed back to *Marie's Bane.* By the time they were halfway to the sailboat, the surf had completely wiped out their footprints in the sand.

Michael O'Connell focused on driving. He had not expected to be attacked in his home, but he had always prepared for the worst. He knew that sooner or later the Russians would see him as less a benefit and more a risk. O'Connell had hoped they wouldn't find him in his beachfront villa. The attack tonight proved that hope completely unfounded. Still, he had survived and had other places to live.

Inside a concealment in the Range Rover was his Irish passport in one of his aliases, a wallet with a European driver's license in the same name, two thousand Euros, lists of his numbered Swiss bank accounts, and an ancient Beretta 7.65mm pistol that had been his father's favorite weapon. In the back seat was a small go-bag that included a set of casual clothes, a set of business clothes, his favorite pair of Italian handmade moccasins, and a small shaving kit. O'Connell smiled. A new life waited for him. He still had the small apartment on Lake Geneva registered in an alias that he hoped the Russians had not identified. He also had an apartment in Morocco. He would have to decide in the next week where he would go. First stop would be Switzerland and his bank.

As he came around the last curve before Croatia, he stopped by the side of the road. He got out of the Range Rover, walked to the edge of the highway, and looked down at the black waves of the Adriatic. He pulled the MP5 machine pistol sling over his head and launched the weapon into the sea. He doubted there would be any border guards on this highway at this time of night, but he had no interest in taking chances. He looked back and could still see his pursuers' headlights approach. It was time to move. He climbed back into the Range Rover and drove at the speed limit into Croatia.

Ten miles along Highway 8, he saw a checkpoint. There was an ambulance, a fire truck and two patrol cars. Road flares and spotlights on the cliff edge suggested a car accident. O'Connell thought of how dangerous the road to Dubrovnik was, especially on a Friday night and especially when the driver had one too many bottles of Croatian plum brandy. He slowed down and followed the police officer's instructions guiding him through the vehicle obstacles. Just as he was about to pull back onto the highway, a police officer walked up his car and tapped on the window with his flashlight. O'Connell rolled down the window. The officer said in perfect English, "I'm sorry, sir. There appears to be a problem with your other side mirror. Can you stop for a minute and explain what happened?"

O'Connell was about to offer his best possible explanation when he looked up and realized that the flashlight had been replaced with a 9mm pistol pointing at his head. It was at that point that he noticed the man at his window was wearing body armor with the FBI logo. There were two men in commando uniforms in front of his car with machine pistols and two more on the passenger side. O'Connell knew immediately that this was probably the last night he would be free. But life is filled with chance encounters and possibilities, so there was no reason to panic or to force these men to kill him now. He put the Range Rover in park and put his hands on his head. Another man came up to the window and said, "Magpie sends her regards."

Barbara received a one-word text message from Beth on the Iridium phone: "Diamond." They had him. She shouted to her mates who had just returned to the sailboat. "All over, mates. They have him." Jake gave Barbara a wave as he, Mutt and Neville stripped off their raid gear and loaded it into a black nylon duffle bag. Jake tied a set of diving weights to the top of the bag, sliced a small hole in the bottom of the bag and dropped it over the side. The weapons, grenades, and clothes disappeared into the sea. Theodore pointed the sailboat north to Dubrovnik. Jake, Mutt and Barbara had an appointment with Beth Parsons.

Just after dawn, *Marie's Bane* docked at Dubrovnik harbor next to a Croatian Coast Guard cutter and a very worn out trawler. The slips next to *Marie's Bane* were taped off with yellow tape marked *POLIS*. Beth was waiting at the dock. "Nice boat. Would the owners like to take us for a ride sometime?"

Jake replied, "Beth, they would be happy to do so anytime. They are very sociable, for Brits."

"I heard that," Neville said as he finished securing his boat. He walked up to Beth and said, "Neville. Happy to help anytime."

Beth was about to say something when she saw Barbara look over her shoulder and say, "What are you doing here?"

A voice that sounded like a younger version of Barbara O'Connell said, "I was just about to ask you the same thing."

Beth turned to see Sue O'Connell, wearing a white jumpsuit and latex gloves. She had her hands on her hips in what Beth remembered as the pose her mother would take when she was caught doing something naughty.

Beth turned to Jake and said, "I think we need to get out of here. This is O'Connell family business." Jake nodded, and they headed up the slip to a waiting Range Rover.

"Mother, what are you doing in Croatia?"

"Holiday?"

"I doubt it. Stacey said you and Beth were involved in a rendition."

"Now, don't exaggerate. We didn't render anyone. He drove into a police checkpoint and was taken into custody."

"I would like to point out that you might have crippled an operation that has taken months to set up." There was no way that Sue's tone of voice could sound like anything but a scold.

Barbara used her most motherly voice as she said to Sue, "And I would like to point out that the guy we captured ordered a creep to use a hand grenade on me. He also killed an asset of mine years ago. This was unfinished business."

Flash walked up to Sue and said, "And at what point are you going to let this family argument go and get back to work? Oh…and hi, Mrs. O'Connell. We like working with your daughter…most days." Flash smiled and then said, "She made me say that."

Barbara noted that Beth was waving to her to join them in the Range Rover. She said, "It was nice to meet you. Sue, I have to go. I have an appointment at the Embassy."

Sue O'Connell was so mad, she didn't know how to respond so she didn't respond at all. She just limped back to her site-exploitation work on the Lebanese trawler.

Once they were through the main gate at the Embassy, Jake, Barbara and Beth dropped off a duffle bag to the Station chief and the RSO. Inside were two computers, three satellite phones, three alias passports and a series of handwritten ledgers, all taken from O'Connell's villa. Terry knew that none of the material would be useful in any prosecution of O'Connell, but he mentioned to the COS that it should be useful for the station or, perhaps, the FBI in their efforts to take apart O'Connell's murder-for-hire program with the Russians. Beth introduced Barbara and Jake to the Ambassador and the COS. They then listened as Jake provided their cover story of the operation. In this version of the story, the team came in from the Montenegrin side of the Adriatic, arrived at O'Connell's home and acted as burglars not raiders. Beth agreed that it was reasonable to leave out parts that would only have created more questions and, perhaps, more trouble for everyone.

The Ambassador said, "Barbara, I'm sorry you missed your daughter. She and her partner Flash are down at the docks and leave for Italy in a couple of hours. I am sure she would have been fascinated by your little private adventure."

Barbara said, "I'm not so sure my daughter would approve."

Beth said, "Oh, I think we can be certain she might have been upset with some geezers trying to do something that should have been the Agency or the military or the FBI's business."

Stacey nodded and said to the Ambassador, "Sir, perhaps Beth is right. She might have been upset. The good news is we are starting out the week with two good stories to tell Washington. Especially good news because in both cases we also advanced our relationship with the Croatians."

"Indeed, Stacey." The Ambassador turned to Beth and said, "I don't want to keep you from your work. I know you and Mr. Longstreet and, I suspect Mrs. O'Connell, have a real job here and we are simply slowing you down."

Beth smiled at Jake and said, "You know, I think we have just been dismissed by the Ambassador."

"That's OK. We do have a real job to do, so I think it is time to start doing it."

On arrival at Camp Ederle on Tuesday morning, Sue O'Connell reported to Smith. As usual, Massoni was sitting on the couch next to the desk.

"So, you were able to work with OGA, complete the mission without any firefights or explosions."

"Boss, it was just like any other HICU mission. Intelligence collection in support of the mission."

Massoni said, "I heard that there were a couple of shots fired."

Sue said, "You can't believe everything you hear from Flash."

Smith wasn't interested in light banter. He said, "Seems you have impressed another COS while you were at it. She has asked me if I would post you permanently in Zagreb."

"Boss, as nice as Zagreb is, I really don't want to work the OGA conventional mission. It is too slow, too boring, and not exactly my cup of tea."

Smith exploded into laughter. "O'Connell, did you think you were going to have a choice? I already told the COS that you were critical to the REAL SUE mission and you were already headed out on another TDY."

"Boss, I hate the unit name."

Massoni said, "Get over it. And, by the way, where is my Croatian wine?"

Smith said, "O'Connell, I already delivered your new target folder to Flash. Get out of my office, go read the folder, get smart and come back at 1600hrs with a plan."

Sue smiled and headed out the door. When she got to Flash's desk, she lightly dope- slapped her partner. "Why did you have to tell them about the gunfight?"

"I thought it added a little color to an otherwise boring TDY."

"Color? Just when I was getting on Smith's good side."

"Really? You think he has a good side?"

"Maybe."

"Hey, while you were hanging out with management, I was going back over our work these last few months."

"Months?"

"I'm tired of trying to explain to Smith why the villains seem to be one step ahead of us. I decided to do some digging on my own. It looks like the problem isn't who is leaking our secrets. It's what is leaking our secrets."

"What?"

"Exactly. Now if you bring me coffee, I will try to explain using small words so you can understand."

Sue turned away before she said something rude. She would get that coffee and sit down to hear Flash out.

Barbara returned to the Chautauqua house after six weeks in Croatia. Her work with Beth and Jake had been fun, profitable and satisfying as they found ways to uncover war crimes that had been buried for over a decade. Waiting for her was postcard from Sue, sent through the military APO mail system. The picture was of a gondola in Venice. On the back was a brief note. Sue wrote,

Mom, the new assignment at Camp Ederle is working out well. I'm not sure when I will get home, but I will let you know by mail. In the meantime, please send letters. Emails and phones are problematic.

Ciao,

Sue

The note was puzzling, but Barbara got the message. For some reason, Sue believed her electronic communication links were compromised. She would send a letter back to Sue using the APO mail to let her know that she understood. She decided the letter would have to include some sort of apology for the Croatian adventure, even if she couldn't include an explanation.

She had expected to hear more than a few complaints from Mary Sanderson and Janice Macintosh. Instead, there was silence from her contacts inside the Intelligence Community. The first call after her arrival was from Terry Reimer. He said, "It appears that the US attorney here has opened a case against a guy named O'Connell. Relative?"

"I hope not."

"Seems the SAC called my boss and asked him if I had done some freelancing."

"And you said?"

"Just a holiday on the Adriatic. Benzinger told me the local FBI thought I might be an obstacle to further cooperation."

"And he said?"

"He told them I had already quit."

"Quit? I thought you liked being a lawman?"

"I do. But, while I was in Zagreb and before we delivered O'Connell to the authorities, Beth offered me a retainer for unspecified operations in the future. Seems she is building her own private army. I agreed, and it would be a conflict of interest to stay with the PD."

"Want to come down sometime and tell me all about it?"

"How about next weekend?"

"You know the way. Call when you leave EA and head my way."

"See you soon, Barbara."

Two days later Barbara did receive a call from Mary. Mary's opening was limited to, "Welcome home." No anger, no finger pointing, nothing but a simple greeting.

After some brief, pleasant banter about Washington, Barbara told Mary of the decision she had made on the flight back from Italy.

She said, "Mary, I think it is time for me to truly retire. I hope you understand. I will drive down to Washington and turn in all of my commo gear at your convenience. I have other things that I want to do with my life. The Andropovich case demonstrated that this is a job for someone a little younger and a little faster. Dodging grenades at my age really doesn't make sense."

What she didn't tell Mary was that, just like Reimer, while in Zagreb, Beth Parsons had offered her a consultancy agreement. Stearns and Mandeville was growing Beth's program and Beth wanted Barbara on her team.

Throughout the conversation, Mary's voice on the other end of the phone sounded tired. At the end of Barbara's resignation, she said, "I understand completely. I will drive up to see you in Chautauqua. I will pick up the gear and we will just call it good. I will expect to have a dinner and some wine and at least one adventure tale."

"I can promise the dinner and the wine," Barbara said. "But you know I'm just a wretched federal pensioner. I don't have adventures anymore."

J.R. SEEGER is a western New York native who served as a U.S. Army paratrooper and as a CIA case officer for a total of 27 years of federal service. In October 2001, Mr. Seeger led a CIA paramilitary team into Afghanistan. He splits his time between western New York and Central New Mexico.

www.ingramcontent.com/pod-product-compliance
Lightning Source LLC
Chambersburg PA
CBHW052046240626
47153CB00006B/2241